Shadow in the Mine

Blue Moon Investigations

Book 20

Steve Higgs

Table of Contents

The Shadow. Tuesday, October 10th 2156hrs

Have you ever had that sensation when you are certain someone is watching you? I think we all get it from time to time. It's an old defence mechanism hardwired into the back of our brains, and it kept humans alive when there were things around that would hunt us.

When we look, twitching our heads around sharply to check for danger, there is usually no one there, or there is someone there and it turns out to be the cute girl or boy from the office that you have been secretly crushing on for months. They have spotted you watching them and have developed a mutual interest – you hope.

But what if when you look there is no one in sight, but your brain continues to insist you are still being watched? What if something that isn't really anything then moves, withdrawing farther into the shadows?

'Did you see that?' asked Wayne, squinting into the darkness.

Wearing ear protectors to stop noise getting in, and because it was jolly cold and they kept his ears warm, Owen didn't hear anything.

When Wayne thumped his shoulder, it made him juggle and slop over half of his freshly made tea.

'What?' he demanded angrily, pulling the right side of his ear protection back so he could hear his partner's response.

'There's something over there,' Wayne nodded his head, speaking up so Owen would hear.

'Yes,' Owen agreed. 'It's a mine.'

They were at the entrance to B face, waiting to be assigned tasks by their charge hand, Gary. Gary was a decent sort, advancing to lead the crew through the basic equation of being older and knowing more.

Fletchers' gypsum mine had been open for almost two years, but had been beset with problems since the start. Safety issues was the most recent concern. Machinery was breaking down even though it was all quite new. A lifting rig snapped just a few weeks ago, sending tons of rock crashing down to the ground where it almost killed three workers. Since then, they had the Health and Safety Executive breathing down their necks. Every shift they were reminded to obey all the safety regulations - as if any of them were daft enough to disobey the rules.

The owners, a father and son team, blamed the recent run of accidents on the residents of a nearby village. There was nothing in any direction apart from that one small settlement just a couple of miles from the entrance to the mine's land.

The locals hadn't said a word when the mine was proposed or when it opened. However, about a year ago, they started making all kinds of noise, protesting and campaigning. The owners believed they were responsible for sabotaging the mine equipment.

Some staff had already quit, taking jobs at other mines even though it meant traveling farther each day. Wayne had no interest in changing jobs – the Fletcher's mine was a convenient driving distance and paid well enough. Even if there was something untoward going on with the locals, he felt confident it would blow over.

'You can't halt progress,' he muttered, still squinting into the dark.

Owen had his ear defenders back on already and was trying to drink what was left of his tea before Gary arrived. Their shift started in a few minutes.

'Hey, there's something out there!' insisted Wayne when the shadow he'd been staring at moved. He shot out an arm to point to it, knocking Owen's arm again just as he was about to take a swig.

Owen replied with a question about the legitimacy of Wayne's parentage.

Wayne heard the insult, but it didn't really register. He'd seen something for sure the second time. It was moving in the shrubland beyond the light cast by the mine's overhead lights. There were wild deer here – they saw them occasionally, but that wasn't what he had seen.

It was only there for a second, popping up as if it needed to check the lay of the land before vanishing again. Whatever it was, it had long spindly limbs. As nightmare creatures surfaced in his imagination, Wayne did his best to quash them.

'It was probably a tree,' he told himself out loud. 'Yes, a tree moving, and the way the clouds were shifting cast a shadow just when I looked at it. It looked like something but …' Wayne looked up at the cloudless sky and swallowed down hard on his rising uneasiness.

Cursing himself for watching too many late-night horror movies – it wasn't his fault, that is what is on at that time of the day and his body clock was all messed up from working nights – he squinted into the darkness again.

'Alright, let's have everyone's attention,' called Gary, wandering out to face the assembled men with a clipboard in his hands. 'Here are tonight's assignments.'

Gary looked up, making sure his team was listening. Faces were looking back at him. All except one.

'Hey, Wayne!' He whistled loudly, putting two fingers in his mouth to create a high-pitched noise.

Owen had one half of his ear defenders off again so he could hear what Gary was going to say. When he looked to see why Gary was shouting and whistling to get Wayne's attention, Owen took great pleasure in jabbing an elbow into his partner's ribs.

Wayne made an 'Ooof' noise as he gasped an unexpected breath.

'Whenever you're ready,' Gary mocked him, nodding his thanks to Owen.

Wayne, rubbing the sore spot under his left arm, listened to what Gary had to say but could not help twitching his eyes across to see if the shadow had reappeared.

I stared into the strangely shaped hole and said nothing. The mine standing behind me, waiting to hear what I had to say. They were two peas in a pod, both sporting beer bellies that jiggled when they walked, both wearing the same clothes even though it wasn't a uniform, and both displaying the same haircut though the father's was going rapidly grey.

They were an inch taller than me which made them just over six feet and quite ordinary looking. They were the kind of men you pass in the street but never notice.

They made the call the previous evening and I promised to visit this morning. I'd been looking into a gargoyle case at a stately home, but we were having a slow week, so Amanda, my girlfriend and business partner, who was working the case with me, carried on alone so I could tackle what sounded like a meatier investigation.

It was meatier. To start with, I had a dead body, not just some petty thefts which I felt sure were going to be down to the staff who worked at the stately home. They were the ones claiming to have seen gargoyles moving about inside the house.

The body was that of a mine worker called Wayne Calder. He'd failed to report in after his shift three days ago. According to Stefan Fletcher, the elder of the father and son pair, his absence went unnoticed until the next shift came in and someone pointed out that his timecard was still live.

A complete search of the one hundred and twenty square mile property failed to reveal his whereabouts. When they couldn't raise him at home or anywhere else, and calls to his parents, ex-wife with whom he had three children, and even the landlord at his local public house, all

5

came back with the same result – "We haven't seen or heard from him" - they called the police.

A further day went by before his body was found and that was where it all started getting creepy.

Wayne's body was desiccated, sucked dry of all moisture and his corpse was completely mangled. I hadn't seen the body, nor read a coroner's report, but I was willing to take Stefan Fletcher's word for it. Worse yet, he was found by other mineworkers in open ground not far from the current edge they were cutting.

They called it a mine, but to my way of thinking, a mine is something underground. This was on the surface or, at least, mostly on the surface.

Anyway, Wayne Calder reappeared, very dead, very dry, and in a place men had been walking only hours before. Someone took him away, sucked out his juices, and put him back.

The killer wanted his victim to be found.

It was macabre. And that, of course, is why they called me.

My name is Tempest Michaels. I am the owner of a paranormal investigations agency which I started after I left the army. It pays the bills.

The hole the Fletchers wanted me to look at was not where Wayne Calder was found. It was inside a cut – what they call the leading face of the open mine. The workers found it the day before Wayne went missing. I couldn't help but stare at it. There were footprints leading away from it, but not man-made ones. Nor were they from any animal on the planet. They were sort of domelike, with a teardrop shape, the point of which was at the back if I was viewing them correctly.

Someone had gone to some effort to set this up.

'What do you think, Mr Michaels?' asked Stefan Fletcher, prompting me to speak because I had been silent for so long.

I thought someone was playing an elaborate trick, but had learned long ago that I cannot simply state there is nothing paranormal going on. Doing so either gets me thrown off the case – hard to make money that way. Or it starts a big argument between the believers and the told-you-soers. Sometimes that argument can rage for days, and it never creates anything productive.

Turning away from the hole, I said, 'It's far too early to draw any conclusions, gentlemen.'

'But you are going to take the case, yes?' asked Stefan.

His son frowned, and for the first time I noticed how annoyed he looked.

'We don't need him, Dad,' Colin Fletcher insisted. 'He's just some charlatan preying on people's superstitions.'

I gave him credit for looking me in the eye when he insulted me.

Stefan came to my defence before I could consider what I might like my response to be.

'No, son, he's the real deal. I've read all about him and he came highly recommended.'

'We can't afford him,' argued Colin, changing tactics. 'We are bleeding money, Dad, and with the workers on strike until we can ensure their safety, we shouldn't be spending anything unless we absolutely have to.' Colin was agitated, his hands and feet twitching as if he was feeling nervous and wanted to be somewhere else.

The older man closed the distance to his son, placing a fatherly hand on his shoulder when he said, 'This is necessary, boy. Mr Michaels is an expert in cases like this. He'll find the culprit and get us working again far quicker than the police. That's what we need and if it costs us a few quid, that's the price we have to pay.'

It was clear his son was not convinced, and wasn't going to be no matter what his father said. Colin glared over his father's shoulder at me, unashamed of his opinion, but silent for now.

Pivoting around to face me again, Stefan asked his question again.

'Will you take the case, Mr Michaels?'

I could hear the sense of hope in his voice. The hole appeared during one of the weekly maintenance shut down periods. Typically, the mine operates twenty-four hours a day, seven days a week, but to perform routine maintenance there was a two-hour shut down every third day. I guess it was that or suffer a much longer shut down when something critical broke.

Apparently, the hole caused some speculation when it was discovered, but the miners' interest in it was only passing – they had quotas to achieve.

When Wayne's body was found they took a closer look at it and called a strike within hours. On top of the safety issues and several near misses that could have been fatal, the loss of one of their own proved too much.

The hole wasn't just a hole, you see. Rather, it was a pocket in the gypsum. A pocket which had contained something vaguely humanoid, and which appeared to have been burst open from the inside.

Something inside had decided to get out and the day after they found the strange hole on one face of their open mine, a man vanished.

I couldn't blame Stefan for wanting to hire me.

A light drizzle began, coming from the east and threatening to bring more rain with it.

I shrugged my shoulders to force the collar of my coat up closer to the skin of my neck. Too often during my time in the army I had been an accepting, yet unwilling victim of the elements. Back then I had no option but to put up with it and tough it out. Now I could go inside if I felt so inclined.

I drew in a deep breath and held it for a prolonged second before letting it go. It was all the thinking time I required. There were scared people, the local police assigned to figure out what happened to poor Mr Calder were most likely stumped by the circumstances of his demise, and there was very definitely something spooky going on.

It was a trademark case for me, and I knew I would choose to investigate it even if they were not offering to pay me to do what I love. There was someone behind this. Someone with ill intent and devious purpose.

Now I just needed to figure who, why, and how.

The radio in the Fletchers' utility vehicle burst into life.

'Boss, this is Angus. She's at it again!'

Having no idea who 'she' might be, or what the 'it' was that she was apparently doing again, I watched the two mine owners to see how they reacted.

Mostly they said bad words. The kind of words my mother automatically crosses herself after hearing if she is in public even though she will employ them herself if she drops a plate or stubs her toe.

Stefan crossed back to the cab of his utility vehicle, leaning through the open window to snatch up the handset.

'Where is she?' he growled.

His son, Colin, was already climbing into the passenger's seat as his father got his answer, the two of them leaving me where I stood to deal with this latest issue. As if suddenly remembering me, Stefan jerked a thumb at the back seat of their truck.

'You'd better come along, Mr Michaels. Sorry, we have to deal with this, but it won't take a moment and we'll take you back to the office straight after.'

I had no intention of letting them go without me – it was over a mile back to my car for a start and that was across churned up, muddy ground. I haven't exactly gone soft since I left the army, but if I don't have to get mud all up my legs and ruin my shoes, I won't.

Also, whoever the mystery lady was, she had the owners instantly hot under the collar and that intrigued me. The hole in the ground was interesting, the desiccated and butchered body of Wayne Calder unexplained, yet I was certain I was going to find a person or persons behind the crime, so checking out who this mystery person was and what they were up to had become an obvious next step.

I got a last look at the hole as the senior Mr Fletcher spun the truck around and roared off over the scrubland surrounding the open mine.

'Who is the 'she' you are racing to intercept?' I enquired.

Stefan swore again. 'Mildred Marchant. She's the head of the local ramblers' society.'

That single piece of information coloured the picture in nicely.

Staring between the front seats to look out through the windscreen, I said, 'Let me guess. They are arguing right of way through the land you now own and are continually breaking through your fence lines to enter areas that are not safe to cross.'

'Bang on,' replied Stefan. 'This is the fourth time this week. They haven't walked this land in decades and wouldn't have either if we didn't erect fences to keep them all safe. It's a mine for crying out loud. If they fell into it or got run over by one of the gypsum trucks after cutting our fence, you can bet they would try to blame us.'

'It's ridiculous,' commented Colin, his voice a low growl.

The Fletchers were not happy, and I understood their standpoint – I would be unhappy too if it were my problem. I offered no opinion, acknowledging that I knew too little about the different sides of the argument to speak my mind. However, I had met with several deliberately awkward people in my time – my mother was one of them – and could see the likelihood that Mildred was just being difficult because she could.

As we bounced across the uneven ground, low scrubby bushes all around but nothing growing higher than a couple of feet, it was easy to make out a gaggle of people in the distance. Stefan adjusted his trajectory to meet them head on and continued to grumble and swear until, skidding to a stop a few yards from them, he jumped out and started shouting.

'Don't mind him,' instructed a woman in the middle of the group. 'Just carry on. We have every right to be here.'

11

I could have guessed the speaker was the infamous Mildred Marchant, but Stefan confirmed it.

'Mildred, we have talked about this. It isn't safe for you to be here.' Stefan was doing his absolute best to keep his cool. 'The police are already on their way.'

'We have every right to roam, Mr Fletcher!' she snapped in his face. 'Even if that does upset your profit churning money machine as it strips the earth of its natural resources.'

The group of ramblers had ground to a halt and were looking about uncertainly.

'Perhaps we should go back, Mildred,' suggested a woman in an orange waterproof coat. She looked to be in her fifties and not all that enthralled to be out in the elements. The sky threatened rain.

'Nonsense, Rosie,' spat Mildred, clearly uninterested in anyone else's opinion.

'But he said the police are coming,' Rosie pointed out, voicing her concern while glaring at the back of Mildred's head.

Mildred smiled as if it were amusing. 'We are not committing a crime. We are the locals here and we have the right to roam.'

'But you do not have the right to cut my fences!' snarled Stefan. 'That's four times this week.'

'Stop erecting fences then!' shouted Mildred, going red in the face.

'It's for your own safety!' screamed Stefan in response. His chest was puffing out and his hands were clenching and unclenching. 'Maybe I should just let you roam, Mildred. Be my guest and walk where you will on my land. Then maybe we'll see what happens to you!'

Worried his father might be about to strike the barmy old bat, Colin grabbed hold of his dad's arm and tugged him away.

'The police are here, Dad,' Colin nodded his head across the scrubland and when I looked, I too could see a four by four with a light bar on its roof heading our way.

Mildred, a smugly satisfied smile on her face, retreated a few yards to stand with her party of reluctant ramblers

There were muttered conversations I could not hear, but they all fell silent when the police off-road vehicle parked, and a local police officer got out.

He was wearing a uniform and no badge of rank which made him a constable. In his late thirties, I felt that made him old to still be on the bottom rung, but perhaps he was late to join the service. Carrying a few extra pounds around his middle and a trim, yet convincing black beard, the Caribbean man looked unhappy.

'This is the fourth time this week,' the police officer pointed out.

Exasperated, Stefan gawped. 'What are you telling me for? Arrest her, can't you? This is getting ridiculous.'

'We have discussed this Stefan,' the officer replied in a bored tone. 'The law is clear, and they have a right to roam. You can appeal but as you already know, it will take a year or more to get a decision.'

'He threatened to kill me,' shouted Mildred, sounding pleased with herself. 'I have witnesses.'

'What?' Stefan's face took on a surprised and guilty expression. 'I never threatened you.'

'Yes, you did,' Mildred came forward, wagging her finger at the mine owner as she closed the distance between her and the police officer. 'You invited me to wander your land and told everyone I would find out what would happen to me if I did. You don't want to pay to put in safe paths for us, so you are going to kill me instead.'

Stefan protested. 'That is not what I said!'

I'll be honest and admit that I lost interest at about this point. The cop met my gaze and rolled his eyes when he thought no one else was looking. I wanted to talk to the local police - they would have pictures of Wayne Calder and an autopsy report, but that wasn't going to happen right now.

I checked my phone, finding a text message from Amanda, and turned away to answer it while the argument about rights to roam raged on.

When they were finally done, Colin led his dad back to their truck as the ramblers carried on their merry way.

The local cop had given them a warning to steer clear of the mine and a sterner warning to the Fletchers to put gates or styles in their fence line, accept they could do nothing about the ramblers, and to carve out safe paths with warning signs to prevent anyone accidentally falling into the mine.

Stefan's knuckles were white as his grip attempted to crush the life out of his steering wheel on the way back to their office, but whatever thoughts were going around in his head, he kept them to himself.

My piqued curiosity to see the people breaking through his fences had waned. I expected to find the murder victim had been killed by a fellow mineworker, but was open to find my first guess proved wrong. Whatever had happened to Wayne Calder it was not at the hands of Mildred or any of her ramblers – they looked like they were fresh from Sunday School.

There were a few formalities to go through before I could get stuck into the case. While I languished in Maidstone Prison a few months ago, Amanda had chosen to hire a new receptionist. Marjory Sinclair was one of those people who live to organise things and she quickly proved to be a real boost to our business.

She was kinda bossy though. Almost forty years older than me, she immediately adopted a maternal position within the firm, taking an adamant stance on the correct filing of reports, paperback, billing, and many other things.

I might have taken exception to her nagging were she not so effective, but also, she had this kindly older lady face that just couldn't be argued with. She wore handknitted cardigans and kept a tissue up her left sleeve. One could guarantee she had a packet of mint humbugs in her handbag, and her hair, though long ago turned to white, had a delicate pink dye and a perm to make it curl around her skull.

The point is, if I didn't get the contract signed and a deposit paid, Marjory would politely message me to enquire about them. I didn't need to be reminded – like I said, I could find myself taking exception – but there were worse things than having a diligent assistant back at the office.

Arriving back at the cluster of buildings that formed the hub of the mine, Stefan and Colin both uttered expletives when they rounded the side of the main office building and found a van marked with Health and Safety Executive on the side.

The HSE were back to harangue them. The Fletchers had admitted their recent run of bad luck, not that Stefan referred to it as such. Unlike many of my clients, he did not believe the strange hole in the face of his

16

mine was the former home of a supernatural creature. His feet were firmly rooted to the planet when it came to such daftness.

Instead, he was convinced the locals were behind his safety problems and blamed them openly for the failing machinery.

'It's just this way, Mr Michaels,' Stefan indicated which way to go with an arm, tilting his head to keep the rain off his face.

We hurried inside, where one of the mine's security guards was keeping a thin, bookish man company.

'Do we have a meeting?' asked Stefan, addressing the man from the HSE. From the tone of his voice, I got the sense Stefan thought he might have forgotten an entry in his diary.

'I do not need to announce my visits,' replied the small man from the HSE with an unpleasant sneer.

Stefan stuttered. 'Okay, I'll … ah. I'll be right with you.'

Mr HSE replied instantly, 'Oh, no, please, take your time. Keeping me waiting won't hurt your report at all.' He was thoroughly nasty, and thus perfect for the job.

It's not that I have anything against health and safety – without it bosses would still be sending children inside machines to free jams while the dangerous moving parts continued to operate. However, I doubted there was any need to be spiteful.

Sounding flustered, Stefan turned to his son. 'Colin, can you please take this gentleman to my office. Get him a coffee and whatever else he wants. I will be there in two minutes,' he checked my face for an opinion and got a nod.

Two minutes was all I needed.

Following Stefan Fletcher as he hustled down the corridor, I was led into a board room. When he closed the door behind me, I was already fishing out my tablet to take an electronic signature and arrange a bank transfer deposit – standard when we take a case on.

'I do hope you can clear this up quickly, Mr Michaels,' mumbled the elder mine owner. The hope in his voice was heart breaking.

'Tempest, please,' I asked that he address me by my first name. 'I can assure you I will do what I can, but can make no promises regarding how long my investigation might take.'

'Well, perhaps it will speed things up to know that Irene Tanner is behind it.'

I noted the name. 'Irene Tanner.'

'She's the matriarch in Playford,' Stefan explained.

Playford was the name of the hamlet just down the road. For convenience I had a room booked there, but that was to place me close to the mine, not because I had any foreknowledge to indicate the locals were involved.

'I don't want to sway you too heavily, Tempest,' Stefan signed the documents where I indicated, 'but they have been vocal about wanting the mine to close for the last year. That Mildred Marchant isn't coming onto my land because she wants to roam, she and her cronies are scoping it out so they can report back. Then they send people in to attack our equipment. It's just not possible to protect it all, there's too much land and security costs a fortune. I've had to double the guards' pay just to

18

keep them here. They all think there's some creature called the Deathling roaming the mine.'

This was the first time he had mentioned it.

'The Deathling?' I questioned.

Stefan sighed. 'Yes, daft, isn't it? There was a case years ago. In the fifties I think it was. A few people died in strange circumstances, their bodies mutilated and drained of blood. There was a huge investigation, but they never caught anyone. The locals claim it was a beast they call the Deathling. Now they are saying it is back. It's why my staff walked out.'

'How long ago did the rumours start?' I wanted to know. I didn't know if this would mean anything, but I was going to have to look into it.

Stefan grumbled. 'Right before Wayne went missing. They killed him. You can bet on it. Of course, I told the police that, but they didn't take me seriously. That's why I called you, Tempest. I need someone who can see through the fog of superstitious, supernatural claptrap and find the truth.'

My chest swelled a little and I had to keep my ego in check when I dipped my head in acknowledgement.

'Dad!' Colin's voice echoed along the corridor. The HSE man was getting impatient.

Hurrying toward the door, Stefan asked, 'Is there anything else, Mr Michaels? As you can see, I really have to go.'

I shook my head.

'I'll let myself out. I'm starting straight away, Mr Fletcher. I'll update you daily with my progress.'

He thanked me as he vanished down the hall, his voice drifting back over his shoulder.

Left alone in the boardroom, I put my tablet back into my bag, made a few notes in my trusted notebook – I had names to remember, and made sure I had all my belongings before I started back toward the car park outside.

A large piece of crystal caught my eye before I got to the door. It was positioned at the head of the long table, right in front of where the chairman of the board might sit. The heavy object was an award – for safety, I noted ironically.

They had received it just a year ago. How things can change.

With the electronic versions of the contract signed and the deposit winging its way to my bank, I left the mine. The next stop on my list was my accommodation for the night.

Marjory had found me a bed and breakfast to stay in at my request, but my satellite navigation system was having trouble finding it. Miles from anywhere, the road I was travelling on didn't exist so far as my car was concerned. I could have travelled back and forth each day, but even though the distance wasn't that great, the slow country lanes between my house and Playford made it a solid hour drive each way.

My parents agreed to have the dogs, so I was staying in The Fox Inn for a few nights. If solving the case took longer than that, I would reconsider.

Spotting the sign for the public house hanging at the edge of the pavement, I angled the nose of my Porsche into the carpark and found a suitable spot in which to leave it.

The pub was the closest one to the mine's main entrance and thus the one I expected to 'accidentally' find mineworkers in when they ended their shift. I hadn't known they were all on strike when I made the booking.

When no one came to the reception desk in the first thirty seconds, I dinged the little bell to attract attention. The bed and breakfast part of the public house was accessed through a different door - my guess that the staff working the bar were the same ones to manage the B&B proved accurate a few moments later when a tall, thin man with a beer-stained shirt entered through a side door.

'Hello,' he called, wiping his hands on a small towel which was tucked into his belt. 'I'm Percy. This is my place. Welcome to the Fox Inn.'

'I have a room booked,' I announced in a distracted manner – my eyes were glued to a bookshelf behind the reception desk.

Seeing my head canted over to one side as I attempted to read the spine of a book, the man followed my eyes.

'You are interested in the paranormal?' he asked.

Ten minutes later, I took a sip from my tea and leafed through the book. It had been left behind by a previous tenant, but the man saw no harm in letting me borrow it from their lost property pile.

If you are wondering what I was doing sitting on my backside in a pub in the middle of an investigation, the simple answer is that, like everyone else, I have to eat. My order of Welsh Rarebit, a slightly indulgent treat I would later berate myself for, would be along soon. In the meantime, I was perusing a book entitled 'Supernatural East Sussex'.

My interest in the paranormal extends to the point of professional curiosity – I find myself fascinated by what some people will choose to believe over a rational explanation. Leafing through the thin book, which might more accurately be called a pamphlet, I found silly ghost stories about haunted houses and spooky graveyards. The author had performed some research to collate tales going back more than four hundred years, but that wasn't why I picked it up.

It had, as I hoped, a section dedicated to the Deathling.

Beneath the title was a crude artist's impression of the beast. The pencil drawing was of a creature from a child's nightmare. Humanoid, but possessing spiderlike limbs and a spider's ugly mouth and eyes, it was standing upright yet hunched over. It was drawn with clothes on – a ragged shirt and trousers to suggest it had transformed from a man into the beast.

On the next page, nestled between the words, was a photograph of the very public house I was staying in. Taken in 1953, the picture sat beneath a caption that read 'Deathling kills five in reign of terror!'. In front of the pub were over two dozen men, all brandishing shotguns and facing the camera as they posed for their image to be captured.

I read the article from start to finish, marvelling at the account. The name 'Deathling' was one coined by the local residents - all farmers - who had banded together to protect their community and attempt to catch the beast. According to reports, it butchered five men plus livestock over a five-week period.

At first, they assumed a large predator had escaped from a zoo or someone's private collection. However, there were odd-shaped footprints – the same ones I'd seen at the mine an hour ago - found in the soft earth at some of the attack sites.

22

There were photographs on the next page showing the butchered sheep, goats, and cows. They were taken in the daylight. Then there was a single grainy, dark picture that was supposed to be one farmer's attempt to capture the beast on camera. It showed something, but it was black on black and too indistinct to make out what it was.

The two farmers who saw it gave statements. Charles Fox claimed they chased and fired their shotguns at what they saw, and that it fled at great speed using four limbs to run like a dog though they first saw it walking upright like a man.

They found a blood trail on the ground, but no body was ever discovered. I did not for one moment believe they had faced down a supernatural creature that was half man and half spider, but they clearly did.

My natural inclination is to dismiss all such stories as daft nonsense, but the geography of the incident could not be ignored.

I wanted to know more. Usually, when I have questions about odd paranormal stuff, I pop around the corner to visit Frank Decaux. He owns an occult bookshop and is basically an encyclopaedia for all things weird. I could phone him, but I already had it in my head to visit the library in the nearby town of Rye. I would check their archive first. If I struck out there, I could bug Frank later.

I ate my lunch, washed it down with the rest of my pot of tea, and shot my cuff to check the time: 1228hrs.

It was time to make a move, and time to make a phone call.

'Hey, butt plug!' trumpeted Big Ben when he answered the phone.

'Good afternoon, Ben,' I replied, not rising to his bait.

'Is it?' he mumbled, sounding confused. I heard him yawn and then two thumps as his feet hit the floor.

'Are you just getting up?' I enquired, my tone filled with disbelief. 'It's after midday.'

'Well, some of us had a lot of top-level shagging to get through last night, Tempest,' Big Ben pointed out. 'These ladies won't satisfy themselves, you know.' There was a pause before he countered his previous statement. 'Okay, I guess they could, but not in the same never-going-to-experience-a-night-like-that-again kind of magic I gave them.'

'Them?'

'Yup,' boasted Big Ben proudly.

I could tell he was about to slip into full regaling mode, and I had no desire to hear about his exploits.

I cut him off before he could get started. 'I need your help on a stakeout tonight if you can spare the time.

Big Ben is an old army buddy and a walking force of nature. At six feet and seven inches of hard, toned muscle, he is a great man to have at my side if we get into a fight. That happens more than you might expect. He is also one of those people who was first in line at the handsome counter and then snuck back into the queue for an extra portion. Women continually fall at his feet and, like the gentlemen he is, he helps them back up and escorts them to his bed.

'I'm in a village near Rye,' I added so he would know he needed to travel.

'East Sussex?'

'Yup.'

'Cool, new territory to explore.' He, of course, was referring to the untapped population of single women the town would have on offer. 'What's the case?'

'Weird murder. A mineworker went missing for three days, then turned up mutilated and with all his body fluid sucked out. Plus, there is a weird hole in the dirt at the face of the mine and strange footprints. It had been made to look like something was hibernating in it and chose to get out. A few mineworkers think they saw something in the dark and the whole lot of them are refusing to work. The owners want me to catch whoever is behind it.'

'Naturally. What time do you need me? Are we staying down there? Are there any cute girls around?'

I rolled my eyes and sighed. 'I'm going to head over to the mine this evening. I have some research to do this afternoon. I am staying at The Fox Inn,' I gave him the address, 'and there are no attractive women in my immediate vicinity,' I added before he could prompt me to answer what he considered to be the most important question.

'Yeah, I suppose you do tend to repel them,' Big Ben acknowledged, being a dick as usual. 'Standby to be at the epicentre of female fineness. When I arrive, they will gravitate to me. They won't understand what is happening,' he remarked wistfully as if he were telling a story. 'They will have no ability to resist it, but their reward will be a night of such unparalleled joy.'

'Do you ever get tired of hearing your own voice?' I asked him.

'No.' The line went dead, Big Ben cutting me off before I could hit him with a stinging one liner.

I swore under my breath and parked my car in the small library carpark.

At the front desk, I waited patiently for the lady there to finish what she was doing. She was sorting through a pile of books with her back to me. A little pear-shaped at the hips, she wore a drab blue woollen sweater that looked to be hand knitted. Beneath it, a faded denim skirt fell all the way to her ankles and hid her feet. Her hair, streaked with grey, had been plaited to hang all the way down her back. There had to be almost four feet of it.

I guess I must have made a noise moving my feet or something, because she spun around to stare at me with a hand on her heart.

'Goodness!' she exclaimed. 'I didn't hear you come in.'

From a table five yards to my left, and from behind a book, an elderly woman's voice said, 'Shhhh!'

'Sorry, Millicent,' said the librarian, her cheeks reddening slightly. 'Is there something I can help you with?' the lady asked in a quiet voice. 'Are you looking to open an account? I don't recall seeing you in here before.'

The book to our left with the elderly woman obscured behind it, twitched, but no further demands for silence were forthcoming.

Now that she was facing me, I could see her name: Linda. It was on a badge stuck above her left breast.

'Hello, Linda,' I whispered in a desperate tone, making a joke of the library's singular customer's need for quiet. 'I have a library card for Kent. Will that work here?'

'Yes,' she whispered back. 'You can take books out and we can hunt you down if you don't return them because your address will be in the system,' she replied with a smile at her own little joke.

I grinned. 'Okay then. I'm hoping to take out any books that make reference to or explore the events surrounding a creature called the Deathling.'

Linda blinked a few times, perhaps surprised by my request and wondering if I was going to add anything. When I didn't, she turned to a keyboard to enter my request.

Frowning down at the screen, which I could only see reflected against her glasses, she said, 'We have four books listed but I'm afraid they have all been taken out already.'

My eyebrows hiked up my head – that was interesting.

'Who took them out?' I asked.

This time I got a more severe look from the librarian.

'That is not the sort of information I can give out.'

'Of course not,' I conceded, wishing she would do precisely the opposite because the name might be a big fat clue.

'We have a research room where you can look the information up,' Linda volunteered, offering me an alternative way to get what I originally came in for.

The research and archive part of the library consisted of a single small room. The lady at the front desk pointed me in the right direction and left me to my own devices. The information was electronically stored, transferred from books to make data access faster, no doubt, and also to make it available without coming into the library.

I was here now, so I sat at a computer terminal – there were three and none were occupied – and booted it into life. Once the screen gave the prompt to start a search, I lifted my hands to begin typing, but got no further because a shocked scream made me jump.

I leapt from my chair, spinning left to face the danger. Expecting to find someone in trouble, I was shocked to discover a surprisingly attractive redhead gawping at me with her mouth open. She was either blessed with naturally pale skin against her lustrous flaming hair, or she was about to faint.

'It's you,' she stammered.

'It is,' I agreed, unsure what other response I could give. 'Is everything okay?'

'Tempest Michaels,' she whispered, her voice barely audible.

I found my right eyebrow cocking itself. I had no idea who the lady was and believed I would remember if I had ever met her before.

'Do I … ah. Do I know you?' I enquired, fearing she might reveal we went to school together or perhaps I once dated her sister twenty years ago.

The redhead had an armful of books, heavy ones at that. Before I could offer to take them and prior to answering my question, she twisted her waist to dump them unceremoniously on a nearby shelf.

Then, smiling in an embarrassed way, and with glowing colour returning to fill her cheeks, she said, 'I'm your biggest fan.'

I blinked, questioning whether I had indeed heard her correctly.

Confused, I repeated her words, 'My biggest fan? I wasn't aware I had any fans.'

Another woman, the one from the front desk when I came in, burst through the door into the research room. She had heard the scream and come running.

'Victoria, is everything all right? Did this man hurt you?' I was being eyed suspiciously even though I was all the way across the other side of the room, a good five yards from the redhead.

'Hurt me?' Victoria murmured, her eyes never leaving my face. 'Only when he stole my heart.'

Oh, boy.

Victoria was in her mid-twenties, boasted a full figure and narrow waist, pouting lips, gorgeous hair, and everything a man could want. Were I not heavily involved with Amanda, she was exactly the kind of woman I would go for.

The lady from the front desk didn't seem to know what to do. She was hanging next to the door, one hand still grasping the frame as she debated whether she ought to press for a clearer answer, or just give up and go back to what she was doing.

Victoria was biting her bottom lip, one incisor leaving a dent as she looked me up and down.

'I had no idea you would be so gorgeous in real life,' she commented.

That was enough for her colleague who chose to close the door behind her as she left. Left me at Victoria's mercy, that is.

Trying to get some clarity of what was happening, I repeated my earlier question, though it was clear from her comment that we had never before met.

'No,' she admitted, 'you don't know me. I feel like I know you, though. I have been following your exploits ever since you first appeared in the paper.'

I was feeling rather shocked by her revelations. I figured there were people who had heard of me; I had been in the newspapers and on TV enough, but it was all minor articles that I expected most people to forget two minutes later. That was not the case with Victoria.

'You're here on a case, aren't you?' she guessed correctly. Then she gasped. 'Is it to do with Wayne Calder? I read about it in the paper, and I knew there was going to be something spooky about his death.'

'I'm afraid I cannot comment about a live case.' That wasn't even slightly true. It was my case, and I could say what I wanted.

'I can help,' Victoria volunteered, coming closer. 'I always wanted to be a paranormal detective. Of course, I'm not brave and strong like you. I wouldn't be brave enough by myself, but with you to protect me, I could be a real asset. Don't you think?'

'Um, sure,' I replied without pausing to engage my brain.

Victoria's eyes flared and she squeaked with excitement. 'Oh, my goodness! I'm going to help Tempest Michaels solve a case!'

Thinking fast, I said, 'I wouldn't want to distract you from your work.'

Quick as a flash she said, 'I'll quit right now if it means I get to work alongside my hero.'

I put both hands up to stop her. 'Whoa, there. No need to be doing anything extreme like quitting your job. I'm … I'm just doing some research into a creature called the Deathling.' I was about to explain what I learned from the book I found, but Victoria was already going around me to get into the computer chair.

'I know all about it,' she boasted excitedly. Her fingers were poised to start typing when two thoughts aligned in her head. 'Oh, my Lord! It's back, isn't it? That's what killed Wayne Calder! Wait until I tell everyone. The mine's official story is that it was a mining accident.'

Jolted back to something resembling my usual level of calm confidence, I knew I had to stamp down her desire to share information and fast.

'You cannot tell anyone,' I stated, making it sound like an order. 'Not if you want to help me on this case.'

She swivelled the chair to look up at me with doe eyes.

'Someone killed Wayne Calder,' I explained. 'Whether they are deliberately playing on an old story or not, I believe they killed him for a reason. Until I find out what that reason is and who is behind it, I want to keep my investigation as quiet as possible.'

'Of course,' Victoria's cheeks flushed again. I was looking down at her face, so I saw when a question formed on her brow. 'Wait, you said someone. I thought you said the Deathling did it?'

Now I was confused. 'Um, if you have followed my cases, surely you must know there is no paranormal. All the creatures I went after had a vanilla human behind them using people's fear of the supernatural as a smoke screen to hide what they were doing.'

Victoria grinned and nudged my arm. 'Of course,' she winked. 'I read the official story each time. I can't believe people fall for it.'

'Um, no, there really is no supernatural out there. It's all just idiots in costumes.'

'Oh, stop it,' she tittered.

The door to the research room opened again, the lady from the front desk sticking her head through the gap.

'Victoria, I'm going on my lunch break. You'll have to cover the front desk.'

Victoria muttered something colourful under her breath before twisting in her seat to offer her colleague a smile.

'I'll be right there, Linda.'

Linda let the door close as she wandered away.

'I'll not be long,' Victoria promised me. 'I've populated a couple of tabs for you to explore until I get back. I just searched 'Deathling' and 'Fletchers' Mine'.

I thanked her and breathed a sigh of relief when she left the room. She was my biggest fan, and currently a problem I could do without.

Slumping into the chair and wondering if I ought to climb out the window when I was done, I clicked on the first tab and started to read.

The reports Victoria found were from the papers at the time of the Deathling case. I scanned the information, trying to find something new and unsure what I was even looking for. There were other reports of men seeing something, but it all sounded like nervous individuals jumping at shadows.

After twenty minutes and half a dozen different reports, I gave up. I was about to go looking for ordnance survey maps – I was going to be on the land around the mine tonight and didn't want to get lost – they would have them for sale in a bookshop somewhere in town, when I spotted the name on the second but last tab.

It was nothing to do with the incident in the fifties.

Clicking it open, I found a story about a conservationist who attempted to shut down the mining activity when he found a beetle. I skimmed over the article, questioning whether it had any relevance to the case.

The rare Wormwood Moonshiner Beetle, one of over four thousand beetle varieties found in the UK, was identified by Darius Cooper of Peckham Lane, Playford. The beetle sat on the critically endangered list so its appearance in a remote area in East Sussex caused an immediate response by volunteers. Using National Lottery heritage funds to fund their campaign, they swiftly invaded the land owned by the mine looking for more beetles.

Quite how that was of benefit to the tiny creature I struggled to understand until I read a little further. The owners were facing a cease-and-desist lawsuit and were accused of burying the nature report carried out prior to mine work commencing. They had been required to demonstrate there were no rare creatures on their land, but it transpired that the original investigation was accurate and there were no beetles.

The single example of the species was insufficient to convince the courts, so despite a team of protesters lining up at the gate each morning, the mine reopened. I wondered how much money the owners lost at the time.

It was almost exactly a year ago. I squinted at the report, aligning the date of the beetle finding with the beginning of the Playford residents' objection to the mine. I had no exact date for the latter, but it had to be very close to when the beetle case fell through.

I noted the name of the man at the centre of the case, but I doubted it had anything to do with Wayne Calder's death. If a connection came up later, maybe … but I doubted it.

I gave genuine but brief consideration to slipping out of the window in the research room and it wasn't just because the windows had safety locks fitted that I chose not to. Honest.

It felt a little like running the gauntlet as I went back through the library. I was leaving – a simple enough task – yet I expected Victoria to impede my exit and worried she might perhaps just throw her clothes off and chase me.

Mr Wriggly had his own thoughts regarding how we should spend the rest of our day. This is because he has no memory and no conscience. He's a live-in-the-now kind of guy. I chose to ignore his thoughts on the subject, reminding him instead how amazing Amanda looks both with her clothes on and naked.

It proved to be counterproductive since all he did was wake up.

Now starting to worry he might be visible, I moved to a bookshelf and picked up a book to distract myself. A few seconds of reading would return him to his slumber.

I checked out the cover of the book in my hand – Confessions of a Call Girl.

I was in the - admittedly small - adult erotica section and the image on the cover was not helping my situation.

Shoving the book roughly back onto the shelf, I glanced right, saw what I needed, and almost ran to the 'classics' section.

Breathing a sigh of relief when I got there, I filled my brain with thoughts of dusty tomes being read by wizened literature professors in quiet halls. Then opened my eyes to see what book I had pulled from the shelf.

Lady Chatterley's Lover.

'*Oh, yeah!*' piped up Mr Wriggly, getting more interested with each passing second.

'Can I help you find what you are looking for?' asked Victoria, her voice right next to my ear and her quiet tone as husky and sensual as a lover's whisper.

I cried quietly, 'Not fair.'

'Is everything all right, Tempest?' she asked. I refused to turn around to face her. 'It is okay for me to call you Tempest, isn't it? I feel like I already know you. I have spent so much time watching you.'

'I'm sorry?' Had I heard her correctly?

Her cheeks flushed a little, and she cast her eyes downward.

'I came to your office,' she admitted. 'I wanted to meet you, but I was too scared to open the door and come inside. I guess I was afraid reality might not match my fantasy.'

'Sshhhh,' insisted a book with a dusting of hair poking over the top at a nearby table.

Her confession was fixing my trouser problem at least. I had a stalker.

Victoria flicked her eyes up to meet mine, an intense look pinning me to the spot.

'I should have been braver,' she murmured. 'The reality is way better than I ever imagined.'

'Sshhh!' demanded the nearby book with a little more force.

She made to step forward, a move that would place her well inside my personal space and bring her chest close enough that I would feel her body heat radiating off it. Mr Wriggly was trying to build up a full head of steam and it was at that moment I chose to run away.

'Gotta go!' I blurted, turning away with my bag held over my groin. The delightful redhead was offering to be my plaything – at least that was how it seemed to me, and quite frankly the idea terrified me. Not because there was anything abhorrent about that as a concept, but unlike Big Ben, I am happy to be monogamous.

A trifling dalliance with Victoria would lead to ruin with Amanda and eternal regret.

'Tempest, wait!' she called after me.

'SSSSShhhhh!'

Victoria snapped, 'Oh, shuttup, Millicent!'

It was the last thing I heard because I escaped through the library door and out into the carpark before Mr Wriggly could convince me to change my mind. There was a car manoeuvring to get into a parking spot and blocking my car in the process. I abandoned my plan to jump in it and hurried away down the pavement instead.

By the time I found a national franchise bookstore where I knew I could find Ordnance Survey maps, my heart rate had returned to normal, and I was feeling much better. I've never let it bother me that I struggle to act rationally around attractive women. I struggle to find the words to ask them out and then stammer through the first hour of any first date.

Given my thoughts, hopes, and dare I say plans for Amanda, I wondered if first date jitters would ever be an issue again. I hoped not.

It took me no more than a few minutes to find what I was looking for, a simple swipe of my company credit card enough to make it mine. In the bag in my car was a prismatic compass, though the topology of the land dictated I would most likely not need such a device – I could read where I was by the gradients.

Armed with information, a map, and a plan, I returned to the library to retrieve my car. I felt like an idiot peering around the corner of the building to check the coast was clear, but I did it anyway. Victoria was a bit too lovely, and significantly too mental, to want to tango with again any time soon.

If ever.

Let's just say I was driving fast when I exited the library carpark.

It had been a couple of hours since I visited the mine and took the case on. I didn't have anything much to lead me one way or another yet, other than Stefan's belief the locals led by Irene Tanner were behind it, but I wanted to speak with some of the mineworkers and I needed to see the mine at night.

The Fletchers were good enough to supply me with addresses for some of the workers – those in Rye - at my request. I would plot a circular course to visit a few tomorrow if needed, but hoped to catch some of them in the Fox Inn tonight. It being the bar local to the mine, and a Friday night, my guess was there would be chaps supping ale right under my nose later. Some of them were bound to live in Playford, right next to their place of work.

However, my first task was to get out on the ground after dark. The mineworkers were too scared to go to work and to me that effect looked deliberate. Someone wanted to scare the mineworkers away and I was going to find out why.

There were a few hours until it would be dark enough to venture out, so I returned to my room at the Fox Inn to sleep and prepare.

What a mistake.

The ability to set my internal body clock to wake at a given time is a skill I developed in the army. To within a few minutes, and only failing on very rare occasions, if I decide to get some sleep and choose to wake myself in time for something else, I need set no alarm clock.

Opening my eyes in the darkened room, I swung my right arm up to check the time on my watch, pleased to find I was bang on for my six o'clock target. Big Ben, if he wasn't already here, soon would be. We would grab something to eat in the bar downstairs and go over the case in rough detail before heading out to see if Wayne Calder's killer wanted to show his or her face.

I'm putting it down to the fog of slumber, but I hadn't noticed there was someone in my room until she spoke.

'You're so sweet when you are sleeping.'

The shock of it made my heart stop and then restart, and I almost squeaked in my fright as I scooted backward across the bed to increase the distance between me and my intruder. It was all automatic reaction, no brain power behind it. In the space of a heartbeat, I went from shocked fear to outrage and anger, and was fuelling my muscles to launch across the room when it hit me.

The voice belonged to my superfan, Victoria. She was in my room, sitting on a chair by the window, and worst news yet, I had chosen to strip off my clothes when I got into bed.

I always do. I haven't worn clothes in bed since I was a child.

'Victoria,' I managed to get my lips working.

'Yes, Tempest?' she replied eagerly.

40

'What are you doing in my room. How did you get in here?'

'Oh, there's a thing downstairs where they hang the keys. I just took the one for your room. I hope you don't mind. Our conversation got cut short earlier.'

I had the duvet clutched in one hand, pressing it to my abdomen as I glanced across the room to where my clothes for the evening were neatly laid out. I didn't want to ask her to pass them, and though it occurred to me that I could just get up and cross the room to show my confidence and disinterest, I worried it might just send her into a nymphomaniac frenzy.

None of those things were going to work and she was getting to her feet.

Seizing control and gaining some gumption, I held up my hand.

'Just stop there, Victoria. This invasion of my privacy is not welcome. Nor is it cool.'

Well, I tried to say those things, but she slipped her dress off her shoulders, and it dropped to the carpet to reveal saucy matching lingerie beneath. The first word died in my mouth, and I could do nothing but gawp at her fine body.

I swear Mr Wriggly blasted a bugle note for the troops to charge and at precisely that moment, my door opened.

Light flooded in from the hallway outside.

'Hey, knob jockey ...' hallooed Big Ben, and, for once, then stopped talking as his eyes took in the scene before him.

I had no idea what my face was doing. Mostly I think it was glad it hadn't been Amanda opening the door – this would have been hard to explain.

Big Ben's face, however, was spreading into a lecherous grin.

'Well, I'll be,' he chuckled. 'Well done, old boy. Well done.' He started to applaud me.

Victoria, flustered for the first time since I met her, was trying to pull her dress back up.

I was still doing the rabbit in headlights thing and could feel the heat coming off my face.

'It's not what it looks like,' I protested.

'It jolly well ought to be,' replied Big Ben with a frown. 'Nothing wrong with a little on the side,' he advised sagely. All Big Ben had was sides. He moved to block the doorway, cutting off Victoria's escape route. 'You should stay, whoever you are. He doesn't get much and, to be honest, he could really do with blowing off some steam. He is so uptight all the time.'

I offered Big Ben my opinion using several colourful terms.

He backed away from the door, holding his hands up as if to ward off my verbal attack and trying hard not to laugh at my discomfort.

Victoria had paused with her dress half up and her heaving bosom exposed. She was looking at me with an embarrassed smile and very obvious intentions.

Big Ben was reaching for the door handle, intent on closing it again so Victoria and I could be alone. I spotted the key in the lock – Victoria said she used it to gain entry. It explained why Big Ben just burst in. He would have asked which room I was in and probably intended to call me. However, upon finding the key in the lock, figured I must be up and about to leave.

I still had the stupid duvet clutched to my groin. I was using it to hide Mr Wriggly from view. He was uncertain about what his next move should be and finding it confusing that we had a man in the equation now too.

Halfway through shutting the door, Victoria glanced up at Big Ben. I think her intention was to thank him, but she froze to the spot like someone who had just seen a ghost.

'Buck?' she questioned. 'Buck Wild?'

My right eyebrow shot for the ceiling.

'Buck Wild?' I echoed Victoria's words.

Big Ben looked at my semi-naked roommate for the first time, his brow wrinkling for a second.

'Oh, holy cow! Victoria, um hey, doll,' he replied, looking a little off balance suddenly. 'Um … how are you?'

'You never called,' she rounded on him, pulling her dress up to cover her boobs. 'You said you would, but you gave me a wrong number and I'm having trouble believing you even gave me your real name. I couldn't find anyone called Buck Wild in the phonebook.'

I blew an exasperated breath that ruffled my lips, cast the duvet to one side, and went to fetch my clothes.

Victoria was in the hallway now poking a finger into Big Ben's chest as he backed away and tried to fight the grin forming on his stupid face.

43

Of course she had slept with him. What woman in England hasn't? Not that it should bother me. I was trying to work out how to get her out of my room when he opened the door, but there was something fundamentally unfair about discovering I had a superfan only to find out she was one of Big Ben's many, many conquests.

Tugging my skin-hugging base layer over my head – we would need layers against the cool autumn air – I attempted to get the grumpy out of my expression before I turned around again.

Big Ben was looking down at Victoria with smouldering intensity. Her ire couldn't fight the power coming from his eyes and she folded into him.

'I'm sorry,' she sighed, laying her head on his chest. 'It's just. No one ever made me feel as special as you did that night.'

Almost a foot taller than her, he had to lean right down to whisper something I couldn't hear.

When he straightened again, Victoria pushed herself away from him and nodded. She smiled up into his deep blue eyes, stood on her tiptoes to kiss his cheek, and turned around again to face me.

I was, at least, dressed now.

'Tonight is not our time, Tempest.' She shot me a sultry smile. 'Perhaps there will be another chance.' I got a wink, and she was gone.

Big Ben turned his head to watch her go, undoubtedly checking out her rump. When her footsteps faded, he turned back to meet my judgmental gaze.

'Is that your usual penis?' he asked. 'Or is it like a compact version because you are travelling?'

I was literally going to kill him.

Crossing the open ground to get to the rough area of the mine proved to be a slog. It undulated mercilessly with deep ruts to turn our ankles or trip us. Where there had been no human activity, the gorse bushes and other hardy plants with evil spikes, had grown to form barriers which proved time consuming and onerous to navigate.

All in all, it took almost twice as long to get into position as I had allowed and much of that was due to our need to move stealthily – we would catch no one if they heard us coming.

There was a rise roughly fifty yards from one face of the mine. It was on the same side as the hole the Fletchers showed me and not far from where Wayne Calder's body was discovered.

It was farther away than I wanted to be from the mine, but that was based on the belief that whoever was behind the murder was somehow involved or invested in the mining activity. If I focused solely on the mine and that first assumption proved wrong, I would waste time looking in the wrong direction.

We settled in to wait. If necessary, we would wait all night, but I doubted that would come to pass. Not tonight, at least. We were here just to get a feel for the land and … well, you never know. Someone might show up and the case could get solved in record time.

An hour later, my hope for a lucky break was fading and cold from the ground was beginning to seep into my bones.

'A beer would be nice,' remarked Big Ben, echoing a thought bouncing around inside my own head.

I expected there to be mineworkers at the pub and that alone made it easy to justify as an alternate venue for this evening's activities. We were out here only on the off chance that something might happen.

Thus far the only people I had spoken to about the case were the Fletchers and they were coming at the case from a very different angle to that which anyone else might take.

Their employees were refusing to work, and I doubted that was a decision they would take lightly. A few might welcome some slack time, but most would be wise enough to fear for their jobs and the livelihood of the mine if they stayed off for too long.

I shot my cuff to check the time, whispering to Big Ben, 'Let's give it thirty ...' the words stopped dead because we both heard something.

It was an eerie low wailing noise. We both froze, making ourselves as still as possible to better hear the noise when it came again.

Just enough time passed that we both started to question if we had imagined it, but before I could speak, it came again.

I twisted this time, looking away from the mine to the west. Could I see something?

The sound was almost like a whine of whale song, an unearthly noise I could not identify. The light breeze distorted it and made the direction from which it came hard to pinpoint. Big Ben and I were both squinting at the dark landscape, however we both knew the chance of spotting anyone was slim to say the least. If they stopped moving, they would be all but invisible.

There are things that give your location away on the battlefield: shape, shine, silhouette, but the biggest of them will always be movement.

And nothing was moving. Not that we could see.

'We need to move position,' murmured Big Ben. 'We covered lots of dead ground coming in.'

He was right. The land the mine occupied rose and fell like waves on a stormy sea. It would be easy for someone to hide from sight, especially with all the thick bushes around. The ground would distort the noise we had heard too.

We had a general area for which we could head, so that was what we were going to do.

I tensed my muscles, intending to back down the rise we were lying against. We would circle around to avoid silhouetting ourselves, but that was when I saw the glint of moonlight on something shiny.

I grabbed at Big Ben, catching a handful of hair where he was already moving down the rise behind me.

'What?' he questioned, slapping my hand away.

The thing was gone, but I hadn't imagined it and now my pulse was starting to crank up. A noise and now movement. Someone was out here, and I could not come up with one good reason why they would be.

I relayed what I had seen.

Big Ben said, 'Perhaps we should introduce ourselves.'

'It would be rude not to,' I agreed.

Splitting up, but staying no more than a few yards from each other just in case the target was armed – lots of people in the country carry shotguns – we stole across the moonlit terrain.

The eerie noise filtered over the open ground once more, a low wail that sounded like no creature I had ever heard. My breathing was becoming laboured, the effort of keeping low to stay out of sight burning calories fast. Even over my breathing, I could make out the strange noise, and questioned whether I could detect something electronic about it.

Like Hollywood filmmakers trying to recreate the sound of a tyrannosaurus or the sound a mythical animal might make, I believed someone was making the spooky sound to scare people off and had used household appliances to achieve it. This would not be the first time we uncovered a genius level of invention behind a crime.

We covered a hundred yards without seeing anything or anyone. The noise came and went – pinpointing its location continuing to prove problematic, but all that became arbitrary when the hairs on the back of my neck went into overdrive.

I got a nanosecond of warning, a primitive sense built into all of us that a predator was about to leap from the bushes, and I sensed rather than saw or heard someone or something attack.

Already in a crouch, I dropped to the ground and rolled, aiming for a gap between gorse bushes.

Something whooshed through the air behind my head. It was almost silent, the sound my ears caught that of the undergrowth being scythed.

Scrambling, I called to Big Ben.

'We have company!'

I got back, 'I know!' and heard a grunt as he too dove through a bush to get some distance from his assailant.

There was more than one and that was not good news. There was no hope of back up and we were not armed. We faced at least two attackers and that to me instantly suggested Wayne Calder's murder was at the hands of a gang. They were out here in force meant organisation. Organisation meant money and probably equipment.

Had they seen us coming? Did they have night vision equipment? In the hour we had laid on the rise watching the darkness, they could have set up this ambush and lured us into it.

Like saps, we had willingly walked into their trap.

I dug my feet in and reversed direction hard.

The person behind me was giving chase and expecting me to continue running. My change in tactics caught them completely off guard.

In one move I was inside their reach and grabbing for the dark shape. Dark shape was the right term too. I could tell it was a person, but they were shrouded in black – head, eyes, and even hands were covered.

The only thing that reflected any light was the sword coming down to cleave my head in two.

Too close to get away from it if I chose to flee, I grabbed their arms instead. They were still moving forward, unable to check their motion fast enough to avoid colliding with me.

I swept my body around, slamming my hip into where I expected their waist to be. I was going to flip them over and onto their back.

It didn't work out for me, and this was partly because whoever I was fighting knew what they were doing and partly because I underestimated their height by a foot.

My hip hit a ribcage, effectively stopping them dead. It drove the air from a set of lungs in a gasp, but they were already kicking away before I could adjust my grip.

The arm holding the sword whipped from my hands, the fabric covering their skin slick and hard to grip.

Now I was in trouble.

'Stop!' The voice – female and excited – rang through the night.

I had my fists up, not that I was sure what I planned to do with them other than offer them up to be chopped off. Breathing hard, my eyes were focused on my assailant, watching to see what they would do. If they came at me again, I was going to be lucky at this range to avoid getting sliced.

They had stopped moving though and in the split second I had to apply some thought to the matter, a small snippet of detail leaked into my head.

My assailant was a woman.

A foot shorter than me, slight, and nimble, and when I first collided with her, it wasn't a pectoral muscle I shoved against.

The excited female voice spoke again, 'Tempest?'

Dots joined in my head.

'Poison?'

My attacker, still sheathed head to toe in black, swore and tore off her hood. It wasn't Poison, but her cousin Mistress Mushy.

Poison appeared from my right.

'Is everyone okay?' she asked. She wasn't. There was blood coming from her bottom lip and she was holding her jaw. 'What are you doing here?' she wanted to know.

I sagged, dropping my fighting pose.

'I'm on a case, Poison. What are you doing here? I'm guessing Hatchett and Bob are here too.'

'I think I've got Hatchett,' shouted Big Ben. 'Or it might be Bob. Hard to tell in the dark.'

'It's Hatchett,' said Bob, arriving behind Mistress Mushy. 'He's out cold.'

'I only tapped him,' protested Big Ben. 'He was trying to cut my head off.'

'Frank dispatched us to kill something called the Deathling,' explained Mistress Mushy.

Poison, a young Chinese woman I hadn't seen in months, closed the distance between us and put an arm around my neck, pulling me into a brief hug. A little more than a year ago, I sort of saved her life, and there had been a promise to repay me using a traditional method hanging over me for many months afterwards.

I resisted her offer not because she is unattractive – she is anything but – but because at her age of nineteen to my wrong-side-of-thirty-five, I felt uneasy about the liaison. Long story short, she met a boy, I fell in love with Amanda, and we are both content to be around each other now.

The bigger issue now was that Frank – remember the occult bookshop owner I mentioned – employs her and her ninja friends to track supernatural creatures. To my knowledge they are yet to catch or kill any.

Not through lack of trying.

'Frank sent you,' I repeated Poison's words. 'Of course he did. Well, I am confident this is a waste of your time. There is no creature at the end of this hunt. Just a man or men. Or women,' I added quickly remembering my need to be inclusive. Did I need to mention non gender specific roles and sexual preferences? I chose to skip that part.

'That's what you always say,' laughed Poison in a tired way.

'We were tracking something,' revealed Bob. 'And it wasn't human.'

'The spooky wailing noise?' I questioned.

'You heard it too?' asked Mistress Mushy, sliding her katana back into its sheath. 'It didn't sound like a man or a woman to me.'

I gave her a half shrug. We could argue all night without ever agreeing and I had neither the interest nor the energy for that.

Big Ben arrived, helping Hatchett along who was at least now awake and walking. He handed him over to Poison and Bob with a muttered apology.

'He'll be all right,' Big Ben tried to sound certain.

'Who wants donuts?' slurred Hatchett.

'In a little while,' Big Ben added, sounding less sure.

'What did you hit him with?' questioned Mistress Mushy, her tone distinctly displeased.

'Just my fist,' protested my oversized partner. 'He popped up right in front of me. It was an impulse reaction. I only hit him once.'

'Wheeee! Pop goes the weasel!' sang Hatchett like a happy drunk person.

'Okay twice,' Big Ben confessed. 'But that's only because he didn't go down the first time.'

Poison adjusted her stance, getting her shoulder under Hatchett's arm.

'I think we'd better get this one checked out for concussion.'

'I can taste twiglets,' observed Hatchett.

'Yeah. Let's go,' agreed Mistress Mushy.

We got about eight feet.

The yelp from Big Ben startled me. The second yelp from Hatchett when Bob and Mistress Mushy dropped him to go for their swords got me again. Poison was at my side before I could even turn around, her sword catching the moonlight as she held it high in a guard pose.

Big Ben was nowhere to be seen which, given that his head scrapes the clouds if they come too low, was more than a little disconcerting.

Before I could call for him, he swore loudly, and his head popped up between two bushes.

'I tripped over something and fell in a hole,' Big Ben explained, sucking air between his teeth as he rubbed his head.

'That's got to be quite the hole,' commented Poison.

He was in it up to his waist which made it at least three feet deep. We came to stand around the edge, me, Poison, and Mistress Mushy using our torches to see inside.

Big Ben chuckled as he clambered out. 'If there is a hole around, you can bet pretty soon Big Ben is going to fill it.'

I closed my eyes and shook my head while the two ladies shot him disparaging looks.

'This is the one you told me about?' asked Mistress Mushy. 'Thinks he is God's gift to women.'

Paying little attention to them, Big Ben dusted off his trousers.

'Babe, I am God's gift. Some choose to resist accepting it, but only for as long as their will can hold.'

I muttered, 'Good grief,' and got to my knees to inspect the hole.

It was three feet deep and maybe two across. Mostly circular, it didn't look to have occurred naturally, but it also didn't look like someone had dug it. Not recently anyway. There were things growing in it.

'It's an old piece of ordnance,' remarked Big Ben. 'At least I think that's what it is. Second World War. What do you reckon?'

We all shifted our attention to what he was looking at. The thing he had tripped over did indeed look like a fragment of an old bomb's outer casing. We were in the southeast of England, where thousands of German bombing sorties flew in the forties. The bomb, if that was what it was, had landed miles from anywhere worth bombing, but there could be dozens of explanations for its presence.

'Wouldn't a bomb make a bigger hole than that?' questioned Bob.

I was no expert on the subject, but I felt inclined to agree. However, it was hardly a subject we needed to carefully discuss.

The stakeout was a bust. If there had ever been anyone out there, and I was convinced there had been, they were long gone now. We made enough noise to ensure anyone within a mile radius would have heard us.

The eerie whining noise remained an enigma to be solved, but I doubted we were going to get any closer to clearing it up tonight.

It turned out that I was mostly right.

'Watch out fellas, the circus is in town!' cackled a man at the bar as I shoved my way inside.

His laughter caused everyone to turn my way just as Big Ben came through behind me. He had to duck to avoid bumping his head on the doorframe and when he unfolded once more to show off his full six-feet seven-inch height, all the mirth ground to a halt.

Big Ben tends to have that effect.

The man who spoke, swivelled around on his barstool, taking keen interest in his beverage to avoid my friend's emotionless stare.

To be fair, we were wearing black, night-ops Kevlar vests over rip-stop fatigues in a distressed black and grey pattern. Our hands were shod in fingerless tactical gloves with Kevlar knuckles, and we had knee pads and shin guards above our black combat boots.

Both ex-military, we were at home in such clothes, but I understood how some would find our outfits strange or disturbing. The addition of black stripes on our faces undoubtedly tipped the balance, though I would defend our war paint as necessary to keep us hidden.

My original plan for visiting the bar where we expected to find mineworkers was to go in normal civilian clothes. We would mingle, offer to buy drinks, and pick brains over for information.

This method was faster.

I looked about the room to find that I did not need to try to get their attention. Everyone was already staring at me. I spotted Mildred Marchant. She was sitting next to a woman in her late sixties and a heavily tattooed man of about the same age. I spotted Rosie too, and the other ramblers I'd seen earlier.

'We've just come from the mine,' I announced, getting the attention of almost everyone in the room.

The riiiip noise of Velcro straps parting preceded Big Ben pulling off his Kevlar vest. He dumped it on a chair and stretched. I saw why a second later as he waved gamely to the young woman behind the bar.

Rolling my eyes, I walked into the centre of the room.

'My name is Tempest Michaels. I am a paranormal investigator.'

'A what?' chuckled the mouthy man at the bar.

Big Ben chose to stand behind him, his presence enough to quash any further comments.

'The mine owners, Mr Fletcher and his son, want me to find the person responsible for Wayne Calder's murder and ensure justice is served.'

'Person?' echoed three different people.

'It was the Deathling, you fool,' scoffed a plump woman in her sixties from her chair across the room. 'Everyone knows that.'

'Aye, everyone who's from around 'ere,' echoed another voice, this time a man with big bushy grey sideburns peeking out from under his flat cap.

This was as I expected it. I carried on as if no one had spoken.

'My success rate with such cases is one hundred percent,' I stated boldly. 'One of your own was killed, but it was not at the hands of a monster, but a man. You can scoff if you wish, and refuse to help me, yet I believe it is in your own interests to …'

'He wasn't one of us,' pointed out the man at the bar before jumping off his bar stool to get away from Big Ben. 'You can both get stuffed.'

Big Ben hadn't moved and wouldn't have done anything to the man. It is one thing to defend oneself with vigour and another entirely to start a bar fight. Dressed as we were, we would be in a jail cell before we knew it.

'Ye'll get no help from us,' spat the man with the bushy grey sideburns. A chorus of agreement swept around the bar.

We had been in the room for ninety seconds and I was still looking around. It occurred to me though, that I didn't see anyone who looked likely to be working at the mine. It wasn't that they were the wrong age – there was a mix of ages present from early twenties up to an old lady in one corner who had to be in her late eighties if she was a day.

It was the demeanour that itched away at my skull. If there were men here, or women, who worked at the mine, they would be clumped in groups. A gaggle of young men here, a table of husbands and wives who knew each other through mutual years at the same firm over there.

I wasn't seeing that at all, and none of them wanted to help me.

'Who here works at the mine?' I asked.

Two minutes ago, I would have been willing to bet more than half the pub's clientele would be employed at the large enterprise less than a mile away. Now I got to see how vastly wrong that assumption had been.

Not one hand went into the air.

It reminded me of a scene from a film where two tourists drop into the wrong bar one evening and end up getting chewed up by a werewolf because the locals scare them into going outside.

Malignant was the correct word to describe the stares coming back at me as I slowly rotated on the spot and met as many eyes as I could.

I nodded to myself.

'My apologies, ladies and gentlemen. It would appear I have addressed my concerns to the wrong crowd.'

'That's right. You have,' agreed the gobby man who then shot another glance at Big Ben to make sure the giant wasn't about to do anything. 'You should hop it.'

I met him with a hard glare of my own and held it until he looked away. I am not a fan of being intimidated – not by anyone or anything.

Addressing the small crowd, whose attention was solely on me, I said, 'I apologise once again for disturbing your evening. I shall adjourn to the bar and trouble you no more.'

'You'll not get served in here,' advised a short, balding man in his forties. He had an impressive pot belly sitting on the belt of his jeans and skinny arms like noodles. I hadn't seen him before, but his position behind the bar and air of authority convinced me he was tonight's bar manager.

Regardless of his position, we were not going to get served.

Big Ben complained. 'I'm not with him. Can I get a pint of lager?'

'You too,' insisted the short man with the pot belly. 'We don't want your kind in here.'

'Our kind?' questioned Big Ben, his voice incredulous. 'You don't want really, really, ridiculously good-looking men in your establishment. I mean, I get it,' he winked at the barmaid who smiled until she saw everyone frowning at her, 'I wouldn't want someone like me around to make you all look bad, but seriously, someone has to step up to satisfy the women of this little hamlet. Who else is going to do it?' He looked around the bar, challenging any of the men to raise their hands.

Big Ben wasn't helping our situation, but it was not his intention to do so. They were stopping him from getting a refreshing drink and he wanted someone to start a fight so he could end it.

No one was that daft.

The behaviour of the locals was beyond odd. I had never witnessed nor heard of anything like it. Miles from the nearest town, stuck out in the countryside, it was almost as if a joint psychosis had overcome them all.

They were acting as if they all believed in the Deathling. I moved toward the door, aiming to head back outside into the carpark rather than through the side door which would take me to the accommodation part of the Inn. If I didn't recognise the people behind the bar, I doubted they knew I was staying upstairs.

You might think seeking alternative accommodation might be prudent, but I wasn't going anywhere. I deal in the weird every day, and this crowd had just swung the meter all the way to its stop.

A quick bit of mental arithmetic added up all the people in the room – if they all lived within the boundary of Playford, then I was looking at more than eighty percent of the inhabitants. Assuming the rest were children too young to be out at this time and I was facing every resident of the hamlet.

That too, was weird.

Outside in the carpark, Big Ben folded his arms and looked back through the window to the locals still sitting inside the bar.

'That was weird, right?' he asked.

I nodded, still trying to piece bits together in my head. 'Yes, it truly was.'

'Weirder than normal, I mean,' Big Ben added for clarity. 'What do we do now?'

It was a question worthy of an answer. I was peckish but had food in my room; emergency rations I always carry for such occasions. Dinner had been light in case we needed to do running and stuff on our stakeout, and like Big Ben I was also quite interested in having a couple of drinks.

Ultimately, I chose the sensible option.

'I'm going to hit the sack, Ben. I have a feeling tomorrow might be just as full of surprises.'

I could not have known how accurate that predication would turn out to be.

I awoke as planned long before the sun came up. Getting a jump on the day by being up before other people was a trick I learned long ago. It suited me, and I got to get my exercise in early today while combining it with exploring the area a little farther.

I'll admit a brief moment of panic as I remembered Victoria letting herself into my room the previous evening and lifted my head to check my surroundings. The chair she'd been in and the room in general were devoid of life. Convinced I was alone, I relaxed.

I rolled out of bed and onto the carpet where I performed fifty good press ups. My muscles only started to tire when I reached the high forties. Once they were done, I sprung up onto my feet to find my running gear.

Outside the air was cold, though not bitterly so. I set off, pounding out the first mile at a sedate pace to let my breathing even out. Though the terrain around the mine was undulating, the road running through Playford was almost completely flat. I ran in one direction until I was out of the hamlet, then turned around and came back on myself to cross the hamlet and leave it again.

Playford was nothing more than a small collection of houses built around a pub. There was a small church with a graveyard to the western edge of the settlement. Centuries ago, when it came into existence, the residents would have been farmers, or worked for a farmer. This was arable land and there were crops and livestock on it even now.

Except for the land the mine owned. Was there something in that? The land around the mine didn't look like it had ever been fields of barley or grazing pasture for cows. An answer would be obtainable if I thought pursuing it were justified.

I ran on, the sky showing no sign of lightening yet, and I thought about the strange behaviour of the residents last night. They said the mineworkers didn't go in there, which seemed odd. What landlord turns away business? With a busy operation like that right on his doorstep, he ought to be doing all he can to bring them in as regulars. That no one in the tiny hamlet worked at the mine was odd too.

Was it just coincidence?

I arrived back at the inn out of breath after running as close to flat out as I could manage for the last ten minutes. Panting and sweating despite the cold air, I put my hands behind my head and walked about sucking in deep lungfuls of oxygen.

Forty-five minutes had elapsed, but the quiet time to reflect on the previous day had given me nothing but more questions.

Regaining my breath, I tugged at the hem of my long-sleeved top and went inside. I wasn't being particularly observant that morning and should have looked around at the cars in the carpark. However, had I done so I might have started running again and not stopped until I got home.

Showered and dressed, I used my laptop to log into work. Breakfast at the inn was served from 0800hrs which gave me more than half an hour to kill.

There were email enquiries from potential new clients – just sifting those and answering the worthwhile ones used to eat up hours of my day, every day of the week. Now, thanks to Marjory, I never read them at all.

I skimmed over the emails to see if anything stood out, checked my personal inbox as well as the business one which we all had access to, and checked to see if Jane had been up to much.

I spoke with Amanda before bed last night as is our custom. It's not always possible – cases and life get in the way – but since we don't live together, a subject I have tentatively skirted around but not yet been brave enough to tackle, we make a point of saying goodnight over the phone.

She was still going with the gargoyle case and had snuck back into the stately home to spy on the staff at night. She was still there now no doubt unless she had caught those responsible and gone home. I had no message from her to suggest that might be the case, so I doubted it was.

Jane had wowed us all yesterday with a case at Buckingham Palace the previous evening – it's not every day a person gets invited to visit one of the most famous buildings on the planet. More than the location, Jane's report of events was what got our attention.

Because there was no report.

All she could tell us was that she had signed a non-disclosure agreement regarding the events and couldn't talk about them. Amanda and I both understood, but it made Jane's adventure in London all the more intriguing.

What she didn't know was that Amanda and I already knew it was something to do with a dragon. She refused to reveal what the case had been about and mimed zipping her lips shut when we pressed her to at least say what the nature of the supernatural creature had been.

Jane had written the word 'dragon' on the chart in my office where we keep a tally of who has gone up against what kind of supernatural beast. It is just a bit of fun, but she hadn't thought to erase that piece of evidence and it was too late to take it back now.

I suspected we would be able to wear her down and wheedle some information out of her over the coming weeks.

At five to eight, my stomach was rumbling, and I was hurrying to finish my current task so I could get to breakfast. There were people in the hall outside, another person or persons making their way to breakfast no doubt. It wasn't Big Ben; he would have knocked for me and not just walked by. They had a dog or dogs with them though, I could hear something snuffling at the gap under my door.

With a final click on the mousepad, I closed my laptop and put it away. The day beckoned and I needed tea.

I got as far as the entrance to the restaurant before my senses caught up with me and a ball of dread filled my gut. I could hear voices ahead, voices I knew, and one in particular stood out.

Fearing for my safety, I peered around the doorframe into the restaurant, and I swear my blood stopped bothering to circulate my body.

'Mother,' I mumbled, disbelief infecting my jaw and lips to make them feel numb. 'What are you doing here?'

My parents looked up from their papers. Bull and Dozer, my two dachshunds, the two dachshunds I specifically left behind, were straining at the end of their leads, and wagging their tails like mad. I was their human and they were super-pleased to see me.

'Morning, kiddo,' hallooed my father in a gregarious manner.

Mother neatly folded her paper and laid it on the table mat in front of her.

'That was a little rude, Tempest,' she chided me. 'We thought we would surprise you.'

66

'Well, you did that all right,' I muttered.

'Seriously though, what are you doing here? I am in the middle of an investigation.'

Here's the thing with my parents, I love them to bits, but they are like a storm at sea. Fascinating at a distance, but you don't want to see it up close because of the destruction you know it will bring.

My mother sings in the church choir, bakes cakes for local charity sales, and does anything she can to make my life more difficult. Dad bumbles through life, keeping himself entertained by annoying my mother. He likes to grow things in the garden, challenge himself with difficult bakes, and get himself into trouble if the slightest chance presents itself.

My mother's brow creased; she was giving me her unruly child frown. As kids it was generally reserved for my sister and rarely deployed on me. Actually, I think my dad got it more often than I did back then.

'We have friends in Rye, Tempest. I thought you would be staying,' she looked around to make sure none of the inn staff were within earshot, 'somewhere nicer. Hearing you were in this neck of the woods, we decided to have a couple of nights away and will be visiting Ellie and Duncan, you remember them.'

'Um, no, I do not.' I truly didn't.

'Oh, Tempest, of course you do. We visited their house several times when you were little.'

'When I was little,' I echoed her words. 'Three decades ago, when my attention span was that of a gnat.'

Grumpily, my mother elected to ignore that I might have a point. 'Well, we are going to have lunch with them and then I thought you could join us for dinner at their house tonight. They know you are a criminal, Tempest, but have agreed to let you into their house anyway.'

I rolled my eyes and tried to keep my rising ire under control.

That I got sent to jail a few months ago for punching a police officer was a source of great amusement for my father and most of my friends. My mother crossed herself twenty times a day and took every opportunity to remind me what a disappointment I was.

Trust me when I claim the police officer in question was well overdue a fist to the face.

I had crossed the room to get to my dogs and given them both a thorough fussing. They were sweet little hounds and demanded very little from me. Leaving them now, and certain they would curl up under the table, I pulled out a spare chair at their table to join my parents.

'Thank you, Mother. I feel, however, that I must repeat my earlier point because I am here to conduct an investigation.'

'You have to eat, Tempest,' snapped my mother, quick to employ irritation as a tactic to bend me to her will. It might have worked three decades ago, but we were long past that now.

'I have to solve a murder case, Mother. That is what I must do. Everything else is secondary.'

The sound of footsteps behind me heralded Big Ben's arrival. Unlike me, he wasn't despondent about seeing my parents. For him this was an opportunity to wind me up.

'Brother Grey Fox!' he called to my father, crossing the room to give my dad a fist bump.

My mother made a point of shuddering and then crossed herself. She hated that my father was an honorary member of a motorcycle gang. It happened almost a year ago, right before Christmas last year when we were trying to solve a case in Herne Bay.

Mum had abandoned dad to attend a Cliff Richard concert with some friends from the church. At a loose end, dad elected to move in with me for the weekend and … well, let's just say things got a touch more adventurous than I intended and mother hadn't let dad out of her sight since.

Dad and Big Ben performed a complicated handshake only just getting through the routine before my mother insisted they stop.

'Won't you join us, please?' I invited my colleague.

Percy the landlord appeared.

'Good morning, good morning,' he welcomed us in a flustered manner. 'Can I get you all started with some hot beverages?'

My phone rang just as my mother twisted in her chair to recite her order. She twisted back to look over the top of her glasses at me.

'Not at the table, Tempest.' She liked to pretend I was still six years old.

I happened to agree in principle with her desire to keep devices out of family time. However, my phone was out, and the name displayed, now flashing insistently on my screen, was that of my current client.

I was going to answer the phone no matter what my mother's thoughts on the matter.

'Mr Fletcher, good morning,' I answered the phone in a calm, professional manner.

'Tempest!' blurted Stefan. 'There's been another murder!'

I was out of my chair and moving before he finished the word 'murder'. I knew a second death was not a failing on my part, but it felt like it anyway.

Seeing me get to my feet, my mother cried, 'Tempest! You haven't had your breakfast yet.'

I grabbed a banana from a fruit bowl set out on a table by the door.

'This will suffice.'

Big Ben muttered several unprintable words under his breath, apologised to my mother, and got to his feet too.

Third to move was my father. 'Duty calls,' he claimed, intending to follow me and Big Ben.

Mum grabbed his arm. 'Sit down, Michael Michaels. There has been quite enough galivanting from you, thank you very much. No more adventures.'

'But, darling, I'm Brother Grey Fox,' he protested as if that would make a difference.

It was time to escape, not least because dad would attempt to sway mum's opinion by involving me if I didn't make myself scarce. However, changing my mind about one factor, I went back for my dogs. They could do with some exercise, and this was the perfect opportunity.

My parents were bickering – they often did though it was mostly good-natured – and I left them to it.

Percy the landlord hovered just outside the dining room. The expectant look on his face made it clear he hoped to catch a word before we left.

I flipped my eyebrows at him, encouraging him to speak while I sorted out the dogs who had managed to tie their leads in a knot.

'Um,' Percy mumbled. 'I heard about what happened in the bar last night. I want to be clear that I do not endorse the behaviour of my bar manager and will be having stern words with him later today.'

I waved him off, dismissing the conversation with a gesture. It had been annoying at the time – Big Ben and I were thirsty and wanted a cold pint – but it had also been informative. The residents of this little hamlet were not only acting odd, they were behaving in a uniform manner. They were all of one opinion and that was as rare as hen's teeth in my experience.

When did you last get three people together and find they could agree on what to eat for dinner? Now multiply that by the residents of a small village. They all believed in the Deathling?

No chance.

'Will it happen again?' I asked.

'I shall ensure that it does not, sir.'

I nodded, plopping Bull back on the floor now that I had finished using him as the needle to unweave the tangled leads.

'Thank you. I am guessing that you are not considered to be a local.'

Percy almost choked – my assumption was amusing to him.

'Goodness, no. I have only lived here all my life. My parents moved in when I was eighteen months old and since none of us were born here, we are still newcomers.'

'What about your children?' Big Ben enquired, trying to wrap his head around the insular behaviour Percy described.

'My daughter wasn't born here either,' he told us. 'I moved down to Rye when I was in my twenties and married a woman I met there. My parents came here to run this place and left it to me, but I wouldn't live in the village. They are an odd bunch.'

That covered the why of his attitude toward me when compared to the residents of Playford, but I was still curious about their shared belief in a supernatural creature.

'Now that I cannot explain,' the landlord admitted. 'I had never heard of the Deathling until a few days ago. When that first poor man was found dead at the mine ...' Percy's eyes took on a faraway look, rolling upward and slightly left as he engaged the memory portion of his brain. 'No, wait a minute. It started before that.'

'What did?' asked Big Ben.

'Talk of the Deathling. I remember it now. There was a conversation in here about a week ago. That was when I first heard them talking about it.'

I pressed him for more, 'What were they saying?'

Percy made a snorting noise of amusement again. 'Not much and they shut up as soon as I asked about it. They know me – I've lived or worked here all my life, like I said, but they still see me as an outsider. Irene - she's one of the eldest and kind of a matriarch around here - she told me the

Deathling was back, and I should be sure to run to my car when I left for the night.'

'Because it might be behind you!' quipped Big Ben in a spooky voice.

Percy smiled at him. 'Yeah. Only, none of them seem to be worried about walking home from the pub at night in the dark. If this thing is out there and they believe it will kill again, why aren't they afraid?'

I had an answer to that question but chose to keep it to myself for now.

Percy needed to get back to his work - my mother would start yelling soon if she didn't get any tea. Big Ben and I were just going to have to manage without.

Shoving the door open with a stiff arm, I directed the dogs to Big Ben's oversized, tricked out, utility vehicle.

Before we could get to the car, my phone started ringing again.

A Second Death. Saturday, October 14th 0831hrs

The call was from Stefan Fletcher again.

'Are you on your way?' he asked, sounding desperate. 'It would be really good if you could beat the police here,' he urged.

Big Ben was driving, his right foot heavy on the pedal but not to the point that we were going to win any races.

'Beat the police? Why?' I asked, shuffling Dozer around a little so he wouldn't slip off the side of my lap. He and Bull got plonked on the back seat, but by the time I had shut their door and opened mine, they were on the passenger seat in the front and wagging their tails expectantly.

Now they were trying to go to sleep on my lap and making grumpy noises because my legs are not big enough for the pair of them.

Stefan didn't reply for a moment and when he did, I thought I was going to have to demand he spit out what he needed to say.

'Well, um, it's ... we've had a look at who the victim is. The guards didn't know, you see. They are all from Rye and not familiar with the locals.'

'Who is it?' I prompted.

'Mildred Marchant.'

The answer echoed in my ear, and I understood why he wanted me to get there before the police – he was panicking.

Mildred twisted Stefan's words yesterday; he didn't intend to threaten her. If anything, he was imploring her to stay away for her own safety, but that was not how she treated it. She made out that he wanted to kill her and did so loudly in front of witnesses.

Less than twenty-four hours later, she is not only dead, but her body is found on Stefan's land.

At the gate, we were waved through by the guard who swung it shut again, jogging with it as if he were trying to stop someone slipping through.

I checked over my shoulder – there was nothing behind us.

Big Ben drove on, his chunky tyres gripping the dirt and trampling the low-lying foliage though he steered around the larger bushes.

He stopped at one point, leaning forward to peer through his windscreen.

'There's another hole.' He pointed.

We were well away from the mine itself and the massive mine vehicles and machines there. Directed by the guards to follow the fence line, we were in open ground and near nothing else at all.

Curious, I motioned for Big Ben to stop when he turned his wheel to go around it.

Getting out, the dachshunds waking suddenly when I grabbed the door handle, I said, 'I want to have a look.'

The hole was smaller than the last one, but just like the pit Big Ben fell into last night, there was an object lying next to it.

Soil from the hole formed a mound to one side. Small bushes grew on it, and one grew through it, proving my belief that I was looking at spoil removed from the ground. The hole itself had less flora than the surrounding area, and less than the one we found last night.

'This one is more recent,' observed Big Ben.

The dachshunds sniffed about at the extent of their leads, picking bushes that required 'watering' before moving on to sniff something else.

Big Ben and I poked about in the undergrowth until my toes stubbed against something that was decidedly more solid than a patch of heather.

Nudging it out with my boot didn't work, so I trapped the dogs' lead under my left foot and dug into the soft sandy earth with my fingers.

What I pulled out were three shell casings. Big ones.

Big Ben skewed his lips to one side, catching one when I tossed it to him.

'Anti-aircraft gun?' he guessed.

I shrugged, looking up at the sky and all around. The vast open countryside could easily have been the scene of aerial dogfights eighty years ago.

'Someone is out here metal detecting,' I spoke the conclusion we had both reached.

Big Ben commented, 'Odd pastime if you ask me.'

I was with him though I would never voice my opinion in public. If I thought I might detect some buried treasure or if I lived somewhere in the world where gold might be found, the hobby might be more alluring, but spending hours waving a metal detector over the ground to then dig up a rusty nail? That didn't appeal at all.

Then it hit me.

'That's what we could hear last night.'

I got a, 'Hmmm?' and a raised eyebrow from Big Ben.

'The eerie low wailing sound drifting in on the breeze. That was someone out here metal detecting,' I nodded my head as I talked, convincing myself as I went along.

'At night?' Big Ben questioned. 'How would they ever find anything? And they didn't have a torch with them,' he pointed out. 'From where we were, we could see miles. If there was anyone out there with anything brighter than a tactical light, we would have seen it instantly.'

He was not wrong.

That someone was on the land owned by the mine late at night, in the dark, and trying to avoid being detected – that is what I took the lack of light to be for – bothered me. Two deaths, both on mine land, an entire village convinced a murderous supernatural creature was on the loose, and now someone detecting on the same bit of land and trying not to get caught doing it.

I couldn't add it up yet, but as mysteries go, this was turning into a doozey.

'Come on,' I started back to the car. 'That's the police coming in.'

More than half a mile away, right back at the gate, the tiny dot of a car now snaking along the same fence line behind us was clearly a squad car. We had beaten it here by a few minutes but then stopped to inspect what I suspected might be a clue.

I had to hold the sausage dogs to my chest as Big Ben drove faster than was probably safe to get us to the scene of the crime as quickly as possible.

There were four men there; two of the mine's security guards and the Fletchers. Their faces were grim.

We parked twenty yards short of where they were standing, and next to the two vehicles they had come out in.

Leaving my dogs in the car to snooze, I made my way over to the body. It was exposed though Colin held a blanket in his hands.

'I wanted to cover her over,' he explained, his voice sounding like an apology. 'But the police said not to when we called them.'

'They want to preserve evidence,' I nodded my understanding. 'Fibres on the blanket could transfer to the body. Have you touched her?' I asked.

'Only to confirm that she is dead,' Stefan promised me, his tone solemn. 'What would she have been doing out here at night?' he wanted to know though it was, of course, a rhetorical question.

Just before I went to the body, I paused to ask Stefan a question.

'Do you know of anyone doing metal detection on your land?'

He cocked an eyebrow. So too his son, Colin.

'I can't imagine why anyone would want to do that,' Stefan remarked. 'There can't be anything of value out here, but they might find plenty of junk.'

It was the answer I expected; whoever was metal detecting at night was doing it so no one would know. Accepting my client's answer, I turned away to focus on the victim.

Going closer, I looked about at the ground and at how the body was lying.

Mildred might have been full of life yesterday on the two occasions I saw her, but there was no trace of it now. Her eyes were open and staring, though the images they recorded were going nowhere. In her

79

mouth, a chunk of rock – gypsum I assumed – had been shoved in to force her jaw open. There were bruises on her neck, dark and disturbing, the obvious signs of strangulation.

What we had was a vanilla murder. No one had dressed this up to make it look like there was a monster on the loose. Wayne Calder had been mutilated and sucked dry, his body missing for three days during the desiccation process.

The killer had changed their method, or it was a different killer. These were obvious conclusions to draw. Neither thing helped me.

A glance in their direction showed me the off-road police car cruising to a stop by the other cars. They would usher me away from the body the moment they stepped out of the car, and I could already see their faces eyeing me sternly through the windscreen.

I stepped back, making my intentions clear, but spotted a piece of paper poking from Mildred's coat pocket. Knowing I would have to be quick, I darted forward to pluck it free.

'Hey!' yelled one of the cops, a detective by the look of him. His suit was sharp to match his young age – an older detective would have given up trying to impress his superiors by looking great – and he was hurrying in my direction. 'Put that down.'

'Sure thing,' I replied, turning to face the victim so my hands were hidden by my body. I took a photograph with my phone, slipped it back into my jacket and placed the piece of paper back in Mildred's pocket.

'Step away from the body, sir,' the detective insisted.

I complied, feigning the hand putting my phone back inside my jacket was there to withdraw a business card which I then offered him.

'I know who you are, sir,' the man said, taking the card anyway and tucking it away without looking at it.

I offered him my hand to shake. 'Tempest Michaels,' I introduced myself even though he claimed to know who I was.

He gripped my hand, unwilling to be rude though it was obvious he wanted me to go away.

'Detective Sergeant Reed.'

His uniformed officer was getting things from the load bed of his squad car: steel rods and tape to create a physical barrier around the body. The medical examiner would be along soon, and the coroner's wagon. Then a crime scene team would appear. The barrier would help to keep people back though there would be a tent over the body soon enough.

'I don't think she was killed here,' I stated boldly. You might question why I would share information when I was being paid to investigate, but the thing is I get paid anyway. That Mildred had more likely been killed elsewhere and carried to this spot was obvious to anyone. She was right next to a rambling route, but I didn't believe for one minute she left the pub and went for a nice countryside walk last night. The state of rigor, even to my untrained eye, suggested she was killed last night and not this morning.

It could be the case that someone had lured her to the mine, but I would bet good money her killer attacked her close to home and brought her here. She was still wearing the same clothes I saw her in last night.

Without looking my way, the detective said, 'Please rejoin the others, Mr Michaels. I am aware of your interest and the rubbish the locals are spewing about some creature. However, this is a police investigation, and I cannot allow your participation.'

81

Arguing wasn't going to get me anywhere, and I had already seen all there was to see. Getting my hands on the autopsy report might be handy but it wasn't going to happen so there was little point giving it any thought.

'What? That's it?' asked Stefan, looking concerned as I walked back toward him. 'Can't you do something to stop them?'

I found myself chewing on my bottom lip and tilting my head to one side a touch as I tried to fathom what Mr Fletcher senior was asking me.

'Surely, you do not believe that I have the authority to impede the police in a murder investigation, Mr Fletcher?'

He threw his hands in the air. 'What the devil did I hire you for then?'

'To identify Wayne Calder's killer and get your miners back to work. That is what you hired me for,' I pointed out. 'Regardless of that, I am a private investigator not the authorities. When faced with a dead body, the first thing I do is call the police.'

'Unless the killer is still around,' Big Ben pointed out unhelpfully.

Stefan continued to fume. For some reason he had convinced himself I could push the police away and investigate in lieu of them rather than alongside.

'I told you before, Dad, we don't need him,' argued Colin. 'He's just taking your money to investigate something the police will solve anyway.' Colin's attitude was not all that unusual, and I rarely bother to fight it.

I made an exception today.

'The police will investigate, Stefan, but they will not be looking at the hole in the face of the mine or attempting to find out who made it.'

Turning my attention to Colin, I said, 'I believe your father is right to suspect the locals' involvement. Someone killed Wayne Calder and then went to a great deal of trouble to make it look like the work of a supernatural creature.'

'It's all just nonsense, Dad,' Colin replied angrily, his eyes locked on mine. 'Don't let him baffle you with his rubbish. Kick him off the case before you waste any more money.'

'No, son,' Stefan shook his head slowly back and forth. 'I want to know what happened to Wayne. The villagers are behind it – that mad bunch from Playford. They'll be behind Mildred's death too, putting her on my land to make me look guilty.'

'Why would someone do that, sir?' asked the detective. He'd been keeping quiet and listening intently.

I held up a hand to stop Stefan speaking so that I could get my advice in first – I have history with the police.

'Tell him the truth, Mr Fletcher. Leave nothing out. It will do you no favours for your ill-timed and poorly chosen words to be revealed by someone else. Especially if the killer chose to target Mildred now because of what you said.'

'What did you say, sir?' asked the detective, keen to hear something that might get his investigation started.

I was going to get nothing much else achieved by waiting around at the site of the second murder, so when Stefan Fletcher took my advice and turned to face Detective Sergeant Reed, I backed away, effectively removing myself from the conversation.

The nature of the second murder troubled me. It was so dissimilar to the first that the possibility of a second killer presented itself as an immediate option. It was that or the killer was smarter than any I had come up against before.

I gave the victim a last look as I turned to go. If the police wanted to talk to me, or get a statement, they would find me easily enough, but there was no shout for me to wait as I made my way back to Big Ben's car.

Behind me, DS Reed was already interrogating Stefan.

'Can you account for your movements last night, sir?

When Colin answered for his father, I stopped walking to hear what he had to say.

'We were both at a theatre in the West End. I've still got the ticket stubs, I think.' Colin rooted around in his coat to find his wallet, producing something I could not see from my angle, but which proved sufficient to satisfy the detective.

'Yes, that's right,' agreed Stefan.

'We left at four o'clock,' Colin explained, speaking for his father once more. 'The train takes over an hour and we wanted to get some food first. We didn't get home until well after midnight.' Colin concluded.

If DS Reed was looking for a suspect, he was going to have to broaden his search – Stefan had an alibi. Colin too for that matter.

I didn't feel I needed to listen to any more of the detective's questions – time was ticking away, and I wasn't going to figure anything out by standing around out here. Getting farther away, the breeze blowing over the open ground began to steal their conversation and the last thing I heard was Stefan yet again accusing the locals of trying to ruin him.

Was it all a big conspiracy to shut down the mine? After seeing the way the locals acted in the bar last night, I could not put it past them. Were they all guilty?

Back at the gates of the mine, the guards were having a tough time.

Showing their solidarity once again, the local residents of Playford – I recognised every last one of them from the bar last night – were shouting and protesting and trying to get into the mine.

'Your boss is a murderer!' spat a woman in her sixties. She had been vocal the previous evening when she argued against my claim Wayne had been killed by a person and not a monster.

The gobby man from last night was also there, and was the first to spot that it was me and Big Ben in the car now approaching the gates from the inside.

He pointed us out, the news travelling through the crowd swiftly.

Eggs appeared.

Someone at the back of the crowd launched one high into the air. It landed with an eggy splat on Big Ben's windscreen right in front of his face.

'I say,' he remarked, turning on his washers and wipers to remove the sticky gunk.

Another landed, and then another.

A guard protested, shouting an instruction to stop. It did him no favours, the eggs instantly finding a new target and the egger – if that is a term I can employ – found friends. One egg thrower became three or maybe five in an instant.

They would run out of eggs soon enough, but not before they coated the guards.

'Should we try to rescue them?' asked Big Ben.

I didn't need to think about my response. 'Stuff that!'

The loud 'Whoooo!' noise of a police siren filled the air and stilled the arms of those throwing eggs. It also temporarily hushed the voices demanding to be let in.

I grabbed my door handle.

'This might be interesting. Come on,' I invited Big Ben to come with me. The locals blocked our exit but through them I could see a crime scene van and an unmarked police car. My guess was the second murder in just a couple of days had attracted someone further up the food chain than DS Reed. I was curious to not only see who that was, but also to hear what he had to say to the residents of Playford.

Clearly he'd had dealings with them before, because he was addressing them by name the moment he got his feet on the soil.

'Irene, this is not legal. You cannot blockade the entrance to a business. I see those eggs behind your back Vincent McGrath. Throw another one and I will arrest you myself.'

On our side of the barrier, two guards were dripping with egg and looked downright displeased with their situation.

'They're all mad!' one shouted to be heard. 'They want to lynch Mr Fletcher. They think he killed that stupid woman who keeps cutting our fences.'

'He threatened to kill her yesterday!' cried a woman from the crowd of villagers, more than one voice backing up her claim. 'We heard him and now she is dead!'

When someone shifted, I saw who had spoken. It was the mousey woman from the group of ramblers. If I heard her name yesterday, I could not recall it now, but she had to be behind the lynch mob forming.

The police officer, a man in his late forties with a trim beard and a receding hairline, advanced across the ground to mingle with the locals. I assessed that he knew them well because he ignored most of the crowd, passing between them to find the ringleaders. One was the matriarch who chose to voice her opinion on the Deathling last night. I was able to pick her out now as Irene.

'I can assure you,' the police officer spun slowly around to meet as many pairs of eyes as possible, 'that whoever is responsible for Mildred Marchant's death, will be caught. They will be brought to justice and punished.' He then raised his voice. 'However, there will be no taking of matters into your own hands. There will be no attempts to get onto mine land to serve justice on your part.'

His voice was commanding and for once the locals were not arguing.

'Now, it is time for you all to disperse. Your cows will not milk themselves, Alfred.'

'Ha! I milked them hours ago,' cackled an unseen voice.

'Your shop is not being tended, Sarah,' the police officer continued making his point. 'Go back to your lives and leave this investigation to the police.'

The locals griped and muttered, but ultimately, they obeyed. As a crowd, once the first few started moving, they turned around and started back down the road away from the mine.

What stood out for me more than anything else was that none of them believed the Deathling was behind Mildred's murder. It further reinforced my belief that a second killer had struck. Perhaps taking advantage of the first death, the second killer chose to murder Mildred Marchant, dumping her on mine land to make it look like Stefan Fletcher might be behind it.

Watching the crowd walk away, the name of the mousey woman came back to me: Rosie. When Mildred talked down to her yesterday, Rosie glared at the back of Mildred's head, and I saw murder in her eyes.

Well, maybe not murder. Something though. I guess my point is that I could see other possible suspects for the second murder. It was the first death I was here to solve though, and whether they intended to or not, the residents of Playford were making me want to believe they were behind the Deathling.

They knew about it, they were promoting it as the only possible answer for Wayne Calder's death, and now they were ignoring any possibility that it could be responsible for killing Mildred too.

Was that because they had killed Wayne but not Mildred? It would explain their certainty.

A cold chill ran up my spine. If I was right, then the entire population of the hamlet in which I was currently residing were murderers. I had no idea what might motivate them to kill, but it was a scary proposition because the first kill is always the hardest.

I wasn't buying that they would kill to get the mine shut down. They might truly believe it was harming the local ecology – I remembered the beetle – but was that a good enough reason to bring together an entire community and have them vote to start killing people?

I couldn't convince myself and that meant their end game was something else.

The thought process that might lead me to an answer got paused because the police officer was coming through the gate and making a beeline for Big Ben's car.

I handed the dogs to Big Ben, who chose to wait in the car – he didn't like talking to police officers unless they were female ones – and stepped out to meet the man coming my way.

He held out his hand to be shaken and met me with a smile.

'Tempest Michaels.' Just like DS Reed, he knew my name, 'I suppose I should not be surprised to find you here. Spooky goings on and all.'

'You have the advantage,' I nodded, pointing out that he had not given me his name.

He chuckled, letting my hand go. 'Chief Inspector Kirkland. I'm glad I got to shake your hand, actually.'

I felt my eyebrows pinch together. 'Oh, and why is that?'

'For punching Ian Quinn, of course,' he replied with a laugh. 'You would not believe the queue of people wanting that pleasure. I recorded it from the television, took a bunch of still frames of it, and have them on the wall in my toilet at home. It is a fun talking point whenever I have someone new come to visit.'

It came as no great shock that my old adversary, Chief Inspector Quinn, was unpopular among his peers. I loathed the man and had been pleased to take the case in East Sussex because it guaranteed I would not run into him.

Since I had Chief Inspector Kirkland's attention, I pushed my luck.

'What's your take on the events here? Could someone in the village be behind Wayne Calder's death and now this one? The local residents claim there is a supernatural beast to blame.'

I got a quizzical look in response.

'Someone from the village? You think those uneducated idiots could mastermind something like this?'

'Are they uneducated?' I challenged. 'How is it that you know them so well?'

DI Kirkland looked uncomfortable.

'I had cause to conduct police business here several times when I was a younger man. There are so few locals, it does not take long to learn a few names.'

I had to acknowledge his point. Memorising names upon first hearing them was a skill I taught myself a long time ago. Okay, it took me a moment to dredge Rosie's name from the back of my head, but I'd thought of her as a minor player at the time.

'Did Mildred Marchant have any enemies?' I asked, knowing that now I was really pushing my luck.

I got a smile from the detective.

'Now then, Mr Michaels, where would we be if I were to start sharing information with you? I wish you luck in attempting to decipher the Deathling case, but I have two murders to solve.' He stuck his hand out again. 'Good luck.'

I shook it, wishing him the same and we went in different directions. He ducked back into his car to head deeper into the land around the mine. He was heading for Mildred's body.

Going in the opposite direction, we were leaving the mine, the egg-covered guards opening the barrier to let us out.

'What was on the note?' Big Ben asked.

I took out my phone to look at the picture. 'You saw that, did you?'

'Yup.'

The note was a list of names, my eyes skimming over them in the half second when I got to look at it. I was hoping there might be something else on the piece of crumpled paper in Mildred's pocket, but there wasn't.

'It appears to be a team list for a quiz night at the pub,' I observed.

Big Ben cut his eyes across the car to see it too.

'Not a clue then,' he remarked. 'Just a piece of paper in her pocket.'

I didn't respond right away; I was reading down the list of names. Grouped into fours, it appeared to have almost everyone in the village. Again, I was making assumptions about the number of residents and discounting children. Certainly, there were roughly as many names as I had seen in the pub the previous night.

'Darius Cooper,' I read the name out loud.

Big Ben glanced again. 'Is that someone I should know?'

I shook my head. 'He made a big thing about a rare beetle a year ago, got the endangered species people involved and they shut down the mine for a while. It turned out there was no beetle. At least, no one else could find it.'

Big Ben's forehead was scrunched in confusion.

'Is that important?'

I could only purse my lips and frown. 'I don't know. It happened right before the villagers all decided they didn't like the mine.' I stopped talking to make a phone call. When it connected, I had Jane on the other end.

Jane Butterworth is the third detective at the business. She is actually a guy and was a guy when I hired him. Or should that be her? I get quite confused about how to correctly phrase things where he/she is concerned. Jane likes to dress up and pretend to be a woman. I think it's called gender fluid because sometimes he turns up as James. Not so much anymore which I think is down to his current boyfriend's preferences.

Anyway, I didn't think Jane had a case currently and she is a whiz at research.

'Tempest,' she answered her phone. 'How's it going at the mine? Big Ben says you have a saucy superfan. Is that right?'

I shot my head and eyes around to glare at my companion.

He started whistling innocently.

Carefully selecting my words in case they ever got back to Amanda, I said, 'I met a person who expressed some interest in my career, yes.' It was bad enough that Victoria had stalked me to my room and let herself in. Amanda did not need to know about that – it would just create unnecessary friction – and she definitely didn't need to know how attractive Victoria is.

Jane sounded amused when she said, 'That's not how Big Ben put it. I take it you are calling because you need me to do something. I'm just sifting through enquiries to find a new case, but if you need help …'

I sent Jane the picture of the note with the list of names and explained briefly what I hoped she could do for me.

'Sure thing. That won't take long. Anything else?'

I was about to say no, but the word caught in my mouth when a random thought occurred to me.

'Can you look into any major battles that happened in the area of the mine?'

'Battles?' Jane questioned.

I tried to explain a little better, telling her about the holes and the old ordnance we had found.

'It might be nothing,' I scratched my head, wondering if I was giving her a daft task that would waste her time. 'Someone is trying to find something, and it looks like they have been looking for a while if the age of the holes is anything to go by.'

Big Ben spoke up. 'How long would it take for ground level undergrowth to reclaim the dirt in a hole? I don't think it is all that long. A few months maybe.'

I noted his observation.

'It could be that there was a second world war battle here and a plane came down. Spitfires and such are worth a fortune.'

'Okay,' replied Jane, her voice sounding thoughtful. 'I suppose it could be someone looking for the body of their great grandfather or something if he was a second world war pilot.'

'Could be,' I conceded. 'Equally, it could be nothing like that and nothing to do with downed fighter planes. All I know is someone has been on mine land looking for something and I don't think they found it yet.'

'Treasure?' suggested Big Ben, arriving back at the main road, and stopping his car to see which direction I wanted to go.

His idea brought a chuckle from Jane. 'Did I just hear him say treasure? The southeast of England isn't exactly well known for buried pirate gold,' she giggled.

Big Ben rolled his eyes and gestured to our left and right.

I jabbed a finger to the right, pointing toward Rye where I planned to find a few miners to talk to.

Talking to Jane, I said, 'I doubt it will be treasure at the end of this search, so don't spend too much time on it. Just a skim search if you can and let me know if anything crops up.'

With the call to Jane ended and Big Ben driving the winding country road back to Rye, I absentmindedly patted Bull and Dozer as they snoozed on my lap and pondered the many pieces of information whirling in my head.

Little did I know we had already uncovered the root cause of everything occurring in and around Playford and the mine.

We were visiting our third miner when I finally asked the right question. Up until then, I had been focused on what the miners might have seen, how they interacted with the locals, and asking them about the hole that appeared in the face of the mine, and the victim, Wayne Calder.

It was almost by accident that I brought up the subject of the local residents' opposition to the mine.

'Come again?' I asked our host to repeat his previous sentence.

In the house of Wesley and Wendy Claridge and their two children Wilson and Wanda – I didn't bother to question why they were so keen on names starting with a double-u – I was beginning to feel quizzing a random group of the mineworkers was a waste of time when it suddenly yielded fruit.

'The locals,' Wesley repeated himself, his mug of steaming hot tea paused halfway to his mouth, 'they didn't care at all until about a year ago.'

'They didn't oppose the mine opening?' I quizzed, wanting greater clarity. Stefan Fletcher had said something about it all kicking off a year ago, but I hadn't realised he meant there was no opposition prior to that point.

Wesley took a mental pace back. 'Well, some might have been against it, but there was no big fuss. We had been operating for almost a year before that thing with the beetle happened and it just got worse after that.'

'In what way?' I had my pen poised and a page empty of notes because until now there had been nothing worth writing down.

Wesley took a moment to organise his thoughts.

'They started protesting about the damage the mining activity was doing to the local ecology for a start. Then they began breaking the fences, though I think that was all to do with ramblers wanting to claim their right of way.'

'Do you remember any names?' I pressed him.

He needed a moment to dredge his memory. 'Mildred something, I think.'

I nodded. News of her demise would circulate later and spread like wildfire through the mineworkers once the first one heard. It wasn't my place to reveal the information and knew it would only prove to be a distraction if I did.

Going back to the interesting bit, I challenged Wesley, 'Mr Fletcher claimed the locals are behind the recent safety issues and blamed them for the machinery breakdowns. He thinks they are sabotaging the mine equipment.'

Wesley shrugged. 'I don't see how that could be true. If they were, we would have caught one of them by now. How could they sneak about around the mine and on the machines without getting noticed? I think the Fletchers scrimped and bought cheap machinery and have been cutting corners with our safety. Also, the locals were friendly enough when the mine opened. They used to wave at us as we drove through Playford. Right up until the beetle thing. After that, it all changed.'

'Changed how? What exactly changed?' I pushed him for detail.

Wesley sucked on the inside of his cheek, thinking about his answer before speaking. His wife popped her head through the door, checking to see if anyone wanted more tea. When she left again, Wesley had an answer.

'It was little things at first. The shop was never open around the time that our shifts changed over. Before, we were always able to pop in and get a paper or a chocolate bar, but overnight we couldn't get anything. Then the pub, which a few of us used to frequent after shift on a Friday or whatever, was always at maximum capacity, and the bar manager wouldn't let us in. We would get turned away at the door.'

Wesley took a last slurp of his tea, placing the mug on top of a Chelsea Football Club coaster on his coffee table.

There was an ongoing policy of exclusion by the inhabitants of Playford. It wasn't just the mineworkers though; Big Ben and I had been pushed away too. The bar manager might let us in tonight, what with the Fox Inn's owner insisting, but how would that play out? I cursed myself for not bugging the place – I might have learned something last night had I been quicker to think of it.

Assuming Wesley's version was accurate, it meant something had changed to make the residents of Playford act differently.

But what could that change have been? What caused it?

Changing tactic I asked, 'Do you know anything about people metal detecting on the land around the mine?'

I got a raised eyebrow. 'Metal detecting? I should think that would be a tough gig. The ground is littered with bits of old metal. One of the chaps found a load of old bullet casings a few weeks ago. He reckoned they were from the second world war most likely.' A new thought made its way to the front of the queue, and I got to watch as Wesley changed his mind. 'Mind you, we're not that far from the Battle of Hastings.'

'1066,' commented Big Ben. I doubted it would be possible to find a person in England who had not studied that period of our history – it was a staple for all schoolchildren.

Wesley nodded. 'There's been important finds not that far away. Maybe if someone were to find the site of a military encampment from the night before the battle …'

'They might find something of value,' I concluded what Wesley was obviously hinting at.

Big Ben repeated a word he'd first said only a couple of hours ago, 'Treasure.'

This time when I looked at him, it wasn't with humour.

We quizzed Wesley a little longer, but ultimately, he didn't know anything about what might have happened to Wayne Calder. When the union voted and his colleagues downed tools, he went with them even though he said he would rather be working. He didn't think the strike was going to last long, but all the talk of a strange creature was making his wife nervous and that alone was keeping him home for now. He would not commit to an answer on whether he believed there was something ancient and deadly stalking the mine, but he looked nervous about going back until the mystery was solved.

There were a lot of other mineworkers to talk to, but I wasn't going to bother. I doubted I would hear anything different from them.

Hearing Big Ben and me get up to leave, Mrs Claridge called her children in from the garden. I heard the collective groan of disappointment – they were playing with my dogs and didn't want their game to end. Bull and Dozer leapt over the bottom sill of the backdoor to land in the kitchen, both puffing, panting, and thoroughly excited.

They would sleep for a while now and would need little exercise for the rest of the day.

As we made our way back to Big Ben's car, my phone rang, the screen displaying Jane's name.

'What have you got for me?' I asked the moment the line connected.

'Nothing,' she revealed in a rather anticlimactic way. 'A client walked in before I could get started and I have been trying to get rid of them ever since.'

'Anything worthwhile?' I enquired, more out of habit than interest.

'Probably not,' Jane replied dismissively. 'Anyway, I thought I ought to let you know that I am on it now.' She was probably worried that the delay was making her look bad. In the hours that had passed since I asked her to do some research, she would normally have compiled a huge folder of information.

I thanked her for the update, my phone clamped between my jaw and collar bone as I scooped the dogs and put them on the backseat of Big Ben's car.

'Next?' asked Big Ben.

When I replied, it was through teeth gritted with determination.

'Back to Playford. We're going to get some answers.'

Big Ben was in the driver's seat, his hand on the ignition key. He paused and turned his head when he heard the timbre of my voice.

'Are we going to ask nicely?' He framed the word 'nicely' so it meant precisely the opposite. He wanted to know if we were about to start hitting people.

I closed the car door, settling into my seat. 'Let's see how they respond, shall we?'

My oversized friend yanked his own door shut with a thunk of steel on steel and mashed the accelerator to match his driving manner to our mood.

I had been pussy footing around with the case and someone else was dead now. I didn't blame myself for what happened to Mildred Marchant – I thought it likely she died as a result of her involvement in whatever the local residents were up to, but it was time to take a direct approach.

Okay, we tried that in the bar last night, but that was the two of us against a mob and the bravery of a mob is a multiple of the individuals in it. Singled out, the same people would not feel anywhere near as courageous.

Traffic on the road back to Playford was light, a few tractors and a double-glazing van the only vehicles we saw. It took seventeen minutes, but in that time, the head of steam powering my sense of righteousness diminished not one bit.

Big Ben parked back at the Fox Inn, and I took just a brief moment to check over my car. Only when I saw it did I question if someone might target it. We were not welcome here, and I remembered my concern that everyone in the village might be involved in conspiracy to murder. Would they decide we were too close and look to remove us?

My car was undamaged, thankfully, which made me wonder if I was getting paranoid. The dogs got dropped off in my room where I was confident they would happily snooze. But the paranoia continued to nip at me, forcing doubt into my mind as I closed the door and left them behind.

I had been targeted before and if something happened to the dogs, I was not sure that I would be able to control the upwelling of rage that would follow. When I thought Deadface the Klown had hurt them, I dropped him to his death.

The memory of his face as he fell haunted my dreams still. Nevertheless, I had a feeling the approach we were about to take might cause some friction and the dogs were safer where they were.

I had no addresses to know who lived in which house, so I walked from the B&B to the first property, some thirty yards along the same side of the road and knocked politely on the door.

'Just a minute,' a woman's voice drifted out through the door.

Big Ben's head appeared by my ear, 'It's a lady,' he pointed out. 'You want me to take this one?'

I rolled my eyes. 'I doubt getting her knickers off will reap the result I need.'

'No harm in trying,' he commented a little sulkily.

I waited patiently, standing a respectful distance from the door, and tried to not look imposing. That was kind of hard with Big Ben's giant form looming over me.

Twenty seconds passed until the sound of someone undoing their lock preceded the door opening inward.

'Hello,' I shot the woman a smile and felt Big Ben's arm waft through the air as he gave her a friendly wave. He probably gave her bedroom eyes too, but I couldn't see his face.

She took one look at us and slammed the door again. Two words echoed back out through the door. I'm sure you can guess what they were.

'Told you,' gloated Big Ben. 'You just don't have the right impact on women.'

I cracked my knuckles and walked across the street to the next house. This time, I was less respectful with the distance I stood from the door and when it opened, I stuck my foot in it.

I was so fast to do so, I hadn't registered who I was looking at until it was too late for them to slam the door in my face.

I leered a satisfied grin.

'Hello, Irene.'

'You've no business here,' she snapped, attempting to slam the door on my foot. Had I been wearing my smart leather loafers, it would have hurt. However, the early morning excursion to see Mildred Marchant's body meant I was wearing heavy boots and the door just banged against them.

Irene yanked the door back a foot and tried to ram it closed again with the exact same result. And now it got tricky because I didn't want to scare the lady, but I did intend to get some answers.

'What's the matter, Irene?' I asked, my tone mocking. 'Care to call the police and report what I am doing?'

That she had no immediate answer was all the confirmation I needed. Glaring down at her, I leaned a little closer.

'What are you all doing with the Deathling? Whose idea was it? Did Wayne get in the way? Or was his death an accident? Just what are you trying to achieve?'

'I've … I've no idea what you are talking about,' she stammered, lying.

Refusing to break eye contact, I said, 'I haven't figured it all out yet, Irene, but I will. The villagers brought an old legend back to life. They made some feet to leave footprints and they spread some rumours, and when that didn't work, they killed a man. You want the mine shut. Why is that? What is out there that you don't want them to discover?'

I'd been able to catch her off guard, but she recovered quicker than I expected. So fast, in fact, that I had to give her credit.

'Ha!' she cackled. 'You've no idea what you are talking about. That thing they uncovered is as real as it gets. We tried to stop them because we feared the Deathling had gone into deep hibernation. My father was part of the original investigation, and he never believed it had left the area. Had it done so, we would have heard about it striking somewhere else.'

'You can drop the pretence,' I growled. 'No one believes your ridiculous monster story.'

Irene's face became an amused grin.

'You don't have to believe, Mr Michaels. I couldn't care less, but when it comes for you, you'll believe then. Stay clear of the mine and all the land around it, death will come to those foolish enough to go out there.'

'Even the person with the metal detector?' I asked.

Her face froze, her eyes widening as she scrambled for a lie that would sound believable. I didn't give her the chance.

'Yes, Irene, I know someone is out there looking for something. You state that anyone going onto the land will die, yet your own neighbours have a rambling society. Led by Mildred Marchant until today, but you don't think the Deathling got her, do you?' Irene's mouth was closed, her lips tight together. 'Yes, I saw you with all your friends this morning. Do you really believe Stefan Fletcher killed Mildred? Why is that? Is it because you know the Deathling cannot be responsible?'

'I know nothing of the sort,' Irene attempted to give a haughty reply. 'Fletcher threatens her, and she is murdered only hours later. It's hardly coincidence.'

'Yet he has an alibi,' I pointed out, shattering her theory. 'He couldn't have done it. So who did, Irene? What is it you want to find on the mine's land?' I repeated the last question because when I posed it the first time, it was just a thing that came to me. Now, though, I thought I might have hit the nail on the head.

'You're a fool,' Irene sneered. 'Interfering in our business will bring you nothing but pain. The Fletchers uncovered something ancient and evil. No one can stop it. Not even those of us who accept what it is. You question what we are doing, well I'll give you an answer, Mr Michaels. We are trying to cut off its food source. If it cannot feed, it will return to the earth. The Fletchers refused to listen and now it is out, and it is going to keep killing.'

There was genuine emotion in her words. I couldn't tell if she was just a great actor, but she made her words sound convincing.

I changed tactic, throwing a verbal left jab to see if I could get her off balance again.

'Where does Darius Cooper live?'

Again, her face froze. How big of a part did he play in all this? Had I seen him in the bar last night? I had no idea what he looked like, so I might have, but if Wesley's account was accurate, everything the villagers had done, had started with his claim to have found a rare beetle. Before that no one cared about the mine. After it, the residents of Playford became increasingly vocal.

Irene just glared at me. She didn't have an answer. Or she did, but she wasn't going to provide it willingly.

I changed tactic again, softening my voice and taking the hard edge from my eyes.

'I can help,' I offered. 'Whatever it is. Whatever trouble the residents are in. I can help. No one else needs to get hurt and if Wayne Calder's death was an accident, the authorities will take that into consideration. Continuing with the Deathling ruse … if someone else gets hurt as a result, the penalty for those involved could be severe.'

I thought for a moment that she was going to cave. Fleetingly there was a spark of hope in her eyes, but it was gone as soon as it appeared, and the hard set returned to her mouth.

'There's none so deaf as those who'll not hear, Mr Michaels. The Deathling is real, and it will keep its own secrets. There's nothing in Playford for you except misery and pain.'

I nodded to myself, accepting there was nothing more to be achieved by prolonging this conversation. Irene wasn't going to crack, but someone else might.

The door slammed home half a second after I got my boot out of it.

'You have such a way with the ladies,' remarked Big Ben, entertaining himself as usual.

I thumped him in the gut as I turned around, making him laugh as he skipped back to exit Irene's garden through her gate.

'Let's talk to a man then, shall we?' I suggested.

'Darius Cooper?' Big Ben sought to confirm. When I nodded my head, he added, 'But I thought you didn't know where anyone lives.'

Grinning, I pointed across the street to a postman happily strolling door to door with the mail.

'I don't. But I bet he does.'

The postie, decent fellow that he turned out to be, did not wish to give the two strange men an address despite the hastily concocted lie about looking for my uncle. He did, however, give it up when I produced a small wad of notes and peeled a few off.

After all, as Big Ben pointed out, he could tell us, or we could just follow him around until we saw the name appear on one of the many pieces of mail in his bag.

Armed with new knowledge, Big Ben and I made our way along the road, turned left down a dirt track as directed by the helpful postman and found ourselves in Peckham Lane.

The row of six tiny, terraced houses were in a mixed state of repair, none of them looking well looked after and none appearing to be about to fall down either.

Darius Cooper lived in number three.

Waiting for him to answer his door, it occurred to me that I ought to know what he looked like. I read a local newspaper report about the rare beetle, but his face hadn't been featured. Was that odd?

I got no further time to consider my thoughts on the subject.

'Help you, gents?' asked a man in his late sixties as his door swung inward and he stepped into the light.

It wasn't the first time I had seen him – he had been in the bar last night sitting with Mildred Marchant and Irene Tanner. I gave myself a half second to take in what I was seeing.

Heavily tattooed, the ink had taken on that blurring one sees when tattoos are a few decades old. Darius Cooper wore brown corduroy trousers beneath a white cotton shirt and a dark red woollen jumper. He was a big man, broad at the shoulder and generally large all over like a super heavyweight boxer. The tattoos extended past his cuffs, down the backs of his hands and onto his fingers. The illustrations also came up past his collar and onto his neck, some then curling around behind his ears. He stank of cigarettes, and when my eyes dropped to check his right hand, I saw dirty yellow stains on his fingers from years of holding the foul cancer sticks.

Meeting his eyes, I studied his face for just a moment, exchanging silent thoughts as we each assessed each other. It ended when his eyes flicked up to check Big Ben.

'You're the two guys the Fletchers have paid to snoop around, right?' It was more of a statement than a question.

'Yes, Mr Cooper, we are. Why don't we cut out a lot of nonsense and just get to the bit where you tell me what all the people in this tiny hamlet want at the mine?'

I got a huff of laughter from the older man.

'There's nothing for you here, boys. You are barking up the wrong tree. Whatever happened to that chap at the mine was nothing to do with us. I should look elsewhere if you want to solve that crime. We're not hurting anyone.'

His response was not what I expected. Thus far, the locals had all been hostile, yet Mr Cooper, the most dangerous looking one of them to date, came across as a man giving friendly advice. It was as if he wanted to help me.

I peered around him and into the dark interior of his house. Noting the change in my focus, Darius pulled the door shut behind him and stepped out onto his garden path.

'Like I said, boys. There's nothing here for you.'

'Is the Deathling real?' I asked him, curious to hear what answer he would give.

The smile came again, an amused grin because, apparently, I had said something funny.

'Oi!'

The shout came from behind and to my left. I turned my head to look, Mr Cooper and Big Ben doing the same thing, so we all saw the posse of men approaching.

At their head was the mouthy one from last night and again this morning at the mine. Then, observing the group dynamics, I realised he wasn't leading them at all, but was backing up a larger man with an angry grimace who was walking at the mouthy man's side.

There were eight men in total. Made more courageous by their superior number, they were striding towards us with purpose. There could be no doubt of their intentions – they were coming to rumble and my first thought was that Irene had sent them the moment we left her place.

It made me glad to have Big Ben at my side. Attacking him is a lot like trying to kick the moving parts of a woodchipper – it isn't going to end well for anyone other than the woodchipper. I have training too, but we would avoid fighting if we could.

Or, to be more accurate, I would avoid fighting. Big Ben applauds anyone who volunteers to be his punching bag and positively encourages it.

'Hey, look, Tempest,' he sniggered. 'It's a gaggle of Nancy-pants. What do you think they want?'

His comment was not what the approaching gang expected. Before they could respond in kind, he was talking again.

'Is a gaggle the correct collective term to use?' Big Ben asked me, feigning seriousness as he continued to mock them.

'Let's not provoke them, eh?' I suggested. 'I'd rather not bring the police here.'

Darius Cooper moved around us, heading for the pavement.

'You are not required,' he addressed the advancing men in a serious tone. 'Go home now, all of you.' Dismissing them as if his simple instruction ought to be enough to deter the men from any further action, Darius turned to face me and Big Ben. 'You too. Be gone and do not return. You've no business here.'

You've no business here. It felt like I kept hearing the same thing over and over again.

The gaggle – correct collective term or not – were not so easily put off by Darius' words. All eight of them arrived at the gate, blocking our path to pin us in place. Their leader, a man I had noticed in the bar last night, was taller and heavier set than me, and had a scar on his cheek plus a misshapen nose that suggested brawling was a pastime.

He looked up at Big Ben. 'You've got a big mouth.'

Cool as anything, Big Ben replied. 'You should see my penis. It's enormous.'

I knew it to be a precursor to what Big Ben would do next. He didn't like being threatened and held with the theory that the best defence was to knock everyone out before they could try to hit him.

Yet as Big Ben's muscles bunched, the three men standing behind the first two all moved as one and three shotguns appeared. One second this was a fist fight; the next, Big Ben and I were staring at the business end of deadly weapons.

'There will be no violence!' shouted Darius. 'I am warning you.' His voice was filled with rage and there was no doubt our aggressors heard him. They didn't move though.

I've stared at the muzzle of a gun before, wondering if I might be about to die, and I can assure you it is not something a person can get used to. It wasn't exactly fear gripping me now though, it was anger.

Big Ben huffed a breath through his nose, probably trying to decide the likelihood that the men threatening us were actually crazy enough to pull the trigger. If I believed the villagers were responsible for creating and populating the Deathling myth, then they were likely already responsible for one murder. That being true, our deaths seemed highly likely.

Equally, even if this was a blind threat, attacking them could easily make a nervous finger twitch and that would kill someone just as easily. Accidentally dead is still dead.

The standoff lasted for a two count and ended when Darius shoved his way through the gap between me and Big Ben.

'Go home, Kevin. I'll not warn you again.'

Kevin, the name of the leader clearly, shifted his gaze from Big Ben to Darius.

'They were bothering Irene, Darius. She sent us to move them on.'

Quivering with rage, Darius Cooper, spoke through a clenched jaw. 'There will be no violence.'

Kevin took a second, making me wonder if he was going to argue. Finally, he relented. 'As you wish.' A wave of his hand made the three men holding shotguns lower them. They vanished from sight, instantly invisible again, just as they had been on approach.

A nod of his head, the gesture indicating they should go back in the direction they had come from, got the men at the back moving. Kevin held

114

on for a moment longer, maintaining his emotionless glare as he stared back at Darius.

He had backed down, but he wasn't happy about it.

'You'd better make good soon, old man,' Kevin threatened cryptically. 'Promises will only get you so far.' I really wanted to know what that meant but I knew no one was going to tell me. I was going to have to figure it out for myself.

Kevin shot me a wink as he turned to go.

'Be seeing you.'

It was a senseless threat, intended only to instil fear. I genuinely hoped we did meet again.

With the threat removed and Big Ben still smarting from not being able to knock some heads together, I shook off the adrenalin pumping through my body and the feeling that my heart might explode to face the man we came to visit.

'Mr Cooper, you hold sway over them, how is that?'

Darius hung his head, looking sad for a moment. However, he didn't give me an answer, he just shuffled back toward his house.

I had to shout my next question; it was the last I got in before another door was shut in my face.

'There never was a beetle, was there, Mr Cooper?'

The door closed with a soft thump, and we were left in the empty street.

'Tempest, what the heck have we uncovered here?' asked Big Ben.

Walking away from Darius Cooper's property, I could only voice the same question. It stuck with me, filling my thoughts until we arrived back on the main road through the small collection of houses. There, the blast of a car horn made me jump.

Spinning around to face the latest threat, I made Big Ben laugh.

'It's your mum and dad, you big doofus,' he chuckled.

Mum, in the driving seat, powered down her window. 'Everything all right?' she asked. 'Tempest you look like you just saw a ghost.'

My heart rate returned to normal while I cursed myself for jumping.

'He's just twitchy because the locals want to kill us,' laughed Big Ben. It was not the right thing to say in front of my mother.

'Well, I'm not surprised, Benjamin. Why you two insist on sticking your noses into other peoples' business I have no idea. I said no good would come of it. Didn't I, Michael?' she prompted my father's opinion and thumped the meat of his nearest thigh when he didn't immediately agree with her.

'Yes, dear,' he winced, rubbing his leg. 'You must have said that many, many times. Fortunately, Tempest stopped feeling the need to heed your advice a couple of decades ago.'

That comment earned him a glare from my mother that would have made lumberjacks wet their pants. However, Dad had built up some armour over the years and just smiled at his wife.

Turning her attention back to me, she dropped the subject at hand in favour of telling us all about what she had been doing.

I held up a hand before she could get up to speed.

'Shall we take this to the inn and have a cup of tea?'

My mother blinked, her face looking confused for a moment before she responded.

'That sounds lovely, Tempest. What's gotten into you?'

Truthfully, I felt the village was no longer to be considered a safe environment and I wanted my parents to leave and take my dogs with them. I would be staying, my presence here like a piece of grit inside an oyster shell. The irritation I caused just by being here would result in a pearl, the analogy in this case being that the pearl was the case getting solved.

Deciding I was glad I hadn't voiced my confusing analogy out loud, I aimed my feet and an arm toward the Fox Inn.

'Shall we?'

My mother would not have noticed but half the curtains in the street moved as we passed them – the locals were reassessing how they thought about me. By going to Irene and then to Darius, I had provoked them, hence the shotgun threats. I declared my intention to catch them. They would be savvy enough to know I was still in the dark, but were they cool enough to continue with whatever they were doing even though I was here and watching them?

If they overplayed their hand, attacking me again, I would call in the police. I could do that already, getting threatened in the street with a deadly weapon is cause for arrest and incarceration, but it would be my word against theirs.

I had a sense that whatever they were up to had an end to it. The comment Kevin made about Darius needing to deliver soon was finite. They were waiting for something and had been doing so for long enough that some were getting impatient.

If I was right, then the residents of Playford were suddenly nervous to have me among them.

Back at the Fox Inn, I sent Big Ben through to the bar to join my parents and went upstairs to collect my dogs. The paranoia I felt earlier proved unnecessary because they hadn't moved an inch since I went out. Indeed, I had to encourage them off the bed where they were warm, content, and wished to be left.

With a dog under each arm, I returned to the ground floor to find my parents chatting with the landlord - they were ordering tea and some biscuits for all four of us.

'How's your day been, son?' asked my father, his tone serious. Unlike my mother, he knows first hand how complex my cases can be and how they have a habit of getting 'interesting'. By which I mean dangerous. When we get close to the person behind the crime and they take exception to my snooping, it often results in violence.

'I think there are two killers,' I announced.

'What!' gawped my mother. 'Tempest what sort of job is it that requires you to constantly be meeting people who kill each other.'

Frowning, I pointed out, 'I was in the army for a bunch of years, mother. That never seemed to bother you. What do you think all the weapons were for?'

'But being in the forces is honourable, Tempest. You get a nice uniform and people respected me when I told them what you did. Now I feel like lying whenever anyone asks me if you really chase ghosts for a living.'

I shrugged my indifference. 'That's on you, mum. I have a flourishing business. Why not just tell people I am an entrepreneur?'

'Because you keep appearing on the news!' my mother hissed angrily. 'Everyone knows what you do. And they know you went to jail.' She crossed herself again for emphasis.

My father complained, 'Leave the boy alone, Mary.'

All he succeeded in doing was shifting her ire in his direction. She swung an arm to thump his shoulder.

'Don't you pipe up either, Michael Michaels,' she snarled. 'His need for danger is all your fault. If it weren't for you, he might be a librarian or a priest.'

I wrinkled my nose, not liking the sound of either alternative career.

'What did I do?' protested my father.

Mum swivelled around in her seat to face him. 'How about galivanting off to join him in his stupid adventures every chance you get. How about that? Remember Cornwall? I got kidnapped.'

'That was your fault,' I pointed out. I was one hundred percent right, too, but mum did not care for how accurate my accusations might be, she was still poking a bony finger at my father.

'How about that dinner at that stupid Lord Hale's house. I told you we should have stayed at home.'

Dad's eyes went wide in disbelief.

'You insisted we had to go. You spent a fortune on a new dress and then complained it was the wrong size when you couldn't fit your big bum into it.'

It was the red rag to the bull.

Big Ben closed his eyes in an exaggerated way, much like a person might if a pyroclastic flow were about to engulf them and they would rather not see it coming.

'Tea,' announced the landlord, strolling back into the room.

Like a pin to a balloon, the wind went out of my mother's sails so when she looked across at the man advancing with a tray and all it held, her face was composed into a sweet smile.

'That's lovely, thank you. Ooh, look, Michael, he broke out the special biscuits. They are covered in chocolate.'

Now that I could get a word in, I dropped a proverbial anchor, and brought the previous conversation to a fast close with the announcement of a new subject.

'I don't think it's safe for the two of you to stay here tonight.' I gave it a two count, in which all my mother did was use a spoon to stir the contents of the teapot. 'Seriously, the second murder this morning suggests there are two killers in this area, each with a different agenda, and the locals are hiding some big secret that I believe they will kill to protect.'

'They threatened us with shotguns,' added Big Ben. 'Which I will make them eat if I get a chance.'

Mother's lips were pursed; never a good sign. The contents of the teapot were now well and truly stirred, but she wasn't stopping or looking up.

In a quiet voice, intended to make her sound wounded and disappointed, she said, 'Why is it that you must bring mayhem wherever you go, Tempest?'

I let a breath go, allowing it to deflate my chest. As my shoulders sagged, I replied, 'I don't, Mother. I just go where the mayhem is. Big Ben and I are getting close, and I worry the locals might do something rash to make me back off. Worse yet, while I am certain they are behind the supposed appearance of the Deathling and Wayne Calder's death, I have no idea what happened to Mildred Marchant last night or who her killer might be. One thing I feel certain of though, is that the two deaths are not connected.'

Since she was listening, I explained about the locals' odd behaviour and how they were all certain the Deathling was not to blame for Mildred's untimely demise.

'We should heed his advice, Mary,' intoned my father when I had finished.

Ignoring him, my mother picked up the teapot. 'Tea anyone?'

This was typical behaviour. Faced with information she did not wish to hear, my mother would pretend she had not heard it.

'I'm going to have one of these,' announced Big Ben, picking up a biscuit covered in thick chocolate. 'I might even have two,' he added as he popped the first into his mouth.

That he enjoyed the discomfort my mother brought was not a subject I could ever berate him for. He lost both his parents in a road accident many years ago and would probably give anything to reverse his fortunes.

I drank my tea quietly, refusing the biscuits' temptation and the worthless calories they represented. My mother would not be moved and dogging her on the subject would only make her dig in her heels.

Resigning myself to keeping an eye on my parents while also trying to catch the local residents red-handed, my train of thought was once again interrupted. This time by someone bursting through the inn's door.

I tensed. My legs, which had been stretched out under the table, snapped back to come under my body as I prepared to launch toward the latest threat.

'Tempest!' blurted Frank as he came into sight, his voice matching the concerned look his face bore.

'Oh, no,' groaned my mother. 'It's that loathsome little man from the comic bookstore.'

She was both right and wrong. Frank Decaux owns a bookstore, which does indeed sell comics. It is a lot more than that though, including a front for a group of nutters who used to call themselves the Kent League of Demonologists. As brave as he is deluded, Frank is the kind of man who would turn up for a fight wielding a magical sword to smite the forces of darkness. That the magic only exists in his head never seems to deter him.

Coming through the door behind him were Poison and Mistress Mushy, who both work in his shop, and the male pair of Chinese ninjas, Hatchett and Bob.

I dipped my head at the group in greeting. 'Hello, Frank. Are you looking for me?'

Frank had already rushed across to our table.

'Tempest you have to get out of here!' he insisted, sounding out of breath he was so desperate to get the words out. 'We've analysed the footprints found near the mine. It seems likely they are from an ancient demon called Quizriel. It was known in the Dark Ages for slaughtering whole villages.'

My mother shuddered and crossed herself.

'Or it's just a chap with some shaped Wellington boots,' I countered.

Frank shook his head vigorously. 'No, Tempest. I know you've been right in the past, but this time you have to trust me. There is a ripple of psychokinetic energy being detected all across Europe and from every point of measurement it is heading here. We have to get you and everyone else out. There is a team coming from Sweden. They will tackle the beast. It's too big for anyone else.'

'A team from Sweden, eh?' I humoured him. Frank is a great guy and driven by the need to do right and protect mankind. Unfortunately, he is also nuttier than squirrel poop.

'Yes, Tempest. They are well funded. They even have their own satellite. They changed its orbit so it crossed this region, and detected a point of energy convergence under the ground near the mine. That's where Quizriel must be sleeping during the day.'

Acting as if I hadn't heard his last mouthful of nonsense, I said, 'Frank, the villagers have invented the rumour of a supernatural beast. There was a second murder last night and it had nothing to do with a demon.'

'Surely, you don't believe that, Tempest?' Frank was all but begging me to see sense. 'Sucking the bodily juices from a victim is classic demon activity.' Mother crossed herself again. 'The dried-out husk Quizriel left is a clear indicator.'

I got to my feet, offering Frank a warm, if sorrowful, smile.

'The second victim was strangled and had a chunk of gypsum shoved in her mouth. It almost certainly happened somewhere in this village. The body was then moved to the mine which I think was a deliberate move, much like the gypsum, to make it appear as if the mine owner killed her. As for the desiccated body ...' I grabbed my mother's hand before she

125

could cross herself yet again – it was becoming an annoying habit, 'I am more inclined to believe a chemical explanation for the lack of moisture left in Wayne's remains.'

My mother yanked her arm away, glaring at me angrily, but I wasn't paying her any attention. I wasn't even listening to Frank as he continued to argue that we were all about to be sucked into hell or something.

My mind was locked in a loop as I explored the chemical thing I had just said. Bombarded and surrounded by clues, and largely on my own because Big Ben isn't a lot of help unless I have someone in need of a thumping or a woman whose clothes I need removed, I had put no thought into how Wayne Calder's body came to be so devoid of liquid.

How would a person achieve that? It happened at a gypsum mine. Is desiccant used to remove the moisture from the raw gypsum? The powdered version we buy to turn into plaster for the walls is completely dry. Do they use chemistry for that? Or heat?

I didn't know the answer but faced with a new angle, there was new research to be conducted.

'Tempest!' Frank shouted in my face. 'Are you even listening?'

'Something about a demon?' I guessed in an apologetic manner.

Frank flapped his arms in frustration. 'You have to take this threat seriously, Tempest. I am leaving the ninjas here until the team from Sweden arrive. They won't get here until tomorrow. They have to finish building the machine that will contain Quizriel when they catch it.'

I looked across at the four young Chinese people. They were dressed in their usual casual black clothes - the kind that are easy to move in. I could not see their weapons, but knew each of them would be armed with

126

something. Their swords, too big to conceal under their clothes, would be outside in a car.

'They are always welcome, of course,' I remarked, unsure what else I was supposed to say. 'However, I hope to catch the villagers involved in the next day or so. Since I now have a running clock, I guess I had better make it happen sooner rather than later.'

Frank had one last go at dissuading me. 'Tempest you have to let this one go. This creature is ancient evil, born long before humankind walked the Earth. Only strong magic will be able to contain it.'

I patted him on the shoulder in a comradely way.

'I'm going to take my chances, Frank.'

The landlord reappeared, coming to check on the new voices he could hear, no doubt. Taking in the four Ninjas and their … alternative fashion, whatever he was planning to say died on his lips.

To help him out, I asked, 'Do you have any rooms left?'

It had already been getting dark outside when Frank arrived with the ninjas. By the time he departed, leaving them behind, it was full dark and out here in the countryside where street lighting is sparse, that really means something. Where the trees grew tall, the canopy shielded even the light from the moon.

I was going to use that to my advantage.

With our tea and biscuits finished, the ninjas moving into their rooms, and my mother refusing to entertain the idea of going home a day early – she had places to explore tomorrow – I went to my own room for a rest.

Tonight, I would be out in the village, snooping and getting less sleep than I wanted and that was mostly down to Jane.

Her call came a few minutes after I closed the door to my room and shut the world outside. It had taken her so long to get back to me because she had been digging hard into one particular person.

I still don't fully understand how Jane finds the level of detail she is capable of producing. The things she can do with internet search engines and social media is staggering to me.

To start with, she explained that there are seventy-eight residents in the hamlet of Playford. Twelve of whom are minors – not to be confused with miners, she joked. Of the sixty-six remaining residents, sixty-five had nothing remarkable to stand them out from the general population of the country. One had an arrest record for driving under the influence of alcohol. It was many years ago and of no interest to me.

None of them had ever served in the armed forces or done anything remarkable with their lives. It was just a lot of background noise and disappointing because I had hoped Jane would uncover ... something.

Of course, then she hit me with the bombshell about the one person who stood out from the other villagers.

'Who?' I had asked.

When she replied, 'Darius Cooper,' I punched the air. I knew there was something off about him. He controlled the shotgun wielding mob with a word earlier. But Kevin left him with a threat so Darius' hold over him was tenuous and weakening. He faked finding a beetle and everyone in the village and their attitude toward the mine changed at the same time.

Settling my excitement, I pressed her for more information.

'Well, basically he doesn't exist,' she stated.

'Doesn't exist?'

'Not until about a year ago,' Jane clarified. 'My assumption is that he is using a false name. He has no social media profile, and I mean none. Not only does he not have his own pages, which isn't all that unusual, he doesn't exist anywhere else and that's not easy.'

My brain was trying to run at faster than full speed, adding this new piece of information to what I knew already.

'You say he popped into existence just more than a year ago?' I questioned.

'September second to be precise.'

I grabbed my laptop and punched it into life. 'Hold on,' I requested, 'I need to check something.'

A few beats of silence followed as my laptop came up to speed. Pop-ups filled the screen when I opened a search engine, but less than twenty seconds later, I had the information I wanted.

On my screen was the same article Victoria accidentally pulled up for me at the library, the one about the beetle. The newspaper article was published on September 7th. Allowing for the paper to only run once a week, Darius Cooper came into being and immediately faked finding the beetle.

The question of why he did it remained to be answered, but now I also wanted to know his real name and where he came from.

'What happened on September second?' I enquired, my brow furrowing because Jane had to have found the date somewhere.

'Oh, er, it was in an online publication of the parish church pamphlet. There was an official church welcome to Darius B Cooper.'

The villagers officially welcomed him. They were completely hostile to outsiders now, but they didn't used to be. It was that change again, from one state to another. Something altered their stance, and it wasn't just one or two of them, it was the whole village. Outsiders are not welcome.

Why?

We went over what else she had found but there wasn't much. Yes, the battle of Hastings occurred a thousand years ago not that many miles away, but there was no record of either army ever setting a camp in the area of Playford. Second World War aerial skirmishes had undoubtedly taken place in the nearby area, but again there was nothing significant recorded. Maybe there was a downed Spitfire fighter plane or something else of value out there, but it was starting to feel like the metal detecting thing was a dead end. Another red herring I wanted to chase.

130

After thanking Jane for her efforts, I settled onto my bed with the dachshunds either side of me. They were content to snooze, snuggled against the warmth of my body, their bellies full from the dinner I gave them half an hour ago.

I awoke when someone knocked on my door. It had not been my intention to fall asleep, and glancing at my clock, I found the time to be 1922 hrs and thus the hour to get working was upon me.

It was Saturday evening, and the Fox Inn was the only place serving alcohol for many miles. There wasn't even an off license where the locals could get something to drink, so we were heading for the bar.

Percy the landlord assured me we would be served this time and the residents of Playford couldn't shut doors in my face if they were in the bar.

Truthfully, I planned to address them en masse, whipping up doubt for whatever plan they are hatching and reiterating my plan to catch them at it. There was some danger in doing so, but as much as I wanted to try to wheedle some information out of them – I would be looking to see who looked nervous – I was also hoping to see who wasn't there.

My expectation was to be shunned by everyone present. That would give me a legitimate reason to finish my first drink and leave. Thereafter, I would sneak around the village and find those who had better, more devious things to do on a Saturday night.

Cunning, eh?

Not so much, as it turned out.

'Where is everyone?' asked Big Ben.

The bar was completely empty. The bar manager had a face like a smacked backside and left through a door behind the bar after giving us a silent scowl. That left the barmaid – the same one from last night – behind the bar where she eyed Big Ben while biting her bottom lip in a sensuous way.

'Cooeee!' called my mother, leaning out from behind a wall. She and my father were in a small alcove where a table for two gave them an intimate space.

I left Big Ben at the bar to check on them.

'Have you been here long?' I enquired, pulling up a chair from another table.

Dad had a rum and coke in his hand – I didn't need to ask or to smell it to know what it was. My father's favourite tipple was no secret.

'Just long enough to get drinks and find a seat,' he replied. 'They don't serve food here, as I am sure you know.' I did. I had vacuum packed rations in my room and some fruit to keep me going.

'So we thought we would get a drink because we were thirsty,' continued my mother, finishing dad's sentence, 'before we head into Rye to find somewhere nice to eat.'

'Jolly good,' I remarked, glad to hear they were leaving the area, if only for a brief period. 'I take it there was no one else in the bar when you came in?' I was looking about to check there were no other hidden alcoves with people in.

'No, son. Not a soul,' replied my father.

I took a moment to consider what that meant. None of the local residents were in the pub – the meeting place they all congregated in last night.

The conclusion was as simple as it was obvious: they were up to something.

In fact, what I suspected they were up to was the mysterious clandestine activity behind everything. The thing that had made them change their attitude toward outsiders, the thing that allowed Darius Cooper to hold sway over local yobs, the thing that made them want to scare people away from the mine and kill Wayne Calder.

'Are you joining us?' asked my mother, an air of hope in her voice. 'We could all have dinner together.'

Her voice penetrated my thoughts, but rather than entice me to do as she suggested, it prompted me to do quite the opposite.

Getting to my feet, I said, 'No, sorry. I've got work to do.'

Mum wailed, 'At this time? Normal, decent people stop work when it gets dark, Tempest.'

I was already on my way to the door, but I turned to face her when I replied, 'Miners don't care about the dark, Mum. Nor do killers.'

'Do you need a hand, son?' asked my father. It wasn't a hopeful request on his part, though I knew he would readily accompany me if I asked him to. It was more that he didn't like seeing me walk willingly into trouble. Somewhere inside his head, I was still his little boy. I got that, even though I had no children of my own to fully understand or appreciate the emotion.

'Oh, no you don't, Michael Michaels,' growled my mother.

133

I dipped my head in acknowledgement. 'Thanks, Dad. I'm sure Big Ben and I can handle whatever comes along.'

Dad shot his eyes toward the bar, emphasising with a nod of his head.

Following his gaze, I found Big Ben was no longer there. No explanation for his absence was needed, for the barmaid was also missing.

I let my head sag, grunting uncharitable words under my breath. In times of extreme danger, I could still rely on Big Ben to let his penis do the thinking for him. With the flip of a mental coin, I decided I didn't have the patience to wait; I was going to manage on my own just like I had many, many times before.

Still muttering under my breath, I shot my father a wave and a smile that didn't make it to my eyes, then pushed open the door and went outside.

A light drizzle had set in, low cloud covering the moon to make it even darker out than I expected. The inn had a small lamp above the door but light from that went no farther than a few yards.

I stopped at my car, doffing my coat to put on my Kevlar vest. The coat went back over the top so now I had an added layer to keep me warm plus some armour if things got dicey.

Looking back at it later, heading off by myself really wasn't all that bright. Not in a village where I suspected every resident was involved in conspiracy to murder. However, if Irene and the others were up to something right now, I was willing to bet it was outside of the village boundary, and thus I was probably safe enough to move around and poke in their houses.

It was with that thought in mind that, keeping to the shadows and moving unseen in the dark, I aimed my feet in the direction of Darius Cooper's house.

As I might have already mentioned, Playford is more a collection of houses than it is a village. Hamlets like this one abound in England. A cluster of houses around some farmland, the homes originally built by the landowner to provide accommodation for the workers in many cases. With a church and a pub, it was enough to warrant being given a name and that made it a mark on a map.

Just over a minute was all it took to cover the distance between A and B, but I approached the property from the rear, ducking down a narrow alley between the houses to find Mr Cooper's garden.

What I had planned was completely illegal; I was going to break into his house. But I had a hunch Darius was using a false identity because he had something to hide, something … criminal, and my hunch included the belief that finding out his real name would blow the whole case open.

There was no sign of life in the house, nor in the houses either side. Two doors up, number one had a television playing downstairs, the flickering light from it shone around the drawn curtains. Twelve children, I reminded myself. They would not be involved, and would probably be heading to bed shortly, at least one parent remaining behind to check they were safe.

I could see no security lights that might abruptly illuminate me, so I vaulted the four-foot-high garden wall, landed in the pond I had failed to see, and cursed my rotten luck.

Darius was not a gardener, and if I had to guess, I would say the pond hadn't been looked at since he moved in more than a year ago.

My feet were squelching as I made my way across the overgrown lawn, the sound audible if anyone were around to listen. I saw and heard nothing, taking that as a sign there was nothing to see or hear.

Finding a poorly hidden spare key took three attempts, the flowerpot in the corner with the plastic plant in it yielding the result when the doormat and handy looking rock failed to.

Inside, the house smelled of cigarettes. The stale stench was strong enough to be almost overpowering. It made me wish I had some chewing gum or a breath mint to hand.

Doing my best to ignore it, I pushed on into the house … and sucked in a gasp of breath through my teeth when my right shin connected with something completely solid in the dark. It was one of those occasions like when you stub your toe and need to scream and swear at the surprising level of pain such a small injury can inflict.

Backing up a pace and carefully bending to rub my shin with my right hand, I wafted my left hand through the air until it found the guilty object.

Cool to the touch, my fingers were feeling something made from metal. It was a shaft - like a broom handle only thinner. I was able to lift it with one hand, judging the weight to be no more than ten or twelve pounds. There was something bulky at the bottom, I felt it brush against my toes and it was balanced by something bulky at the top too.

I didn't want to use the torch on my phone; it would cast light in a manner that would look unnatural to anyone who could see the house. I also didn't want to use the light switch because then I would be illuminated.

The chances of anyone seeing me might be slim, but there was a row of houses that backed onto these and anyone inside them would see me instantly if they happened to be looking in the right direction.

Faced with little choice, I clambered gingerly over the odd metal thing, and flailed around on the wall either side of the door leading to the rest of the house until I found a light switch.

I flicked it on for a one count and flicked it off again.

Then I flicked it back on and left it that way.

I was visible now but too absorbed by what I could see to care.

The bruise on my shin came from a metal detector. I have never used one myself, but I knew what I was looking at just the same as anyone else from a civilised nation would.

Carefully, I picked it up again, looking it over this way and that before placing it back where it had been left. I didn't want to mess with it and leave any sign that I had been in the house, but I did take a photograph.

It wasn't something I could use in evidence – I doubted it could be used in court since I would have to admit breaking in first. However, on the box at the top end was a plastic hoop to put one's arm through and a handle below it to grasp. A battery box slung under the top end would provide power and one third of the way down the wand was an LED screen.

I was tempted to turn it on, yet managed to resist, instead taking pictures of the device and especially the letters embossed on the side: OMK GPX 6000.

It was something for me to look up later, though my heartrate was speeding from the discovery. Finding a metal detector in his house didn't conclusively make Darius the person out hunting for something buried at the mine, but it sure pointed the finger firmly in his direction.

My decision to break the law had already paid off. I killed the light, left the detector where it was, and left the kitchen to explore the rest of the house.

I hadn't found anything in the kitchen that might have suggested what Darius was looking for, but that wasn't as important now as finding out his true identity. In the man's lounge, I set to work rifling drawers and inspecting scraps of paper.

I needed to have a tactical light with me, but hadn't thought far enough ahead to stuff one in my pocket before I left. Making do by using the dim light from the screen of my phone rather than the bright light of the torch, I still found nothing.

After a few minutes, I concluded there was nothing to find.

Darius lived like a hermit, or whatever the correct term for a person with very few belongings is. The living room contained one old sofa on which two people could sit. It appeared to have somehow escaped the seventies if the pattern on the material was anything to go by and had to be second hand. Pieces of silver duct tape held one corner of the seat together.

A small table, the varnish for which had long since given up, stood by the couch, and an old television, the kind that comes with its own stand and would have been a prime model in 1988, dominated the opposite corner.

Whatever Darius had done for a living or whatever he did to bring in money now, wasn't working for him. If the contents and décor of this one room were anything to go by, he was flat broke.

I moved on, finding the same in the small dining room and in the only occupied bedroom upstairs. The house was a simple two up, two down configuration, with a set of wooden stairs set between the two downstairs rooms and two bedrooms, one to each side, at the top.

Hoping to find a bill that would show the real name of the occupant, I found nothing. It was as if he didn't get any bills.

I checked in the wardrobes and the drawer in the nightstand, but there was nothing to find. Trudging back downstairs, I questioned where else he might stash items of interest his metal detecting found. Anything that might provide the slightest clue to what he was looking for.

He was broke, so was he pinning his hopes on finding Roman gold? That was a longshot, but it kind of vaguely fit the shape of the mystery. He turns up promising the locals a fortune if they take him in and says there is treasure on the mine land.

However, the Fletchers own the land so if he digs it up and they know about it, he would get nothing or next to nothing. But if he finds it without them knowing, by going out at night, he can then claim to have found it elsewhere.

The rare beetle was his first attempt to hold up mining activity but that probably backfired when all the environmentalists arrived. So he concocts the story of the Deathling, resurrecting an old legend from the area's past. The villagers know all about it. Heck, maybe one of them even suggested it.

Heading for the back door, I ran the basic scenario through my head. It fit, sort of, but I just couldn't get myself to believe it. No one would kill for the promise of some Roman gold, or any other kind of treasure for that matter.

If the whole village were behind the Deathling's reappearance and Wayne Calder's murder, I was yet to find the cause.

I slipped out the back door, making a note to call Detective Chief Inspective Kirkland in the morning. He said he wasn't going to disclose any details about the investigation, but it was worth asking a few questions, nevertheless. Maybe I could find out what killed Mildred Marchant and find out if the forensic guys had found traces of desiccant on Wayne's body.

So wrapped up in my thoughts was I, that I didn't see the shadows step out from the lee of the last house in the street.

Fight. Saturday, October 14th 2002hrs

The scuff of a foot on loose gravel spiked my senses, flooding my bloodstream with adrenalin as I spun around to face the threat.

'Well, well,' said Kevin, his tone filled with fake amusement. 'What do we have here, boys?'

The mouthy man from the pub last night was by his side as usual, being brave because the numbers were on his side.

'I'd say we have someone who has already been warned enough times, wouldn't you, Kevin?' he replied, the same mocking tone filling his words.

Kevin continued their witty double act. 'Oh, yes, Terry, I should say that was exactly what we have.'

The pair of them were backed by the same rabble of idiots as before. Did they have their shotguns with them? Very possibly. The bigger question was whether they intended to use them.

Facing them, there was no sound coming from behind me. It meant I had a possible route of escape and the sensible choice at this point was probably to turn and run. I'm fit and I run regularly. If they didn't have someone who could catch me in the first hundred yards, they probably wouldn't catch me at all.

Running, though, might provoke them to shoot so I did the one thing they wouldn't expect. The one thing that made no tactical sense.

I attacked.

I didn't bother with a clever line, but only because none came to me. Eight sets of eyes went wide as I drove off with my right foot, shedding my coat in a single move before leaping into the air.

141

I might not be a great fighter – mostly because I don't like people hitting me – but that comparison is made against people who are good at fighting. Against a gang of dopey farm hicks, even vastly outnumbered, I figured I stood a chance.

Plus, I just don't like running away.

Kevin had the sense to take a step back which meant all my energy came down on the mouthy man - the one I now knew as Terry. He was trying to backpedal, but had already bumped against the man behind him who was trying to come forward.

A hard elbow to Terry's face followed swiftly by a blow to his groin and a strike to his throat took him out of the equation. That was good, but it wasn't great because, as suspected, he was only in the group for comedy value. The other guys were the fighters.

Kevin hit me with a right hook that snapped my head around to the left. It was a sweet punch that made my teeth rattle. Had he followed it with another, he might have put me down right there and then, but mercifully for me, his friends got in the way.

All wanting a piece of the action, they surged forward, but in doing so each of them blocked another from delivering a worthwhile blow. I was the only one with free reign to lash out and that was precisely what I did.

I didn't even need to aim. Not really. There were so many targets it was like throwing darts at a board ten feet in diameter.

A round house kick to a set of ribs brought about an outrush of air just as I ducked a haymaker that sailed harmlessly over my head. Snapping back up, I converted my motion into an uppercut that created a hole in the sky where a head had been a moment before.

They were coming forward as I went back, too dumb to break off and circle to get behind me. In the first five seconds two more joined Terry in taking a backseat, but I would be wrong to claim they weren't getting through.

A kick to my right leg only just missed parts of me I really do not like to have kicked and the blow knocked me off balance.

Lashing out, I found an arm, and gripped it. I wanted to convert the movement, fold the arm down and around to throw him into at least one of the other men but my left knee went out as someone kicked it from behind and I heard Kevin's shout of triumph.

Ultimately, there had been too many of them to fight off and all they needed was one lucky strike to slow me down. One hit that could stun me or reduce my capacity for defence and they would be able to press their advantage. That was all they had needed, and they had it now.

The punches and kicks came fast. Another kick from behind dropped my knee to the pavement and from there on it was all downhill.

Darius had saved me earlier, but he wasn't here now, and I doubted he would intervene if he knew I had just been snooping through his house.

A shoe hit my mouth, the taste of my own blood filling it the next second, and I questioned at what point they would stop. Did they plan to just kick me to death?

A scream filled the night air, the torrent of kicks stopping instantly. I knew the voice behind the scream, it was my mother, and her scream was one of utter terror.

My attackers were twisting to see who was there, taking their attention away from me. I hurt all over, but it was time to get myself moving.

If mum was here, then so was dad. The two of them must have decided to come looking for me, but whatever the case, they were here and that gave Kevin and his cronies no choice but to deal with them too. If I couldn't get myself off the pavement and back into the fight, they were going to kill all three of us, and I wasn't about to let that happen.

Of course, grit and determination will only get you so far when your abs are on fire from being kicked repeatedly and you are struggling to get your legs back under your body.

Yet more fuel to get back in the fight arrived in the form of my dogs. Their insane barking filled the lull and the sound of their fast paws told me they were about to get into the fight.

They are foolishly brave and terrify me every time they pick a fight. There's just nothing to them. Sure, they can open an ankle like no one else, but that's about the full extent of their arsenal.

Before I could twist myself around to spot them, an almighty thwack noise, like a tree punching someone in the face, echoed off the buildings around me and Kevin sailed clean over my head to land on his back between two of his friends.

I spun my head around to find my father standing with his fists up and a nervous/angry expression on his face. He was holding two dog leads awkwardly, his left arm looped through their lead to hold them in check. They continued to bark and lunge and look generally mental.

Next to him was Big Ben. He was shirtless and shoeless, showing off his ripped chest and abdomen.

'Who's next?' Big Ben asked, adding, 'You'll do,' before anyone could respond. He lunged forward, whipping his right hand up and around in an arc which ended at someone's cheekbone. The punch had enough energy to knock the man into the man next to him and both went down.

Then, before my disbelieving eyes, Big Ben flexed his muscles in a classic Incredible Hulk pose and growled like an angry bear.

I had to turn my head again to confirm the stampeding feet I could hear was the rest of Kevin's group running away.

'I'm calling the police,' gasped my mother, rummaging in her handbag to find her phone.

'No!' I shouted to stay her hand. 'No police.'

Mum bustled over, shoving my father to one side. Big Ben was inspecting the unconscious men, making sure none of them were dead or dying.

'Now just you listen here, Tempest Michaels, this isn't a playground tussle with Reggie Markum,' she named a boy who sent me home with a black eye when I was six. He was eight at the time and though it took me more than a year to even the score, I made sure to do it in style. 'Those men were hurting you,' she pointed out.

'Yeah, I noticed,' I muttered, accepting my father's hand to get up and wincing at the pain being reported back from all over my body. I spat out some blood. 'How did you find me?'

Big Ben laughed. 'We followed the sounds of someone getting their butt kicked.'

'They were using terrible language,' complained my mother, still gripping her phone and looking ready to make the call.

145

'No police,' I reiterated. 'I just broke into someone's house,' my mother threw her arms in the air, 'and I'm pretty sure they saw me. Getting the police involved will do me no favours.'

Stuffing her phone back into her handbag and scowling at me, mum began wagging a finger.

'This is not how I raised you, Tempest. You were brought up in a nice, Christian household. All this running around at night, sleeping with random women, and breaking the law ...'

'Hold on a second,' I held my hand up and tried to control my frown. 'What random women have I been sleeping with?'

'She means Big Ben,' explained my father. 'You're just guilty by association.'

My mother stamped her foot. 'She didn't even have a bra on when she came running back into the bar.' I assumed she was referring to the barmaid.

Big Ben grinned. 'Nope.'

Dad attempted to fill in some of the blanks. 'I sent Brother Sasquatch a text telling him you had gone out alone.'

'I read it after round one,' said Big Ben, 'and figured you probably needed a hand. You tend to find trouble if you can. Hey, can we head back to the inn? It's a little nippy out here.'

'Round one?' gawped mum. 'Round one? What does that mean?' She stuck out a hand, palm first. 'No, forget I asked. I have no desire to know.'

Dad offered me a shoulder for support, and I held it as we started back toward the main road and the inn.

'Are they all right to be left like that?' asked my mother, looking at the four figures lying in the street.

Big Ben shrugged. 'None of them are going to die. I didn't hit them that hard. And the one Tempest knocked out … well he never hits anyone hard enough to do any real damage.'

A chuckle escaped my lips, Big Ben was being his usual self, and I regretted it instantly as my battered body rebelled.

I had found the metal detector and knew who was using it. I could figure out how that fit with everything else shortly. Right now, I needed a sit down, a change of clothes and a belt of rum. Not necessarily in that order.

The hit of rum eased the tension coursing through my veins, but did nothing to diminish the tenderness emanating from the multiple injury sites all over my body.

My mother continued to grumble about my willingness to break the law and the frequency with which I seemed to find myself involved in altercations. She did so at a volume just loud enough for me to hear and kept glancing at me to make sure I was listening even though her body was turned away in the pretence that she was talking to herself.

I let it wash over me. In truth, I knew she was right, and I gave her too much cause to worry altogether too often. However, to be fair, she only knew about the current events because she had chosen to insinuate herself in my life again.

Dad was inspecting the visible wounds – those on my face where I likely had a black eye forming and a cut to my chin from someone's boot that could do with a stitch or two.

The dachshunds were under my chair, quiet and calm now that the excitement was over.

Big Ben reappeared with a med kit from my room. He'd also found his shirt and shoes and had his jacket hooked over an arm. The plan for this evening had been to annoy the locals in the bar, see what answers we could scare up and then head out to scour the village before scoping out the land around the mine once more.

That plan had been changed by the residents of Playford when they elected to avoid the bar and, in turn, us. I still wanted to find out where they were though. They were congregated somewhere, I felt certain of it and that had to mean they were currently involved in their criminal enterprise.

News of my altercation with Kevin, Terry, and their friends would have reached them by now. I was certain of that too, so the question was whether they would now abandon what they were doing, believing I was out looking for them, or whether they would believe the injuries inflicted, which Kevin and friends would exaggerate to make themselves feel better, were sufficient to deter me from any further activity tonight.

I was willing to bet it would be the latter. Gratefully, I took a pair of paracetamol and two ibuprofen from Big Ben, which I downed with the last of my strong rum and coke. He got me to lift my chin so he could clean up the cut and apply a couple of steri-strips to close the wound.

I hadn't gone looking for a mirror – I had no desire to see my reflection at this time. It was bad enough that my mother had to see it. Getting to my feet, I performed what I call a 'basic body systems' check: my arms and legs worked, I could see and hear, and none of my teeth were loose. Stiffness and soreness aside, there was nothing wrong with me which meant I had no excuse to call off my plan to ruin the locals' plans.

Mum looked aghast when I picked up my coat and slid it over my shoulders.

'Surely, you're not going out again, Tempest?'

Knowing it was the right thing to do, even though she is a pain in my butt, I knelt down in front of her chair, so my head was at her eye level, and offered her an apologetic smile.

'They attacked me because they know I am onto them, Mum. They are nervous, and that is going to make them slip up. The very fact that they are not here, and the village appears to be mostly deserted, tells us all that they are engaged in whatever nefarious plan is behind the daft Deathling shenanigans. This is my chance.'

'Tempest,' Big Ben called to get my attention.

When I looked up, he was already moving toward the window, my father too. Both were looking outside, but there was no mystery as to what might have caught their attention. The flashing lights of several police cars had just whizzed by.

I left my mother in her chair with a quick kiss to the top of her head and ran outside to join Big Ben and my father.

Big Ben murmured, 'They're heading for the mine.' It was like a prediction coming true only I had been too slow to do anything about it. My belief the villagers were actively engaged in doing something tonight should have propelled me to find them and catch them in the act, but getting rumbled by Kevin and his crew ...

It hit me like a cold bucket of water. The niggling question about why they were not with everyone else had been stuck in my head for the last half hour. Now I knew. They were left behind as a rear guard to stop me or slow me down if I dared to poke my head out of the inn.

They had achieved that most effectively. Given Darius' stance on violence – which was still surprising to me – their brief had probably been to watch me and intervene only if I looked to be heading in the right direction to cause them a problem. They either chose to disobey that simply because they wanted to, or they really were watching as I broke into Darius' place and got the green light to kill/give me a beating.

Either way, the tactic worked. I missed my chance to stop them or catch them before they carried out tonight's crime. It wasn't too late to act now though.

'Come on, Ben,' I snarled. 'Let's get out there and get them.'

I ran to his car, holding my gut with my right hand because that made it hurt slightly less. Big Ben plipped the doors open and was sliding into the driver's seat before I could open my side. Our doors thunked shut with determined thumps, but then the back doors opened.

'We are coming too,' stated my mother in the same voice she used to employ when she wanted me to tidy my room.

I snapped my head around to find her fighting with the seatbelt on the backseat of Big Ben's twin cab. Mouth open to start arguing, I changed my mind before the first word could form.

If I knew where she was, I could know exactly how much danger she was in. My parents had a dachshund each, Bull standing rigidly on my mother's lap, his little body poised and alert. Craning my head around to see Dozer, I found him licking his bottom on the seat next to my father.

My command to 'Punch it!' caused a spray of gravel from the back tyres as Big Ben mashed his accelerator pedal and threw us all back into our seats.

The swathe of light from his headlamps was the only illumination anywhere once the dim light from the Fox Inn and Playford were gone from the rear-view mirror. The flashing strobes of the police lights were far enough ahead that they had all but faded into the distance, swallowed by the cloying darkness and obscured by foliage.

Big Ben used them as a reference point but that wasn't where we were going. If Irene or Darius or whoever was leading the rabble of villagers on their ill-advised quest was now trying to get off the mine land without being spotted or caught, they would not be heading for the mine entrance.

No, they would be heading for a breach in the fence that ran for miles around the outside. They could pick any point, obviously, and make a new hole, but why do that when you have a known route? The rambling made sense suddenly. They had a route into mine land that ran right by the cut faces of the mine itself. It was well worn by traffic and thus easy to follow, and even if the owners had repaired the fence since Mildred's most recent vandalism, it would be easy to break again and claim it was nothing more than enforcing their right to roam.

Sensing the urgency I felt, Big Ben kept a heavy foot on his gas pedal. That is until he hit a sizeable rut and Bull found himself propelled from my mother's arms and into the air. I caught sight of him over my shoulder as he reached the apex of his upward trajectory, hung there for a second and then began falling.

His ears stayed where they were for a moment, his head seemingly sinking between them. Swift to react, my father caught him, if a little awkwardly, and plopped him back onto my mother's lap where she held him all the more tightly than before.

Big Ben drove a little slower after that.

The last half mile was driven slowly, and with the headlights off. It felt dangerous because it was. We had no way of knowing if there were any deep ravines we might fall into, but our luck held to deliver us to the spot I wanted in one piece and the right way up.

Following the line of the fence, it had been easy to find the hole again.

Sliding from the car, I whispered into the darkness of the backseat, 'Stay here. We'll scope it out and come back for you.' I was lying through my teeth. I was going to vanish into the dark and come back when I was done. Once they lost sight of me and Big Ben, my parents would have to stay with the car.

On the ground, the two of us moved like ghosts, just the way we had been taught so many years ago. Keeping low, staying out of sight, and weaving through the undergrowth, we made it to the hole in the fence and onto the Fletchers' land.

The fence sat on one of the rolling high points which gave us some advantage. If the Playford locals were yet to make it this far – I was banking on it – then they would skyline themselves as they came over one of the other ridges stretching out between our position and the mine itself some mile and a half in the distance.

The horn on Big Ben's car blasted into life, sending a flock of sleeping birds into the night sky and shattering any hope we had of ambushing anyone. I wanted to step out as the villagers came near us, startling them as we caught them red-handed with the daft Deathling footprint boots and whatever else they had, or maybe hauling along something they had dug up.

Not much chance of that now.

We ran back to his car, cursing and swearing all the way. My belief that having mum in the car would mean I knew she was safe had backfired completely. Five yards from his truck I could hear the argument raging inside it.

'I did see it!' snapped my mother.

'That's no reason to sound the horn!' raged my father.

Mum argued, 'How else would they know?'

'How else would we know what?' I demanded, yanking the front passenger door open. 'What is it that you think you saw, Mother?' I was trying quite hard to keep my tone in check though I mostly wanted to bash her on the head with a handy rock.

'There's something big out there, Tempest,' mum revealed, pointing a shaking finger through the windscreen to the darkness beyond.

'Yes. It's me,' supplied Big Ben unhelpfully.

I huffed out a sigh and hung my head. If the people I wanted to catch were anywhere within a mile radius, they would know exactly where we were now. The point of coming out here was in the toilet now and any chance of catching them gone up in smoke.

'Really,' mum insisted. 'I saw it move the bush over there.'

She was pointing again, and I could tell she believed what she was saying.

Dismissively, my father said, 'It was probably a rabbit.'

'No, it wasn't!' mum snapped, pinning him to the backseat with a hard glare. 'Rabbits don't move entire gorse bushes, Michael.'

He raised his hands in surrender and turned his head away to look out the window.

The choice now was whether to pack up and head back to Playford with the forlorn hope we might find the villagers there, or stay and get mum to drive Big Ben's car away to make anyone out there think we had left. If the horn blast made them go to ground, they would want to get back up and move once they believed the coast was clear.

154

I nodded at the plan, but never got to explain what I wanted to happen because Bull bounced onto his feet, sniffed the air once and leapt from mum's lap. He leapt across from the back seat to the glove box thing between the front seats, across the passenger's seat and through the gap by my legs before I could shift my body to block him.

'Tempest! Wash your mouth out,' remarked my mother at the expletive that slipped through my lips.

The tiny dog had vanished the second he hit the floor and now I was urgently hissing his name and demanding he return even though I knew he wouldn't. Far more headstrong than his brother, the elder dachshund had the scent of something, probably a bunny, in his nostrils and was on the hunt.

Dozer struggled in my father's grip, my dad fast enough to catch the little blighter before he, too, vanished into the night.

'Stay here,' I repeated my earlier instruction, flaring my eyes at my mother to show how much I meant it. 'Do not sound the horn unless you are being attacked. Do not get out of the car, and do not turn on the lights. I will be back once I have found my dog.'

Mum had something to say about her son's attitude, but I didn't get to hear it because I closed the door and walked away.

'Bull!' I hissed as loudly as I dared. 'Bull, come here, you disobedient little monkey!' Okay, the word I employed wasn't monkey, but I was feeling like everyone and everything was conspiring to make my life harder.

Big Ben was ten yards away, doing the same thing, both of us calling then pausing to listen because Bull's movement was going to give him away quicker than anything else.

A rustle from my left drew my head and eyes around. He was on the other side of the fence already!

I clicked my fingers once to get Big Ben's attention, but he was already moving, fast strides taking him on an intercept course with the hole in the fence.

I met him there, sidling through the gap after him to spread out again on the other side. Or I would have spread out if he hadn't grabbed my sleeve.

Pointing silently across the ground toward the mine, he drew my attention to the distant sound of a vehicle.

'Someone's coming,' he whispered.

He wasn't wrong, but more interestingly, they were being stealthy about it. Their lights were off, just as ours had been on approach, and they were keeping their engine noise quiet by not revving it hard.

This was better than expected. They probably hadn't heard the blast of horn if they were inside a vehicle. And if they had, I doubted they would have been able to pinpoint the direction it came from.

We might just catch them yet.

Buoyed by that hope, I thumped Big Ben's arm to jolt him into action.

'Let's find that stupid dog.'

He tapped my shoulder in acknowledgement and we returned to the routine of quietly calling for Bull to return. Time was tight. Even though the approaching car was moving slowly, they couldn't be more than a mile away and we had only a few minutes to find my dog and prepare an ambush.

A sound from my left, far too big to be made by a miniature dachshund and sounding nothing like a dog or a human, sent a chill up my spine.

Fighting against the natural reaction, I swivelled around to see what might be there. Ahead of me at the level of the scrubby brush covering the ground, all I could see was black against black. The bigger gorse and bramble bushes would have cast shadows if there was any worthwhile light coming from the sky or anywhere else.

Holding still, I squinted my eyes, trying to work out if I was jumping at shadows. I hadn't imagined hearing something organic a moment ago, and I didn't imagine it when the sound came again.

This time my feet twitched, my brain attempting to override my motor functions to make me run away. It was a grunt of sound, the noise of a beast.

My skin crawled.

Big Ben was yards away, calling for Bull and using inventive names my mother would not approve of.

My breaths came in nervous lumps, and though I told myself to stop being scared that there might be something lurking just a few feet away watching me in the darkness, Frank's haunting voice kept on whispering warnings I chose to dismiss.

Quizriel, a demon who could suck the moisture from a victim's body to leave nothing but a dried husk. I hadn't seen Wayne Calder's body and I was jolly glad about it. I had enough nightmares haunting my dreams without adding fresh images to the catalogue of things that would wake me in the night.

The clouds parted above my head, sending a shaft of moonlight down to spread a soft glow across the land. In that first moment of vague illumination, I picked out a cloud of warm breath being exhaled by the thing looking at me and the twin glowing orbs of its eyes.

I sucked in a breath to shout a warning to Big Ben and that was when it charged.

I'm going to claim I didn't squeal like a frightened girl, but I worry that might have been precisely what happened.

The thing was squat and low to the ground, yet also big enough to give the impression it was larger than me. Instincts bred into the human race many thousands of generations ago kicked in, propelling me backward and away from the hideous monstrosity now in full attack mode.

Bull appeared just as I got my body facing the opposite way. He was running toward it, his lips drawn back to reveal his tiny dagger-like teeth as he barked a threat.

I heard Big Ben shout something that sounded like 'Time to dig!' but I knew the thing behind me wasn't going to give the chance to quiz my colleague for clarity. I powered on, the bruised muscles in my legs and gut protesting about the latest demand I placed on them.

Bull charged, the sausage-shaped missile streaking over the ground to kill the beast on my tail. He was going to shoot straight by my legs and get himself killed. You might think me foolish, but I tried to stop him.

Letting Bull distract whatever it was – it wasn't a villager in a costume – might have bought me the time I needed to get away, but that thought never crossed my mind. I ducked to get my hands down, aiming to scoop him up so I could run with him like a rugby ball against my chest.

A root, a rock, or something jutting up from the soil had other ideas, catching the toe of my lead foot to send me sprawling just when I was about to make a grab for the speeding wiener.

Bull shot through my hands, and I bit the dirt, stuffing my head into a gorse bush, and reopening the cut on my chin with a tug of pain from my torn skin.

I rolled, yanking my head from the thorny entanglement, and gaining fresh scratches for my efforts. Mental calculation placed the thing right on my backside. It ought to be filling my vision as it bore down on me, but bringing my feet up to defend myself, there was nothing there.

I caught a flash of movement as something large vanished back between two gorse bushes with the sound of Bull's incessant barking right on its butt.

Hard, panting breaths formed a cloud of mist in front of my face, my heart banging in my chest yet again and I fought to make sense of the last ten seconds.

'That was fun,' chuckled Big Ben, appearing in front of me and offering a hand to get me off the ground. 'That's the biggest wild boar I have ever seen. Why didn't you catch it? We could have had a hog roast.'

'What?' I mumbled my response, confusion making me question what he was saying. 'That was a wild boar?' So that was what I heard Big Ben shout. He'd called out, 'It's a pig, not time to dig.'

My heartrate was slowing, climbing down out of the clouds but doing so cautiously, and checking below constantly to see if it needed to go back up again.

Big Ben whistled loudly for Bull to return, then commented, 'You need to warn me next time you plan to scream like that. I need a few seconds to get my phone set to record. Smile,' he requested, snapping a picture of my startled face because he is a complete dickhead.

My night vision completely shot, I slapped at where his arm had been and missed completely because all I could see was the dwindling corona left behind by the flash.

'Hey, here he comes,' announced Big Ben in a jovial fashion. 'Did you get it, Bull? Did you bring down the pig, you little predator you?'

Struggling to believe how badly everything tonight had gone, I pulled out my own phone, intending to check Bull over for injuries. My phone didn't work though. Angling it toward the light coming through the gap in the clouds, I could see the smashed screen. I could feel it too with my finger. Whether it was terminal or not I would find out later.

I stuffed it back into my pocket, picked up Bull, who I could now just about see as the blinding light in my eyes faded, and started to stomp back to Big Ben's car.

I was muttering most of the way.

Bull's heart was banging away in his chest, the little dog having the adventure of a lifetime chasing the giant boar no doubt.

The sound of the car sneaking over the land to get to the gap in the fence was still there. Despite the bedlam of the last minute and, apparently, my screaming, they hadn't changed course. It meant there was still opportunity to achieve something tonight.

I could dump Bull back in the car, find a place to lie low, and be ready to intercept whoever was in that car when they got to us.

However, as I reached the fence, and was about to pass through it, I realised the hole was far too small for a vehicle to get through. I could walk from one side to the other without the edges of the fence touching

161

my shoulders, but the locals trying to escape the mine in the car were going to have to abandon it.

That made no sense.

Mentally scratching my head to reconfigure my thoughts, I heard the soft, yet unmistakable, squelch of a radio in the near vicinity. That was the only warning I got before lights came on to blind me once again.

Brighter than the sun, headlights from a car filled my vision. Big Ben swore a foot from my shoulder as he too shied away from the painful light. The same thing came from behind us as the car we'd been waiting for arrived in a sudden flurry of movement, its own headlights pinning us in place from the other side.

'Police!' shouted a man's voice. 'Stay where you are and put your hands in the air where I can see them.'

Big Ben, because it is what he does, started disco dancing like John Travolta. Left hand on his hip, his right hand pointed skyward and then back down to the ground. He stopped when I elbowed him hard in the gut.

'I'm Tempest Michaels,' I shouted blindly toward the lights. 'I'm holding a dachshund,' I explained why my own arms were not aloft. 'Um, it's not loaded,' I added.

We could hear multiple sets of feet on the ground behind us and more to our front. The man who had issued the command to stay where we were, muttered something unprintable and then issued a command to whoever was inside the car to our front.

The headlights dimmed, changing from full beam to dipped. It was a vast improvement.

162

'I say. What's going on?' asked my mother.

'Holy …!' gasped the cop, caught totally by surprise. He hadn't noticed Big Ben's car hidden off to one side in the dark.

'I know I look dangerous, but don't shoot us, okay?' requested Big Ben. 'I promise I won't sleep with any of your wives.'

'They're British cops, dummy,' I sighed. 'They don't have guns.'

My mother had more to say. 'Why is anyone getting shot? We're the good guys,' she pointed out. Then, as if a question had just occurred to her, she added, 'Aren't we?' in an uncertain voice. 'Tempest, we are the good guys, right? Or did your breaking and entering earlier make us all criminals?'

A shadow moved in front of the headlights of the car on our side of the fence – someone was coming towards us. There were voices coming from behind us as well on the mine side of the fence which made us the epicentre of interest.

'Breaking and entering, eh?' asked Detective Chief Inspector Kirkland. 'Am I to assume you are now going to deny all knowledge of said crime and claim the lady over there is simply confused?'

'Yes. Please do exactly that,' I requested, wishing I had a piece of rock to hand. I wanted to use it to knock myself out. Maybe that way I could skip all the frustrating problems my mother seemed hell bent on causing, and just wake up in a cell at the local police station.

DCI Kirkland came close enough that I could see his face and didn't have to rely on the sound of his voice to identify him. With the headlights behind him, he was nothing more than a black silhouette until he got within a few feet. At that point, he stepped to my left and into the light coming from the other car, the one behind us.

'Good evening, Mr Michaels.' He tilted his head to the left, inclining it and frowning slightly as he took in my appearance. 'You appear to have been having an adventurous evening. Would you care to enlighten me as to the nature of the events that led to the injuries on your face?'

'What happened at the mine?' I countered, acting as if he hadn't posed a question first.

It brought a snort of amusement from the senior officer.

'You don't disappoint, Mr Michaels. When I met you this morning, I spoke with an old colleague in Rochester. He said you were a slippery customer and difficult to pin to anything.'

I took it as a compliment.

'He also said, you were almost certainly breaking the law, but to give you enough rope and see if you succeeded in hanging yourself. In his opinion, you are a useful tool to be employed carefully. I think he meant that you would lead me to the real criminals so to that end, I shall overlook my concerns about ... whatever you have been up to.'

'He's a good boy really,' insisted my mother, arriving in our small circle with my father holding her arm to stop her tripping in the dark and Dozer straining at the end of his lead. 'He used to go to church every week.'

'Because I was ten and you took me,' I raised what I felt was a valid point though none of this was germane to the situation.

'It's this silly job of his. It gets him into all sorts of trouble all the time.'

164

'Mary,' my father's voice cut across hers and he raised a finger to his lips. 'Shhh. Let the nice policeman talk now.'

DCI Kirkland waited a couple of seconds, checking to see if he was going to be allowed to continue. When my mother looked back at him with an expectant expression, he shifted his gaze back to me and cast his eyes upward, trying to remember what he was saying before mum interrupted him.

'I'll tell you what, Mr Michaels. Let's exchange some information and see where that leads us.'

I cocked an eyebrow, surprised by his offer.

'I'll even go first,' he added. 'The incident at the mine this evening appears to be the guards jumping at shadows. They have allowed the bedtime stories of a local monster to spook them and took to arming themselves.'

'Guns?' I questioned.

Kirkland shook his head. 'Crossbows, a few knives and bats. One of them thought he saw something in the dark and fired his crossbow.'

I tensed, wondering what the detective chief inspector was going to say next. Had one of the villagers, dressed as the Deathling, or wearing the boots to make fresh marks, been shot with a crossbow bolt? Had the mystery already been neatly sewn up?

'He hit one of his colleagues as he returned from a patrol. It's not life threatening, but the panicked cry for emergency help came through garbled and we were scrambled to check it out. I was just about to leave the mine when we heard a horn in the distance. It's surprising how far noise travels out here at night, isn't it?'

I shot a look at my mother.

'Given all the recent mysterious activity around the mine, I thought I had better investigate. So I sent some of the mine's security chaps to this location with one of my constables; they stayed inside the wire, so to speak, while I circled around outside. We are less than a hundred yards from where Mildred Marchant's body was found this morning.'

Mum swore, the shock of his statement catching her by surprise, and she crossed herself twice while looking embarrassed.

DCI Kirkland shot her a questioning look, perhaps checking she had nothing further to say before once again bringing his attention back to me.

I was admiring how well he'd manoeuvred me. The offer to share information had filled me with momentary hope that I might learn something, or that this daft case might actually have been solved without need for more involvement on my part. Alas it was not the case and he'd only offered to exchange stories because his was worthless.

The guards were spooked. Big Deal. That told me nothing of use and was precisely why he was prepared to let me know about it.

I took that as my cue to be equally unhelpful.

'Most of the residents of Playford have vanished this evening,' I revealed, getting a raised eyebrow in response. 'I spoke with several of them earlier today, but expecting there to be a gathering in the Fox Inn, much as there was last night, I found the bar to be empty. On scouring the village, I can report very few signs of life.'

'You believed they were on mine land attempting to cause trouble,' Kirkland concluded, guessing that was my reason for being out here.

I nodded. 'We followed your lights, actually. Seeing your roof bar strobes heading toward the mine, I guessed there had been another incident and hoped I might head them off as they escaped through the hole they made for rambling.'

'Still convinced the locals are behind Wayne Calder's death, eh?'

Sensing an opportunity to pick his brain, I chose to challenge him. 'If not the locals, then who?' I studied his face wondering how he would choose to answer.

He in turn studied my face, checking to see if I was serious.

'Mr Michaels do you seriously believe that a small collection of farm workers could be responsible for the dried-out husk we found here this week? I admit I have not yet determined an alternate suspect, yet I can find no connection between Wayne Calder and anyone in Playford. I put it to you that the only connection the locals have is their dislike of the mine.'

I accepted what he was saying even though I had to wholeheartedly disagree.

'It would appear, Detective Chief Inspector, you and I have reached an impasse. Inevitably one of us will be proven correct and I must say that I do not care which of us it is, so long as this mystery is solved. If there is nothing further, I think perhaps I would like to return to my lodgings, it is cool outside tonight.' I waited to see what he would say but did not think that he would argue.

Kirkland appeared to consider it for a few seconds, before nodding his head.

'You are free to go, Mr Michaels. I trust I shall hear no further incidents of breaking and entering or anything else related to your name. I am sure I do not need to remind you that you are a civilian and must obey the laws of this country.'

'Oh, I shall see that he does,' chipped in my mother helpfully.

There being nothing left to say, I tapped Big Ben on the arm, dipped my head at the DCI in acknowledgement, and made my way back to the car.

Mercifully, my mother also had nothing further to say and my father was not forced to gag her with his hand. Bumping across the open land just moments later, I considered my evening and just how fruitless it had been. Since arriving in Playford just a day ago, my investigation had yielded little in the way of clues, my phone had been smashed and might be dead, I had taken a beating, and I was mostly wishing I hadn't taken the case.

All in all, and considering none of us had managed to eat dinner, unless you counted the rations I foraged from my bag, I should have taken my mother up on her invitation of going out for dinner in Rye.

I did however have one thing to investigate when I got back to my room.

Because everyone was hungry, Big Ben drove a circuitous route to get back to the Fox Inn, stopping at a takeaway fish 'n' chip shop in a nearby village.

To avoid leaving too much stench in his car we kept them wrapped and in the load compartment behind the cabin until we returned to the inn. There, I bade my parents goodnight, thanked them and Big Ben for their assistance this evening, and retired to my room with my two dogs. Bull and Dozer were thoroughly excited by the scents emanating from the package I held, and because they'd had an interesting day too, I shared some pieces of fish with them.

Munching on chips, and wiping my greasy fingers on my trousers since they were filthy from rolling around on the floor anyway, I used one hand to poke and prod my phone.

It was dead.

I could not even get the screen to come to life. This was a temporary problem, easily resolved when I could get hold of a new phone and exchange the SIM card in the back. However, for now, it prevented me from contacting Amanda, meant that she was probably trying to get hold of me and having no luck, and more pertinently to the case, meant I could not access the photograph I took earlier.

To resolve one issue, I opened my laptop and sent Amanda an email. In it I chose to omit details of my altercation with Kevin and his pals and stuck to wishing her a good night. I also told her how difficult this case was proving and explained that I had broken my phone while leaving out details of how it had become broken.

With that vital task complete, I opened the search engine, and dredged my memory for the code I had seen on the side of the metal detector in Mr Cooper's house.

It took me two attempts to get it right, but when I entered OMK GPX 6000, the search engine immediately found what I was looking for. The page presented me with images of the exact same device I had seen propped against the wall in Darius' kitchen.

Bull barked at me, the unexpected loud noise jolting me and making my heart jump. I had not finished my chips. So absorbed was I in the information on the screen before my eyes, that I had one hand poised above the still warm pile of greasy, soggy, yet unctuous chipped tubers.

Both dogs would decide it was bedtime as soon as there was no further food to be eaten, so I chucked them both a couple of chips instead of giving them their usual bedtime biscuit, then shooed them into their bed as I finished the remaining few.

This time, rather than wipe my hands on my trousers, I went to the small bathroom where I washed them in the sink - I did not want a greasy keyboard. Back at my laptop, and using my tongue to work small pieces of potato from the crevices between my teeth, I stared in disbelief at the price of the device in question.

The metal detector cost roughly the same as a high-end German-manufactured car. That was interesting in itself, especially given the nature of the furnishings and decor in Mr Cooper's house and how he appeared to be flat broke. Either he had stolen the device, someone had bought it for him, or he had money, but simply chose not to spend it on his house.

Whichever of those it was didn't particularly matter. What I found more interesting was that this particular metal detector was specifically designed to find just one material. According to the manufacturers, there was no finer metal detector available on the planet for finding gold.

Gold!

That someone had been using a metal detector in the search of something of value had already occurred to me. Indeed, I think Big Ben was the first to bring the subject up though I am certain he was being ironic or ridiculous at the time. However, with the discovery of the metal detector and its purpose, I could no longer question that someone, namely Darius Cooper, and whoever was working with him, believed there was something of worth in the ground around the mine.

Now I had motive. It is a universally held truth that most murders occur for one of just two or three reasons. Love and money are right at the top of that list. How many people across the centuries had died in the pursuit of riches? Treasure was a word that would drive people crazy, and it gave instant explanation for the strange behaviour I had seen from the locals.

I also now had an explanation for Darius Cooper's rare beetle find and the fact that it then proved to be erroneous. He had been trying to bring a halt to mining activity so that he could hunt for what he thought was out there. He hadn't found it yet, clearly, and now the rest, or at least the majority of the villagers were also involved.

This explained Kevin's comment when he expressed his impatience, and the promise of riches, if indeed there was any gold here, would be enough to unite all the people in this tiny postcode.

I pushed back from my laptop and stared up at the ceiling, linking my fingers behind my head as the full revelation of this discovery washed over me. I will admit a certain sense of satisfaction stemming from the

171

belief that I was the only one who had made the connection. I was certain the police had no idea.

I probably ought to tell them. But I wasn't going to do that. Not until I had amassed significantly more evidence than the circumstantial placement of a metal detector I discovered through an illegal search.

Pressing the kettle into service, I make good use of the room's tea and coffee facilities. The instant coffee did not appeal, not that the instant milk substitute enticed my taste buds particularly either, however I plumbed for tea and let my brain fizz for a few moments until the water in my mug became sufficiently murky.

Settling back at the small table and chair in one corner of the room and taking a sip of my tea, I cracked my knuckles. It was time to get into some serious research.

I started with attempting to determine if gold had ever been found in the UK. To my great surprise, for I expected to read that there had never been any found, there were deposits all over Great Britain and Northern Ireland. It wasn't exactly plentiful, and the nearest discovery was over one hundred miles from my current location. However, I could not dismiss the possibility that under my nose might be a gold mining operation.

With each article I read, I became more and more convinced Darius Cooper, whoever he actually was, had come to this area because he knew there to be gold here. Whether he then revealed his discovery to the locals because he needed their help or they found out what he was doing and demanded a cut, was another detail that did not matter.

My working hypothesis was that Wayne Calder stumbled across Darius, or someone else, in the process of prospecting or possibly even finding gold, and had been silenced permanently. That his death coincided with the sudden appearance of a hole in the face of the mine and the rumours of an ancient creature returned to wreak bloody havoc, could be no coincidence.

A yawn split my face and I shot my cuff to check the time: 0022hrs.

That it was after midnight came as no particular shock, the ache from my eyeballs from staring at the screen was sufficient to tell me I had been doing so for several hours. I wasn't done though. Not even nearly.

If I sacrificed sleep now, grabbed a couple of hours before breakfast, and entered the new day with answers and the ability to close this case within a few hours, then I would sleep happily in my own bed when it was done.

Nevertheless, my backside was getting sore, and my shoulders stiff from hunching to stare at the screen. I pushed the chair back and got to my feet. I was still wearing the same clothes I had been in all day. I was dirty from sweating, had leaf litter and dirt in my hair, and grime under my fingernails. To give myself a screen break and revitalise my senses before fatigue overtook me, I stripped off and headed to the shower.

Five minutes later and standing naked in my room while I towelled the moisture out of my hair, I heard a floorboard creak in the corridor outside. Instantly alert, I flicked my eyes across to my pile of clean clothes. There was no time to find pants to put on, so I swiftly wrapped the towel around my waist.

The floorboard creaked again, or more accurately, another one did, and it told me whoever was outside had just paused outside my door. I was thankful for this, for it meant the would-be attacker was here for me and not my parents.

Then a worrying thought gripped me. What if it was Victoria returned? Was she here for another attempt to seduce me?

Oddly, I found myself hoping that it was a killer outside. Somehow, even wearing nothing but a towel, that seemed easier to deal with. Not only that, but I was also about to catch them by surprise, and that would give me someone to question.

I didn't want to turn the light in my room off because it would alert the person outside that I was awake. I assumed the hallway was dark so light from my room would be shining out underneath the door.

Moving stealthily, and hoping the floorboards would not creak beneath my careful feet, I stole up to the door. With a few deep breaths to charge my body with oxygen, I gave myself a two count, gripped the door handle, and ripped it open.

The person outside yelped in surprise. They were in the dark and now had unexpected light streaming into their eyes, giving me every advantage I could have asked for. My eyes were not on their face, for that is not where I expected any threat to come from. Instead, I was looking at their hands, checking for weapons.

It took only a nanosecond to determine the hands were indeed empty, so before the initial yelp of shock had died away, I was already grabbing my latest assailant by the front of his jacket. Behind me, both Bull and Dozer leapt from their bed, barking and snarling to repel the intruder.

I lunged forward, breaking the person's balance, before thrusting backward and swivelling off my rear foot. The combination of confusing motions combined with a lack of preparedness, ensured my attacker swiftly became my victim, and airborne, yelped again as I spun him around and threw him down hard onto the carpet in my room.

He landed on his back, the air whooshing from his lungs.

Now was the time to follow up with a blow to throat or groin or gut to ensure whatever fight he had left was swiftly quashed. However, it was at this point that I discovered the man on my carpet was my client.

Colin Fletcher's eyes were wide with fear and his hands were coming up to ward off the inevitable blow. My right hand was pinning him to the floor and my left was drawn back ready to strike when I recognised who it was.

The dachshunds, probably thinking they were helping, had both leapt on top of the man now lying on my carpet, where they were trying to bite his arms. It was a good thing then that I did not want to do him any further damage because they were about as in the way as they could be.

There were already noises coming from elsewhere in the inn as the sounds of our activity woke Big Ben and probably my parents.

'Tempest!' called my former army colleague as he burst from his room into the corridor.

'What is it?' questioned a woman. She was in the corridor too, following Big Ben from his room.

He skidded to a stop at my door, racing to get inside and help me, though by then I was standing upright once more and giving Colin a hand up.

The dogs whizzed round his feet, then onto the barmaid, for she was big Ben's companion for the night, then back to Big Ben, across to me, and then back out into the corridor when they heard my parents coming

'You scared the bejesus out of me, Mr Michaels,' wheezed Colin as he attempted to get his breathing under control. 'Is that how you usually answer the door?'

Standing back to give myself some room as Big Ben, the barmaid, and then both of my parents joined me in my room, I folded my arms, unfolded them again to check my towel was securely fastened around my waist, and hit Colin Fletcher with a questioning look.

'To what do I owe the pleasure of this late-night visit, Colin? Were I not engaged in research following up on a clue I found this evening, I would be asleep. Did you not think to call me?' Having asked the question, I then realised the problem with it and let my shoulders sag. 'Sorry, yes, you probably did, but my phone broke earlier this evening.'

'Did you get into a fight?' Colin questioned, while staring at my face.

'What's going on Tempest?' my mother wanted to know. She was standing in the doorway with my father in front of her, both in their nightwear. Just like Big Ben, they had run from their room at the sound of Colin impacting my floor.

I shot my mother a tired smile and said 'It's nothing, Mother. This is my client for this case. One of them, at least. We have a few things to discuss, and you should get back to your room and return to sleep. All of you, that is.'

Big Ben stayed in place, narrowing his eyes slightly in question as he checked to see if I was just trying to get rid of my parents. I shook my head, letting him know that he was not needed and gestured towards the door with both my hands. I shooed Big Ben and the barmaid, who appeared to be wearing nothing but Big Ben's shirt which she was clutching closed with one hand, back out into the corridor.

'Get some sleep,' I suggested. 'Or... whatever, I guess.'

The barmaid, whose name I was yet to learn, though I doubted Big Ben had bothered to learn it either, giggled at my remark, and held out a hand to take Big Ben back to bed.

I closed the door, leaving just Colin Fletcher and me in the room with the two dachshunds.

'If you'll be so kind as to excuse me for a moment, Mr Fletcher, I'm going to get dressed.' I did not bother to wait to hear his opinion on the subject. Thus far our relationship had been tenuous to say the least. He had been vocally against to his father's desire to employ me and borderline unpleasant on several occasions. I was curious to hear why he wanted to visit me at this late hour, but it could wait until I at least had underwear on.

Grabbing a handful of clothes, I went into the bathroom and closed the door so I could get dressed in peace. Choosing cotton jogging trousers and a thin tee shirt to go over my boxers, it took but a moment to get dressed, and I started talking before I opened the door again.

'So, once again, Mr Fletcher, what is it that brings you to my room at this late hour?'

'My apologies for the intrusion, Tempest, I suppose I did not think things through. When I was unable to get hold of you, I began to fear something might have happened. There was an incident at the mine last night, I'm not sure if you heard about it.'

I pulled the bathroom door open stepping back out into the main room with my arms folded across my chest. I wasn't trying to look impatient, yet there was something about his desire to check on my health that didn't feel entirely honest.

'Your guards decided to arm themselves, and poorly trained as they are, one managed to shoot another in the dark. I am aware of the incident, is the guard in question okay?'

Colin looked a little embarrassed or perhaps flustered might be a better word. His behaviour gave me the impression that he wasn't saying something. Pinned in place by my gaze, he had to give an answer.

'Um, yes, yes. Thank you for asking. I am told the injury is not life threatening. However, it would appear he requires surgery. My father is at the hospital now.'

'And you are here,' I pointed out, letting the words hang on the air because they required him to fill in a blank.

He looked flustered still, searching for words and giving me the impression that he was having to think on his feet to provide an explanation for his presence.

'Well, yes, as I said, I called earlier after we heard about the incident. It felt prudent to check that you were not somehow involved or endangered by their activities. You did say that you would probably be staking out the mine at night.'

'Yes, I did say that. You were here then only to check on me?'

As if grasping the chance I had just given him, Colin nodded his head vigorously.

'Exactly that, Mr Michaels. I'm sorry if I came across as gruff yesterday and again earlier today,' he added. 'I still don't agree with my father's desire to employ you. We are haemorrhaging money and can ill afford any further expense. I for one do not believe any of this supernatural nonsense regarding … what is it they call it?'

178

'The Deathling,' I supplied.

'Yes, that's it. Superstitious nonsense for country folk,' Colin remarked.

It was one thing he and I agreed on, at least.

Wanting to wrap things up and get back to the research I had been conducting before the latest interruption, I was about to invite Colin Fletcher to leave when a question occurred to me.

'As you can see,' I waved a hand at my face, 'with the exception of a few scuffs,' I ignored the visible bruising on my ribs, legs, and arms, 'you can see that I am in fact in one piece.' Watching his face carefully to gauge how he reacted, I asked, 'You would have had all manner of geological surveys conducted prior to buying the mine land, yes?'

'Naturally,' reply Colin, fielding an easy question.

I nodded, happy that I got the response I wanted. 'Was there any gold found in the ground that you bought?'

Colin Fletcher coughed and snorted in a sort of choking manner. My question had caught him by surprise, but I had been watching his face to see if my question would startle or scare him because he was hiding something, and he was not.

'Gold?' he repeated the word. 'There's no gold in these parts. There's no silver either. Or tin, or copper, or anything much else that could be considered a valuable mineral. There's money in gypsum, but you need a lot of it, and you need to be able to work it fast. Which is precisely what we're not doing and will not be able to do until this mess is cleared up. We need to get our workers back.' Eyeing me curiously, he added, 'Why do you ask about gold?'

179

'Just curious,' I lied. 'It came up on a quiz at my local pub just a week or so ago.' I hadn't got the answer I wanted or possibly the one I hoped for. Colin knew nothing about gold unless he was a very convincing liar, and I really didn't think he was. To stop him from questioning me any further I aimed an arm towards the door. 'If there's nothing else ...'

Colin's feet twitched, a moment of indecision as he tried to work out what he wanted to do. It made me once again question why he had come to my room. However, before I needed to prompt him again, he started towards my door as invited.

I stepped out of his way, allowing him to open my door and leave. He didn't bother to close it behind him or bid me goodnight. He simply walked back to the stairs and out of sight, his footsteps retreating until I could hear them no more.

I was on the wrong side of the building to see him get into his car, yet in the silence of the night I was able to hear his engine start and the soft crunch of gravel as he pulled away.

Closing the door and turning back to the bed, I found a pair of dachshunds on it staring at me. Now that I was meeting their gaze, both wagged their tails. So far as they were concerned, this was a fresh bedtime - they'd been up and done stuff and now it was time for another bedtime biscuit.

I rolled my eyes, wagged a finger at them, and tucked them under my duvet.

The shower, fresh clothes, and then the excitement of a late-night visit had driven my fatigue away. Coupled with the excitement I felt over digging further into the possibility that I had now uncovered what was behind the deaths and the villagers' odd behaviour, I was wide awake.

Settling back into the uncomfortable chair in front of my laptop, I did my best to mentally prepare myself for several more hours of research.

Land Registry. Sunday, October 15th 0112hrs

I started by returning to the search for gold. None had been found here before and all the thousands of years that people had lived on this island suggested that was because there wasn't any here to find. Jane's research, because I knew she would be thorough, eliminated to a large extent the possibility that there was something like the Saxon Horde here to find.

Certainly, I believed it more likely that rather than buried treasure, there was in fact a gold seam here. It was that or Darius Cooper was pulling some kind of scam on the entire village. If that were the case, it had cost a man's life, and given Mr Cooper's apparent aversion to violence, it seemed strange that he would still be here instead of choosing to run away.

Nevertheless, I explored the possibility that there might be gold in the ground. I made a few notes in my notebook to that effect - trying on a few theories. Nothing I could come up with sounded more likely than my initial belief that Darius Cooper knew something no one else did.

Once I had exhausted enough web pages to convince myself that there was no information out there worth finding, I made a fresh cup of tea in the hope that the caffeine would keep me going. Back at my desk, I started a new line of research.

Warming my hands against the cup, I let go with my right, and using two fingers to type, I opened a new tab for the Land Registry. Land Registry in the UK is that organisation which acts as a repository for information about who owns which piece of land. When you buy a house or when you buy a piece of woodland or whatever, Land Registry is where the new ownership is recorded.

Still sitting at the centre of this mystery, Darius Cooper was an enigma and I wanted to know more about him. Since I'd found nothing in his house to indicate his true identity, and all Jane had turned up in her attempt to identify him was that he didn't exist, I was opting to work backwards.

There would be a name recorded against the property in Peckham Lane. I was certain the name would not be Darius Cooper, but who would it be?

I have used Land Registry before to find information, so I already knew when I filled in the information search enquiry and paid the small fee to get an answer, that it would be not until the next working day that I received my response.

With the enquiry sent, I finished my tea. Holding the empty mug in my left hand while I drummed the fingers of my right on the desk, I questioned if there was anything else I could do.

There were several things still bothering me. Chief among which was exactly what had happened to Wayne Calder. Someone had murdered him, removed his body, used a chemical process - if my guess was correct - to desiccate his corpse, and then returned him to the mine as a warning to everyone else.

That singular act did everything to reinforce the villagers' story of an ancient beast roaming the area, and was responsible for scaring away the workers which in turn caused the strife the Fletchers were now enduring.

Irene, Darius, Kevin, and whoever else from Playford was involved in this conspiracy, were guilty of the crime. Or at best were protecting the person or persons who had murdered poor Wayne.

In the morning when the sun came up, not now because I was bone tired and sore from the events of the day, it was my plan to investigate some of the farm buildings in the nearby area. It felt a little like clutching at straws, because there were so many farm buildings. Yet I believed the killer or killers could not have taken Wayne very far when they removed his body.

That was pretty much my last thought, as I drifted off to sleep still in my chair, awaking almost an hour later with a stiff neck, a sore back, and an overwhelming need to empty my bladder.

Sleep took me quickly when I clambered into bed just a minute or so later, and I stayed that way until I was rudely awoken by a hammering on my door.

As usual, my sausage dogs ran across the room to repel the person outside. My door was locked from the inside, but that just meant that the person outside continued to hammer.

I didn't have to wonder who it was for very long because they announced themselves.

'Tempest? Tempest, are you awake?' my mother called through the door. 'It's after nine thirty, Tempest. If you don't get up soon, you're going to miss breakfast. And you'll be late for church.'

Groggily, I lifted my head from the pillow and squinted at the door. Was it really that late in the day? When I crawled into bed, I hadn't given much thought to what time I needed to get up, and it had been so late, or perhaps early depending on one's point of view, that I'd fallen into a deep enough sleep that my internal body clock had failed to wake me.

'Tempest?'

'I'm awake,' I called back.

'Can you let me in, Tempest?'

I shuffled my body around, getting my legs and arms pointing the right way so that I could get out of bed. Reports coming in from all over my body reminded me of my fight with Kevin and gang just a few hours ago. The bruising was coming out, and it would do no favours to let mother see it.

'Just give me a second, mum. I need to put something on.' I hopped on one leg and then the other, slipping into my jogging bottoms and then covering my top half with the same thin tee shirt I'd had on before I climbed into bed.

Both dogs were snuffling at the gap underneath the door, eager to see my mother and probably eager to get outside as they would want to do their business.

I scooped them both, unlocked the door, and swung it open to let my mother in.

She waltzed into the room as if she owned it, a suit carrier hanging from her left hand.

'Have you anything suitable to wear to church today, Tempest?'

'Huh?' I was still trying to get my brain up to speed and questioning why it might be that my mother thought we were all going to church. It wasn't as if this was even our parish, not that I went to the church in my own parish.

Without being invited to do so, my mother opened the wardrobe in my room, rolled her eyes when she found nothing in it, and hung the suit carrier, operating the zip to expose what was inside.

185

'That's one of dad's old suits,' I observed. 'I have no desire to go to church this morning mother. I'm in the middle of an investigation. Besides, there's no chance that thing will fit me.'

'Oh, Tempest, it's been so long since we went to church together. In fact, we don't really do anything together anymore.'

My mother was laying the guilt on thick. She'd been doing it my entire life, and thus had gotten quite good at it.

With a sigh, I said, 'Mother, surely you realise there are more important things than attending a church service? Two people have died here, and there are all manner of screwy goings on. I think I'm getting close to figuring out what it is the locals are up to.' I didn't want to tell mother about the gold. Experience had taught me that telling my mother as little as possible about absolutely anything was always the best policy because she had no ability to keep a secret.

Were I to reveal what I believed I had discovered, she would be blurting it to everybody within minutes.

My stomach rumbled, the naughty fish 'n' chip supper from the previous evening digested and now forgotten. Breakfast was my first priority, and then I needed to get out and explore. The end to this mystery, and finding the evidence that would deliver me the persons behind Wayne Calder's death, was now tantalisingly close. I could waste no time on trivial pursuits and that included doing things that would keep my mother happy.

I hooked a pair of socks out of my bag and then donned my shoes. My first activity, as it is almost every morning, was to take the dogs out for some exercise.

'If you'll excuse me mother, those little dogs are dancing because they want to go out. Have you had breakfast yet?'

'No, Tempest, not yet. Yet again, I was hoping we might all have breakfast together,' my mother replied in a pointed manner. Adding a flare of her eyes, she dared me to disappoint her.

There really was no point arguing or fighting about it. As she pointed out, it was nearing the time when the landlord would no longer wish to serve breakfast, and I was hungry.

'I'll see you in the dining room in just a few minutes, Mother,' I replied with a smile to reassure her. 'Now, if you'll excuse me, I really must take these little dogs outside.'

It might be because they are well trained, though I think it more likely they are simply driven by the desire to get back inside for their breakfast. Whichever it is, my two little sausage dogs got on with the task of signing their names on the rock wall outside, and ran back to the door to be let in again.

Thus it was, less than ten minutes after rising, I was coming into the dining room to find my parents. It was, however, to my surprise, that Big Ben was sat with them. Yet more surprising was his attire.

When he isn't clothed in combat fatigues because we're off doing dangerous stuff at night, Big Ben can usually be found wearing sportswear or will perhaps be dressed in an outfit suitable for a round of golf if that is what he is doing with his day. In vast contrast, he was wearing a suit with a shirt and a tie.

'What are you wearing?' I asked as I pulled out the remaining empty seat at the table and sat down.

Big Ben grinned at me. 'My Sunday best, of course.'

My father held up the pot of tea as a question, and at my nod, filled my cup. I bade both my parents good morning even though I had already greeted my mother in my room a few minutes ago.

'You don't go to church,' I pointed out, thinking that to be quite a pertinent factor. 'Where did you even find a suit that would fit you at such short notice?'

Big Ben bit into a piece of toast, shuffling it to one side of his mouth so that he could attempt to speak around it.

'I never leave home without a decent suit,' he claimed. 'One never knows when it might come in handy. As for church,' he glanced at my mother to see if she was listening and gave me a sly grin, 'there are always single women in any congregation. I like to pop along for a service every now and then so I can answer their prayers.'

I closed my eyes and unconsciously prayed for someone to deliver me from the situations I found myself in.

There were thickly cut slices of toast on a rack in the centre of the table. I helped myself to two triangles, slathering them both in butter. The toast had gone cold, yet that did not diminish the pleasure they gave. Having eaten greasy, naughty fish and chips last night, I ought to be out trying to burn off some calories this morning and eating extra carefully. Instead, I was stuffing my face with carbs and fat.

I figured I could get away with it. Just for today.

A buffet table set against one wall provided fruit, granola, yoghurt, cereals, and other breakfast delicacies. I filled a plate and returned to the table.

188

'Has anyone seen the ninjas this morning?' I asked.

Big Ben mumbled around another bite of toast, 'I heard them getting up. It was just after six. Trisha said she had to leave to get things set up ready for breakfast.'

Whether Trisha was in fact the barmaid I'd seen Big Ben with in the middle of the night, or a different woman, because that would not be unusual for him, I chose not to investigate. What surprised me most was that my mother let the comment pass without remarking.

'Is everything alright, Mother?' I enquired.

'Yes, thank you, Tempest,' she replied. 'You are questioning why I'm not berating Benjamin for his womanising, yes?'

Frowning slightly, I said, 'It is somewhat out of character for you, Mother.'

'Yes, well, Benjamin is coming to church this morning where I am quite sure he will beg our Lord and Father for forgiveness. It shames me that the same cannot be said of my own son. Will you be out breaking more laws this morning instead of attending church as you should?'

I had my mouth full of yoghurt and granola and thus couldn't reply immediately. It was another one of those occasions where I really felt like saying something rude. However, the delay in answering allowed me to get my brain up to speed. If I went to church, how many of the villagers would I see there? All of them? Would I see those who I wanted to see? How would they react to my presence? Better yet, would it be the case that some were visibly absent?

I wanted to poke around, but since I had no idea where they might have been last night, the church, potentially, was as good a place as any other to start.

Decision made I announced my intention to accompany my parents to the small chapel at the edge of the village.

My mother beamed a smile, a typical response when she believed she had gotten her own way, and her entire demeanour changed.

'Now you get to beg for forgiveness in person, Tempest. That's so much better than me doing it for you. God loves a sinner,' she reminded me.

I remained quiet, which was a good policy considering that I had a half plan to sneak out part way through the service. This mystery wasn't going to solve itself, and like I already said, I was getting close to uncovering the truth.

The regular Sunday morning service was due to start at 1030hrs; my mother had already checked the board at the front of the church. With breakfast finished, it left me with approximately fifteen minutes to get dressed.

That, of course, presented a fresh challenge, for my father's suit, ignoring that it was three decades out of style, was not the right size for me. Like many of my generation, I had grown taller than the one before. I was also more muscular than my father had ever been and wondered if I could even get my shoulders into the jacket.

It turned out that I could. Worse yet, I had omitted to lock my door, so my hope that I might claim that it did not fit even if it did, went to ruin when my mother put her head through the gap and spotted me wearing it.

One of the reasons it fitted, was the eighties style for huge shoulders.

'Oh, Tempest, you look lovely,' remarked my mother in an enthusiastic manner. 'Michael, Michael, come and look at your son. He's wearing your suit and he looks splendid.'

My father arrived at the door a moment later looking over my mother's head. He had to fold his top lip over his bottom to stop himself from laughing. The suit fit. But only sort of.

The biggest issue in my opinion, if one is to ignore the style, the shoulders of which made me look like an American football player complete with armour, was the small fact that the trousers stopped a full four inches before they reached my ankles.

The same could be said of the jacket sleeves which were so short on my arms that it looked to be a fashion statement. I didn't have a shirt with me unless one counts a polo shirt which was what I was now wearing.

Essentially, I looked ridiculous.

A loud guffaw of laughter filled the corridor when Big Ben arrived behind my father and looked over the top of his head.

'Hey, nice outfit, butt monkey!' he exclaimed. 'You look ready to audition for a kids TV show.'

My mother elbowed him hard in the ribs which had about as much effect as whacking him with a cushion and only served to heighten his amusement.

'You are not a very good friend,' my mother attempted to chastise my tall friend.

My father shook his head and walked away. 'It's just banter, Mary.'

'Men,' my mother muttered as if that summed up the entirety of all that needed to be said on the subject. 'We really need to go, gentlemen. Come along.'

I messed about, faking a need to settle the dogs and take them out again before we could set off. It was a deliberate tactic on my part, not because I wanted to mess my mother around, but because I wanted to arrive late and have all the churchgoers from the village already there.

My hope was that they would all be inside, and I could avoid any unnecessary nonsense outside where I worried they might actually try to block our entry. It sounds like such an unlikely thing to happen outside a Sunday church service, yet the villagers had been ... shall we say, unwilling to be friendly at any point thus far. I wanted to avoid exposing my parents to further unpleasantness.

So it was just gone 10:30 when, with my mother hurrying us along, we approached the church. Mother was tutting and grumbling because we could hear singing coming from inside and that, of course, meant the service had already started.

The small chapel was largely hidden from view by trees and shrubs until one turned the final bend in the road, but when it came into view, it was not the church that drew my eye, but the cars parked outside it.

There were dozens.

Why would anyone drive to a church that was only a few hundred yards away? On both sides of the road, parked on the grass verges and bumper to bumper, car after car sat waiting for the congregation to collect them again after the service.

I paused for a second, staring at them until my mother hooked her hand into my elbow and yanked it.

'Come along, Tempest. We are already late!' she complained, hauling me along like a disobedient child.

Our entrance to the church went largely unnoticed because the congregation was singing. A verger, not someone I recognised, greeted us, and pointed to an empty pew at the back.

A few heads turned, eyes widening when they saw who it was, and then a ripple which started a few feet from us spread across the church.

My mother, a regular churchgoer for her entire life, did not need the hymn book to know the words and had begun singing before we took our seats. I was not singing, I was working. Almost everybody in the congregation had turned to look at me, and that allowed me to see them.

I made several observations in the first few seconds. To start with, Kevin was nowhere to be seen. I spotted two of the men who were with him last night, both were those who managed to escape relatively unscathed. Terry the mouthy man from the bar was nowhere in sight. But all of that was background noise because standing together in the front pew, were Irene and Darius.

That they knew each other came as no surprise. In such a small community, I felt it certain there were few secrets, and everyone knew more or less everything about everyone else. However, that the woman I took to be the matriarch of this community, and the man I believed to be at the centre of the mystery were standing side by side, seemed significant. It was the second time I had seen them together.

The term 'thick as thieves' echoed in my head.

The hymn came to its conclusion and the residents of Playford sat once more, though the suspicious glances over their shoulders continued. My mother was oblivious to it, or perhaps able to simply ignore it. She was focused on the vicar as he moved to the lectern to read a piece of scripture.

His words washed over me, my brain unable to focus on two things at once and already locked on the mystery I was trying to unravel. Darius and Irene knew that I was looking at them. They checked over their shoulders a couple of times to see if I was still watching before finding the control to stop looking.

I found myself chewing on my lip, mulling over this latest minor clue, and wondering what it meant. It was going to upset my mother if I left before the end of the service. She undoubtedly planned to stay for tea and cake or whatever the local practise was. There was a small church hall just across the graveyard to the front of the church and perhaps the congregation would migrate there.

However, there was no chance I was hanging around. Ignoring the hostility the locals constantly displayed towards me, and my concern that they might do the same to my parents, I was going to depart shortly. If these people were here, then they were not wherever it was they were keeping the gold or where they stashed the props used to fake the appearance of the Deathling. With me breathing down their necks, I had a hunch they might well head there when they got out of the church.

If I could prompt that by leaving early, and increase the nervousness I suspected they already felt, perhaps I would be able to tail them. I believed it was worth a shot at least.

The second the muscles in my legs tensed, my mother placed a hand on my arm.

'Where are you going, Tempest?' she hissed at me.

When an old lady sitting in front turned her head and scowled, her expression intended to make my mother quiet, my mother shot her a pleasant smile. The moment the old lady turned back around to face the vicar, my mother scowled at me again.

'You're not leaving this church, Tempest.' Mother tried to melt my face with her eyes.

I tapped her hand, sliding my backside across the wooden pew to get away.

'I need to use the little boys' room, Mother. I know, I know, I should have gone before we left.'

Okay, so I was lying through my teeth to my dear mother in church. If you believe in a forgiving God, then I'm sure I will be okay.

Without another word, I got up, crouching slightly, and ducked around to get back to the door whereupon I swiftly exited the church.

Now I had options. I wanted to see if members of the congregation would soon sneak out, I also wanted to then be able to follow them. However, I was on foot, and I had to assume they were all going to jump into their cars after the service. I needed my car if I planned to see where they went.

I also wanted to have a proper scout around the village and the surrounding farmland. I could not do all these things at the same time, and I was still dressed ridiculously.

Choosing to deal with the least important thing first, I ran back to my room at the B&B.

Bull and Dozer lifted their heads as I came into the room, looking surprised that I was back so soon after leaving. The lazy monkeys did not get out of their bed, the sum total of their response a half-hearted attempt at a tail wag from Dozer before both dogs put their heads back down and closed their eyes once more.

I had shucked dad's jacket as I jogged up the stairs to my room and now, with the door swinging shut behind me, I was already peeling off everything else. Grabbing fresh clothes from the bag next to the bed, I reached across to the desk and tapped the on button for my laptop. While it booted up, I sat on the bed and slid my legs into my ripstop combat trousers.

I was picking an outfit more appropriate for the likely events of the day.

My computer, much like most others I'm sure, has a feature whereby it populates new emails in a corner of the screen to advise the owner that they have some. Spotting that, I opened my messenger tab and was surprised to find one from Land Registry.

I had a reply to my inquiry already.

Questioning my luck - I didn't think they worked on Sundays - I nevertheless opened the email. Thinking that perhaps they had changed the working hours, or perhaps working practises, I scanned down the information until my eyes screeched to a halt upon seeing the one piece of detail I needed.

Number three Peckham Lane was not owned by Darius Cooper. Of course, I knew that already. It was not going to be his name displayed because his name was fake. I expected to see a different name, but for it to still be a man's name. Instead, number three Peckham Lane was owned by Irene Tanner.

That's the same Irene Tanner, who was standing at the front of the church next to Darius Cooper. She owned the house that he was living in. So what was their connection?

I was half dressed – trousers on but not my belt, socks on but not my boots. It had been my absolute intention to get back across to the church and have my car tucked out of the way ready to go should I need it. Now though, I found myself lowering into the chair, the need to explore this connection further my latest priority.

Expecting that she was up and awake, and would have her phone to hand, I sent Jane a message via social media. That done, I opened a web browser and started searching for Irene Tanner.

Jane responded so fast the search engine didn't have enough time to respond before her Sunday morning greeting popped up in the corner of my screen.

'Good morning, Tempest. You're using social media? You always text me. Did something happen to your phone?'

I typed my response. 'I broke it. Can you do two minutes of research? I have a lady here called Irene Tanner who owns the house of Darius Cooper - the man you identified with the fake identity. I need to know more about her. I'm going to try from my end, but you are better at this than me.'

In response I got several emojis. I wasn't sure what all of them were. One appeared to be a head laughing while crying and tilting to the side. Another might have been popcorn? I'm just not that down with the kids.

Mercifully, her response ended with some words. 'I'm on it.'

Keeping my eyes on the screen and scanning down line by line, I looked for a likely hit that might give me some information, whilst simultaneously finishing the process of getting dressed.

Apparently, searching for Irene Tanner is too broad. I had pages of hits but none of it looked likely to be to do with the particular Irene Tanner in question. I refined the search by placing a plus symbol and the word Playford immediately after her name, then jabbed the return button to make it search once more.

This time, I got a whole load more responses, but they were still not what I was looking for. My search was now too narrow, causing the machine to just find what it could to do with Irene Tanner and ignoring the Playford connection.

Back in my chair as I tied my boots, I questioned how else to attack this. What would Jane do?

What Jane would do, apparently, is beat me to it.

A textbox popped up at the bottom of my screen as Jane started a fresh conversation.

'I've just sent you an email,' she announced. 'I think this might be the smoking gun you've been looking for.'

I clicked the tab for my emails, holding my breath and attempting to still my excitement. What had she found?

The email bore the title 'Is this him?' and I could see there were attachments to it. My eyes could barely move fast enough as I attempted to absorb everything that she had written. Not that she had written it, she had simply grabbed chunks of information from wherever she had found it.

It started with Irene Tanner and the fact that she was a widow. I knew this already for I am observant and had seen the wedding band on her finger. That there was clearly no man around, combined with her age and the wedding band told me all I needed to know about her marital status.

However, this was where it got interesting. There was nothing remarkable about her spouse, at least that was not what Jane was highlighting. Not unless you counted the fact that he had a famously criminal brother.

Jane had found the connection in a minute or maybe slightly more. There was nothing particularly unusual about this, she had always had a way of finding information no one else could.

I was staring at a picture of a younger version of Darius Cooper. There could be no question that it was him because I could see some of the ink on his face and neck. It was a mug shot from a newspaper article. He had been jailed for murder forty-two years ago and released just weeks before the beetle story emerged.

I was too young to remember the crime, however, I had heard of it. Known as the United Banks Robbery, a gang of armed men had hijacked a gold bullion transport and got away with an unfeasibly large amount of gold. It was the kind of story, a bit like the Great Train Robbery, that got romanticised by the press and lived on in infamy.

Itching away at the back of my head while I read about Darius, who had been christened Joshua Curly, was a little voice that was trying to make itself heard. I ignored it to press on with the story I was reading.

Joshua Curly was the only one of the gang to be caught. The police caught up to him as he attempted to get to Dover. That the men had never been caught, and the gold never recovered, was one of the factors that made it such a famous case. A security guard was killed in the robbery, and it was that crime for which Joshua Curly had been convicted. That he had never given up the identity or whereabouts of his fellow gang members was undoubtedly a factor in the length of his sentence.

But now I knew why he was out on mine land attempting to find gold - that was where he hid his share! I did not doubt my guess for one second. He wasn't prospecting for alluvial gold. There was no ancient seam of gold hidden beneath the soil and gorse bushes around the mine. No, Joshua Curly, perhaps sensing he was going to get caught, chose to bury his gold.

At the time the land was almost certainly just a forest, and he had chosen a place that he believed he could return to, and which would not be found by accident. How dismayed must he have been when he was finally released from prison only to discover the landmarks he must once have relied on were no longer there?

For the last year he had been searching for the gold. I read further into the story, confirming my belief that he was not originally from the village of Playford. Joshua Curly, and indeed his brother, originally hailed from Leicester, but Joshua had been taken in by the local residents and was treated as one of their own. I knew why - he had many millions in gold and was willing to share it with them.

That was why he came up with the rare beetle story. That was why the villagers got behind the idea of the Deathling and promoted the story. They wanted to search for the gold but had to do so in a secretive manner.

I pushed back in my chair, a sense of both relief and awe washing through me. Wayne Calder must have disturbed them when they were looking for the gold a few nights ago. Perhaps they'd been searching systematically and had eliminated many of the areas away from the mine, forcing them to come closer and closer to where the mineworkers operated.

I had them. I felt certain of that. But it was not yet time to call my clients. I did, however, feel it would not be jumping the gun too greatly if I were to reveal the probability now of a swift conclusion.

Tapping the button to start a new email I sent a quick message to Stefan Fletcher, in which I outlined that I knew now who had killed Wayne Calder, and hoped to be able to give them a full report within a few hours. It was suitably vague, but given the drama at the mine last night, I felt sure both owners would be grateful to hear something positive.

The little voice in the back of my head which I had been ignoring for several minutes now, demanded I pay attention. When I finally listened to what it had to say, I almost fell off my chair.

Jumping to my feet with such suddenness that I woke the dogs, I began looking frantically around the room. The scrap of paper in Mildred Marchant's coat pocket had listed the quiz teams from the village and it was on that piece of paper that I first saw Darius Cooper's name.

I didn't have the piece of paper, I remembered. I had put it back into her pocket, but I had taken a photograph. Of course, I couldn't look at the photograph because my phone was broken.

Closing my eyes, I visualised it in my head. Joshua Curly had chosen to disguise his identity, hiding from the world in a small village while he searched for the gold he stole. In my head I could see the name as it was written.

Darius B Cooper.

DB Cooper.

The man had been laughing at me the whole time.

That the name he picked was that of an infamous American thief who allegedly got away with a vast amount of money should have occurred to me days ago.

'Better late than never,' I muttered to myself.

I shot my cuff to check the time: 1053hrs. It was time to get going. The church service would end in a little over half an hour, but if people were to sneak out early, I wanted to be there to follow them.

Quickly performing my usual routine of patting my pockets to make sure I had everything, and satisfied that I did, I grabbed my jacket and was ready to leave the room. Bull and Dozer took this to be a cue for going out, both bouncing from their bed, their little tails wagging. I was about to put them back under the blanket but stopped when I acknowledged I could not be sure when I would return.

You will remember that I did not want to bring them with me on this case, and in fact chose to leave them with my parents. They were going to get in the way of what I was trying to do today, but I wasn't content to let them suffer for that. I could leave them in the car at times, and perhaps I would meet up with my parents and be able to trade them off.

Accepting the situation for what it was, I clipped them onto their leads and opened my door. Outside in the corridor I found Poison. She was heading my way, a determined gait to her stride.

'Oh, hey, Poison,' I waved to her in greeting and moved my body to block her route. She needed to hear what I had to say.

'Hi, Tempest,' she replied, sounding a little tired. 'Sorry, I have to go. I'm meeting some people. The Swedish are here already. They were able to finish building their machine far more swiftly than anticipated.'

'I've got to the bottom of what's going on, Poison,' I revealed, failing to step aside. 'This is nothing to do with a monster and everything to do with a forty-year-old crime. There is a man in the village who stole gold bullion and I believe it is buried somewhere in the ground close to the mine.'

'Gold bullion?' Poison repeated my words, failing to hide the surprise in her voice.

I nodded my head. 'The local villagers brought an old legend back to life in the hope that they could explore the ground close to the mine. They needed to get the mineworkers out of the way and my guess is they killed Wayne Calder because he found them or spotted them.'

Poison seemed to be considering what I just told her, her delicate features scrunched up slightly in thought.

'But ... the Swedish have found something. Frank said they diverted a satellite to check the area and they found something under the ground.'

I think we both realised what that meant at the exact same moment for we simultaneously blurted, 'They found the gold!'

Picking up on our excitement, both my dogs barked. A noise from farther down the corridor behind Poison turned out to be Hatchett opening the door to his room.

He stumbled out into the corridor scratching his head and looking sleepy. They had probably been up half the night, scouring the ground around the mine. That they had not accidentally run into Darius or anybody else from the village out there looking for the gold came as no great surprise, the land around the mine covered hectares.

'What's going on?' he mumbled.

Poison twisted around at the waist to look back down the corridor at him.

'I'll explain on the way,' she said. 'Get your clothes on. We need to go.'

Another door opened just a couple of yards behind Hatchett, this one revealing the scantily clad form of Mistress Mushy. Like Hatchett, she appeared to have just woken up having snatched a few hours of sleep.

She asked the same question, 'What's going on?'

Hatchett, sounding a little flippant, turned to Mistress Mushy when he said, 'She'll tell us on the way.'

Frowning in confusion, Mistress Mushy asked the obvious question, 'On the way to where?'

Poison waved her hands, indicating that they should scurry away and get dressed. Her urgent gesticulations having the desired effect after a couple of seconds.

Turning to me, she said, 'The Swedish team should be pulling up outside any moment now. They were coming here to collect us.' She brushed by me, calling over her shoulder, 'Come on.'

At the bottom of the stairs, we both turned right to exit the building and I heard the sound of a man humming somewhere in the background. I suspected it was the landlord, going about the daily business of running a pub. Knowing what I now knew, he was almost certainly on the outside of the conspiracy and knew nothing about it. Had he done so, he would have stopped taking in guests.

I thought back to the congregation in the church, and to those who were not there. It wasn't just Kevin and Terry who were missing, I estimated that there were perhaps twenty to twenty-five percent of the residents not in attendance. It could just be that those persons did not go to church; nothing unusual in the twenty-first century. Yet I suspected they were not in church because they were actively engaged in trying to hide what was going on.

I was running by the time I hit the door, shunting it open with a flat palm. There was a sturdily built off-road vehicle in the car park. It wasn't the kind of thing you could hire or buy; this had been built for a specific job. A man with blonde hair was next to the driver's door, talking to whoever was inside the cab.

He heard us coming and broke off his conversation to greet us. I wanted to do this fast and get back to the church, so I was talking before we even got to him.

'Hi, I'm Tempest Michaels. There is no monster here. Poison will fill you in on the details.' I touched her arm to get her attention. 'I'm going to the church,' I told her, 'All the people involved are there. I think it's probably about time we called the police, but I broke my phone. Can you do it?'

Assuming she would do just that, I didn't wait for her answer, and broke into a jog. My parents were at the church, and though they were with Big Ben, and therefore relatively safe, Big Ben is not bulletproof.

My dachshunds skipped happily along the road, tugging at the end of their leads even though they had no idea where they were going.

The distance to the church couldn't have been more than about two hundred and fifty yards, however, I was still fifty yards shy when I started to get a sinking feeling.

The cars were no longer parked outside the church.

Worry made my pace increase, my dogs matching it so they continued to tug me along the road. I reached the path from the pavement to the front of the church, running its length as it wound beneath ancient trees. I already believed my concerns were well founded, but when I got to the door, and confirmed it was locked, my heart sank.

The service had ended, the villagers had all left, and my parents were nowhere in sight.

I yelled for them. Bellowing their names as loudly as I could before listening, but no response came back. The integrity of the door was tested by my boot when I kicked hard at the lock to see if it would give.

It didn't budge.

The door was made from oak, the fittings from steel forged many decades ago and my body would give in first.

I ran around the church looking for another way in. In truth, I doubted they were in there, but I had to check before moving on.

Wherever they were, they had Big Ben with them, but that just meant he was in trouble too. Sucking in a few lungfuls of air, I spun myself around and started running back to the inn.

There were people gathered in the car park outside the pub. Poison was with three people bearing distinctly Swedish features. They all had blonde hair and they were tall. Even the woman was taller than me, and the tallest man had to be close to Big Ben's height.

They all looked my way as I approached. Their expressions were curious, undoubtedly questioning what I was up to having just run one way, vanished, and then come running back again.

By the time I got back to them I was out of breath and slowed my pace to a walk for the last fifteen or twenty yards.

Seeing my face, Poison asked, 'What is it, Tempest?'

Between gasps of air, I managed, 'They've gone. They've gone and they've taken my parents.' I wanted to make a joke about how they were probably going to give mother back, but this was the wrong audience.

'Who?' asked one of the Swedes, a man in his early forties. He was the one I'd seen talking to the driver of the van when I first left the inn. 'Who's gone? Who are we talking about?'

The new arrivals were way behind the curve on current events.

Before I could answer him the three remaining ninjas exited the inn, Mistress Mushy leading the way. They were still sorting out their clothing having rushed the job of getting dressed, but they were ready, and I knew that they could be relied on.

They still didn't know about the gold bullion. The Swedes, however, did.

'Is this something to do with the gold Poison mentioned?' asked the female member of the Swedish team. She was very thin, with glasses that distorted her features a little.

'What gold?' asked Bob.

I had no time for any of this. My parents are missing and almost certainly in the hands of people I knew to be capable of murder. My anger was rising, a full head of steam building up. Soon it was going to burst, and by then I hoped to be in a position to exact some justice.

Raising my voice, I expressed what I felt needed to happen next.

'I'm talking about the residents of this village,' I explained. 'They invented the creature you have erroneously been sent here to capture. It is nothing more than a ruse.'

'We'll still need to check that out for ourselves,' remarked the taller of the two Swedish men.

I could have argued that it would be a waste of his time, but doing so would have been a waste of mine, so I skipped forward to the part where we achieved something.

'The locals have killed at least one person and it is all because one of them stole millions in gold a long time ago. It's buried on the land near to the mine which came along before he could come back for it. They will kill again to protect the gold and they have just kidnapped my parents and my colleague.'

'They've got Big Ben?' Poison wanted to confirm.

'Yes, and they'll probably choose to kill all three of them and make it look like the Deathling got them. We don't know where they are,' I pointed out. 'They were all in cars. At least, there were a whole load of cars parked outside the church before and now there are not. So I suggest we go to the one place on the map we can identify.'

'Where's that?' asked Poison.

I shifted my gaze from her to the three Swedish people. 'Your satellite found something, yes?'

My belief was that the gold was yet to be found. Based on Kevin's comment to Darius yesterday, it dictated that if we could get to it, and I was right that it was indeed the gold the satellite had found beneath the ground, then I would have everything I needed to force the villagers' hands.

I was in the front cab of the Swedish scientists' off-road vehicle. Poison and the ninjas were following behind in Mistress Mushy's car, a little Suzuki off-roader. It hadn't taken me long to learn the Swedes' names: Gable, Hagan, and Babette. Gable was the tall one, his blonde hair pulled into a ponytail. Both men had beards, and they were the most muscular scientists I had ever met.

Before we set off, they questioned how best to get onto the land owned by the mine and were a little startled when I suggested simply driving up to the gate. With me on board they had legitimate access to the mine.

On the way there, I explained who I was, taking no offence that they had never heard of me. My refusal to believe in the supernatural was treated with amusement, until of course I had fully explained a few of my cases and exactly what it was we were walking into this time

To say they were disappointed there was no monster for them to find was understating things quite severely. The back load bed of their vehicle was filled with a strange device. I could only imagine its purpose - the multitude of electronics, cabling, hoses, and what looked to be an enormous emerald mounted behind a screen, had been built for some strange supernatural purpose.

I could, of course, have asked them, but then they would have spent time explaining something I didn't need to know about. Much like Frank and the ninjas, the three Swedish scientists were from the school of thought that believed in all things arcane and paranormal. They all worked in research, Gable explained, adding that his grandfather had been killed by a troll. He made it sound as if it was something to brag about.

Steering the vehicle as best he could, Hagan manoeuvred across the rugged landscape at a sedate pace. I wanted them to go faster, but they dared not in deference to the delicate machinery they brought all the way from Sweden.

I think they were secretly hoping I was wrong about everything so they would get a chance to test it on something ancient and evil.

The satellite navigation system mounted on the front dash - not a standard item, but something they appeared to have built themselves, was taking us to a point marked on the map. The map itself was featureless, there being no roads anywhere near us.

As we came closer, the distance to target ticking down steadily, I was able to gauge just how close the mine had come to accidentally discovering the gold. Had the mining operation continued onwards, eating up the ground as it continued to bore for gypsum, I estimated that it could have been no more than a few weeks before they would have made a startling find.

Cresting a rise, my eyes torn between the satellite navigation screen and the landscape ahead, I performed a double take when I got a first look at our target.

There were two cars, both battered off-road vehicles undoubtedly owned by the local residents for their farm work, parked exactly where we were heading. Completely hidden from sight until a second ago, they were in a natural trough in the landscape. No one at the mine would see them unless they came out here looking.

It was people from Playford. They had beaten us to it!

My heart rate spiked, the two sleeping sausage dogs on my lap both reacting as they somehow picked up on the change in me.

My companions were babbling in Swedish again, speaking animatedly, and clearly discussing that there were people in front of us.

'Didn't you say these people were dangerous criminals?' asked Babette.

A head popped up at ground level, the face of the person looking at us showing their shock when they realised the vehicle approaching was not the one they expected.

We were ten yards away when Hagen took his foot off the accelerator and let the vehicle cruise to a stop. My colleagues were still discussing what they should do, not that I could understand what they were saying, the tone of their words was enough to make it obvious.

This was not what they came here for. They were here to find a monster or to catch a demon or something equally ridiculous. Now faced with humans - humans who were probably guilty of murder - they wanted to go back to Sweden.

I was having none of that.

Before they could argue, I reached across Gable, grabbed the door handle, and shoved it open.

'I'm getting out, chaps,' I told them with iron in my voice. 'If you wait here, you will be perfectly safe.'

However, it transpired that I'd misunderstood what they were talking about. Yes, they had been arguing about what to do, but they were also very curious about the potential for there to be gold in the ground and how badly it had skewed the results of their satellite. Thinking scientifically, what they wanted to do was investigate so that they might tune their instruments to read more accurately.

'We are coming with you, Tempest,' Gable assured me, swivelling his legs around to get out.

Following him out was easier than clambering over him. The two dachshunds wanted to come too, but I shut them inside, promising that I would not be long as I closed the door on their disappointed faces.

Disturbed by our appearance, three men and a woman from the village had clambered out of the hole. They were looking scared, none too surprisingly, and glancing around furtively as they questioned what their next move might be.

I recognised three of them. Two from the altercation last night, one of whom was Kevin, who I must say I was very pleased to see again. The third was Rosie. They were all a little grubby, and looked to have been working hard.

Kevin held a gold brick in his hands, dismissing any question that I hadn't got this part of the mystery right.

With the three Swedes hard on my shoulder, and the four ninjas hurrying to catch up, Rosie, Kevin, and the others were outnumbered and knew they were in trouble.

I drew level with the back of one of the old, battered off-road vehicles, my eyes flaring in surprise when I saw just how much gold they had already recovered.

Kevin dropped the gold brick and grabbed a shovel, lifting it to shoulder height as his face contorted into a grimace. He meant to fight.

I did not need to turn around to know that the sound I just heard was four swords being drawn. Poison and her friends didn't need to say anything, the startled expressions from the four locals said it all.

'Drop it,' I growled at Kevin. 'You're all in enough trouble already. Don't make it any worse.'

Apart from climbing out of the hole in the ground, they hadn't really moved since we got out of the cars. They were rooted to the spot, caught red handed, and they had no way out.

'Where are my parents?' I aimed the question at all four villagers.

None of them answered, but I didn't think they were playing dumb. Wherever my parents had been taken, it had happened when they left the church, and these four hadn't been there. They had been out here recovering the gold.

Two more strides took me close enough to the edge of the hole that I could see in. What I saw blew my mind.

Looking down into the freshly dug hole, then back at the gold already stacked inside the two vehicles, the equation didn't balance. I could see where the gold had been. Neat rectangular indentations in the soil showed where brick after brick had been removed and what I was looking at in the back of the vehicles was just a small fraction of the whole.

My brain needed only a moment to get up to speed. Joshua Curly hadn't buried just his share, he buried everything they took. That was why his accomplices had never been caught and the gold had never been recovered. I could only guess that perhaps he had killed them all or maybe they had escaped. Maybe it had always been his intention to double cross his accomplices and keep it all. Whatever the case, all the gold from the United Banks Robbery had gone into this hole where it had lain hidden and untouched for more than four decades.

Poison came to my side. 'What should we do with them, Tempest?' she asked.

I huffed out a frustrated breath. 'I still need to find my parents. And Big Ben,' I added, remembering that he was also missing. Aiming my next question at Kevin, Rosie, and the others, I asked, 'Where have you been taking the gold?'

'We haven't broken any laws,' protested Rosie.

I almost choked at her lie. 'Try telling that to Wayne Calder.' I scoffed. 'I'm sure you did not all play a part in his murder, however someone in this village did, and the rest of you are hiding it. On top of that, you have been disrupting mining operations, for which I am quite certain the owners would like to sue you, and do you think that gold in your hands is yours? You know Joshua Curly stole it and has been looking for it ever since he got out of jail.' Glaring at Rosie since she had been the one to speak, I drilled into her with my eyes. 'Tell me where the gold has been taken.'

I think she was genuinely about to reveal where all the villagers had been gathering, but she didn't get a chance because somebody shot her.

The bullet hit her high on her right shoulder, spinning around and throwing her backwards as blood from the wound shot into the air. There was a half second of stunned silence, in which I think everybody just stared at her. Then the crack that always comes after the shot reported across the landscape, the echo of it fading away to nothing.

Everyone was shouting in an instant. Reacting fast, but not fast enough to stop another bullet from finding a target. This time it was Gable who was hit, the round hitting his ribs low and on the left side.

Babette screamed, losing her mind at the horror of our new situation. My own pulse was through the roof, the instant danger an unknown shooter presented sufficient to get me into fight or flight mode.

I was crouching, looking around and trying to find where the shot might have come from. The length of time between the bullet striking Rosie and the audible crack of the shot was sufficient to tell me it came from four or five hundred yards away.

There was nothing within that distance apart from the mine. It was an obvious place for a sniper to set up, but why shoot Rosie? Like a blow to the skull, I realised it had to be another one of the people from Playford. They were not a great shot, but were positioned as overwatch to kill anyone who came to disturb the gold extraction. Now that they were at the most critical part of their plan to get rich, they would stop at nothing.

It also meant they were not shooting at Rosie and Kevin, but at me and Poison and anyone else who was not on their team.

I could not be certain the shots had come from the mine, but one thing was for sure, we could not stay where we were.

I was not the only one who had come to that conclusion. Leaving Rosie where she lay, Kevin had charged to the vehicle nearest him and was already firing the engine into life.

To my left, Hagen and Babette were helping Gable to get back to their vehicle. The four ninjas were going with them, their weapons and expertise of no use against a long-range sniper.

As Kevin's vehicle tore away, the other two men who had been with him grabbed onto the sides and the rear door, clambering inside with the gold, some of which spilled out to land on the dirt. Shouting emanated from inside the vehicle, the men arguing about whether they should go back for it or not.

In the driving seat, Kevin got the casting vote and kept his foot flat on the accelerator.

There had been no further shots after the first two, but that was no cause for hope.

I gave up trying to spot the shooter and turned my attention to Rosie.

She was trying to get up, bleeding heavily from her wound, and whimpering in a pathetic way. If I didn't help her, she was going to die. With that in mind, and keeping my body as close to the ground as I could, I scurried across the soil and plants to get to her.

My heart was banging in my chest, and a small voice of doubt kept warning me that I could die at any moment. I wasn't going to let fear stop me from doing what was right, but I would be jolly annoyed if it cost me my life.

'Let me help you,' I begged. The wound needed dressing. Had it been a limb that was injured I might have applied a tourniquet. High on her shoulder as it was, there was no good way to stem the flow of blood and she was losing a dangerous amount.

I needed to get her into the remaining vehicle and hope there were keys in it. It was the closest thing to us. Though just as I thought that, the sound of an approaching car drew my eyes around.

The ninjas were coming to me!

Mistress Mushy was behind the wheel, piloting her little Suzuki over the uneven ground. It slewed to a stop right next to the hole, spilling dirt back down onto the few remaining gold bars at the bottom. It was going to be a squeeze. Mistress Mushy's vehicle only fitted four and really didn't have a boot. We were going to have to make it work anyway.

I scooped Rosie, keeping her injured side away from me. However, mindful of the shooter still out there, I ran and all but threw her into the car. It had no back doors, which meant Hatchett in the front passenger seat had to get out just so the rest of us could get in.

Before Hatchett could even get his butt back onto his seat, Mistress Mushy stomped on her accelerator pedal, blasting her car away like a scalded cat.

We were all hunkered down, none of us brave enough to raise our heads up to look out of the windows. Even Mistress Mushy, driving the car and attempting to steer around the gorse bushes and holes that dotted the landscape, had her head as low as she could get it. It was futile, of course, because the side of the car would no more stop a bullet than a piece of gauze.

I held my breath, imagining that I probably wasn't the only one in the car doing so as we rocketed over the ground. The car angled suddenly as Mistress mushy found a slope.

She yelled, 'Everyone hold on!'

I raised my head just enough that I could see what was happening. Mistress Mushy had found us some cover. To our left and right were banks of earth high enough to keep us from sight.

With relief washing over me, even if it was temporary, I pushed myself back to something resembling upright. Doing so gave us a little more space if nothing else. Bob and Poison followed my move, all three of us looking down at Rosie where she lay across our laps.

My heart jumped until I felt her pulse. She had lost consciousness, though for a moment I thought she might have died. We had to get her to help really fast.

From the front seat, Mistress Mushy shouted over her shoulder, 'Who shot at us? Was that more of the same people?'

'Yeah,' chipped in Hatchett. 'Were they aiming for her?' he asked, nodding his head to indicate Rosie. 'Or aiming for us and just missed?'

I had an answer for them. Though I admit I had no idea who was behind the trigger. We would have been easy to spot from an elevated position on top of one of the larger buildings at the mine. After a year of searching, and in Joshua Curly's case, four decades of waiting, they had found what they were looking for.

Right on the cusp of achieving their dream, I turned up and ruined it all.

They intended to kill me to protect their fortune. At the very least, they wanted to scare me off so they could recover the last of the gold. What they planned to do with it now was anyone's guess, but I suspected staying in the area would not be possible. They would need to leave the country and find somewhere where they could spend their haul.

The land rose again, spitting Mistress Mushy's car back out into the open. We were heading away from the mine and going in completely the wrong direction to get Rosie the help she needed. Of course, if I was right about the sniper, we couldn't go back that way.

I could not see the other car, the one the Swedes had arrived in. I was worried about them, especially the injured Gable, but there was nothing I could do to help them at this time.

Worse than that, there was no sign of Kevin's car either. If I had been able to see him or follow him, he might have led me to where I would find the rest of the villagers and my parents. I had an image in my head of them all gathered in one place divvying out the gold.

Thinking fast, I leaned through to the front of the car and pointed through the windscreen.

'Go that way,' I jabbed my arm in the direction of some trees ahead. 'There is a gap that way.' I didn't mention that it was only wide enough for pedestrians. With no other way out, we were just going to ram it and hope for the best.

'Her pulse is getting weaker,' Poison alerted me. 'We need to get her to help soon.'

'Where the heck are the police?' I questioned. 'It's been ages since you called them,' I pointed out.

Poison blinked twice, her face filled with questions. 'You actually wanted me to call them?'

It took me a second to work out how to respond, my jaw flapping as I struggled for words.

'Of course I wanted you to call them. You're seriously telling me that you didn't?'

Poison shook her head. 'Tempest you never want the police involved. I thought you were being flippant or perhaps just making it sound like you were doing the right thing in front of the scientists from Sweden.'

Still reeling from this latest revelation, I made sure this time to be clear.

'I would have done it myself, Poison. But like I said, I broke my phone. Besides, I always call the police once I figure out what's going on. I can't do the arresting, can I?'

I shut up then, falling silent so that Poison could make the vital call.

'We're not gonna fit, Tempest!' Mistress Mushy screamed when she spotted the gap in the fence.

I placed a hand on her shoulder and gripped it, leaning forward to bring my head closer to hers.

'Make the hole bigger.'

Mistress Mushy uttered some choice words, moaned about what all this adventure was doing to her car, and then squealed that we should all find something to hold onto.

She hit the fence at forty miles per hour, aiming her bonnet to strike dead centre of the hole. The steel mesh fence parted instantly where it had already been cut and folded back though it clattered and scratched against the sides of the car.

Now on the other side, Hatchett wound down his window and looked out.

'That's not going to buff out,' he observed.

'I'm still making payments on this car,' Mistress Mushy scowled at me in her rear-view mirror. She didn't slow down though, and it took only another few minutes to get back to a road.

Finally facing in a direction that was going to take us back towards the village, Poison directed emergency first responders to meet us at the inn. That task complete she was put through to a police dispatcher.

I tapped her on the leg. 'Get them to contact DCI Kirkland. This is his case. Tell him it is all about the United Banks gold robbery. Then get hold of the Swedes and get a grid reference for that hole we were just in. Tell them to send everyone, they've got a lot of people to arrest.'

I was full of nervous energy, my right leg jiggling and refusing to sit still. I knew what this mystery was all about now, and I knew why Wayne Calder had been killed. That brought me no joy right now though because in the process of unravelling it all I had lost my parents, I had lost Big Ben, and now I had lost my dogs. Not only that, I didn't know where any of the villagers were and I believed they would kill to defend the gold.

Mistress Mushy was driving fast, speeding to get us back to the Fox Inn. Lying on the back seat and bleeding was doing Rosie no good at all and none of us wanted her to die in our arms. However, when I spotted something through the trees, I knew I was going to delay her arrival at the inn.

'Stop the car!' I yelled. 'Stop the car, I need to get out!'

Roughly five seconds later, the little Suzuki was once again rocketing into the distance, and I was standing at the side of the road.

From the corner of my eye, I had seen a barn door closing. You might be thinking that that's not a whole lot to go on and you would be right. Perhaps I was going to be wrong, but I was betting that inside that barn I was going to find a whole load of people.

We were a quarter mile outside Playford and there was nothing around us but farmland. The only people living around here were the people in Playford, so a barn door closing was like seeing smoke rising from the barrel of a gun.

'Shall we?' enquired Poison. The nimble little Chinese minx had insisted on coming with me. And since she was coming, so too was Bob. I'll admit it felt good to have a little backup.

Without feeling a need to vocalise my reply, I pointed my feet towards our target and started to hustle. I went in a straight line, weaving through trees and jumping a low fence when I got to it.

The area was quiet, no real noise at all apart from the wind whistling through the trees. But then there is nothing for miles around with the exception of the mine.

Approaching the barn, my confidence grew - we could hear voices coming from inside. There were people in there and they were talking loudly. The corrugated steel walls of the barn muffled and distorted the noise, yet it was clear they were arguing.

Feeling fired up, what I really wanted to do was kick in the door and storm the building. That was just going to get me killed though, plus Poison and Bob along with me. None of that would do my parents any good.

So I was gonna play this cool, find a way to confirm who was in there, and then bring the police to us.

Like so many of my plans, it did not go to plan.

In a scuttling run as I crossed the ground close to the barn, I got caught in the open when someone inside came out.

There was no way she could have missed me. I was less than five yards away, had a sword wielding ninja to my left and to my right, and above all I was acting suspiciously. Of course, she already knew who I was, just like everyone else in the village.

There was a frozen second when the woman stared at me, and I stared back at her. I was already running, and questioning whether I could get to her and clap my hand over her mouth before she raised the alarm.

I could not.

'He's here!' she screamed.

I did not know the woman's name, nor did I think I was ever going to learn it. She was just another resident of the village. Someone's daughter or someone's wife, but just as invested in getting rich with all the gold as the rest of them. And just as guilty of murder.

She ducked back inside the building before I could get to her, throwing the door wide as she went. The action gave me a glimpse inside - the barn was full. In that brief moment when the door flew wide and clanged against the side of the barn, I saw a sea of faces staring back at me.

I didn't get the chance to pick out many individuals, but I spotted some children among them and was willing to bet that everyone from Playford was in the same place. We needed to reverse direction and run away. We could get the police and we could bring them here, but we couldn't do that if we were captured or murdered.

However, to my great regret, as soon as I reversed direction to get away from the barn, it was already too late to escape.

Shouts, audible curses, and screamed instructions all followed us as once again the barn door smashed open. A shotgun went off, the loud noise driving a spike of terror through my heart.

'Stop where you are!'

It was an order I expected, and one which would spell my doom if I chose to obey. I glanced at Poison, glad to see that she hadn't been hit. And then at Bob, confirming that he too was still in one piece.

To my great disappointment, they were both coming to a halt, and raising their hands in surrender. In so doing, any hope that one of us could escape and raise the alarm evaporated. I couldn't leave them behind, and now they had stopped, they were sitting ducks to be picked off.

Reluctantly, I accepted my fate, hoping that maybe I could stall them for long enough for Mistress Mushy and Hatchett to send help back to find us - they knew the general direction we were heading in when they left us at the side of the road.

I turned around to find it was Kevin holding the shotgun. His face was drawn into a satisfied grin, and he had the ugly weapon pointing straight at my centre of mass. If he sneezed and pulled the trigger, it would cut me in half, and he wasn't the only villager holding a gun. Looking along the line of local residents now standing outside the barn, I counted no fewer than seven.

'That's enough!' roared Darius, forcing his way through the mass of people to get outside. 'Put the guns down,' he commanded.

Kevin's eyes never even twitched. 'He's been nothing but a pain since he arrived, Darius,' he remarked, speaking from the side of his mouth with his eyes locked on mine. 'He's going to ruin the whole thing.'

'Why don't you just call him Joshua?' I asked, doing my best to sow doubt and draw things out.

Darius stiffened – he hadn't expected me to have figured out who he was.

Sensing an opportunity, I continued talking.

'I'm sure you all know his real name, just as you know his past.' I dismissed Kevin, turning my attention to Darius. It was a dangerous gamble – Kevin could so easily be the one who killed Wayne – but there was clearly disharmony within the group, and I wanted to use that to my benefit.

Speaking as if I were addressing a class, I raised one hand to gesticulate and took a pace to my right.

Kevin tracked me with his gun, refusing to obey Darius' command.

'Joshua Curly served his time. However, the conviction for murder really is an indelible stain.' I made sure to watch his face, but was aware of all the other faces watching me.

'I didn't kill anyone,' Joshua Curly stated. 'I was the getaway driver. I never even went inside the building. They gave me a gun, but it never left the vehicle. The judge considered me to be complicit and therefore equally guilty. Since they hadn't been able to catch or even find any of my

227

accomplices, he happily levied the full scales of justice at the one man they had in custody.'

I listened when he talked and watched his face. I gave myself a moment to think about his words but decided that I believed him. His actions in stopping Kevin on two occasions now backed up his claim to have not participated in the murder.

That did little to explain what happened to Wayne Calder.

Behind Joshua and Kevin, the locals we're becoming agitated. I could hear enough of their mutterings to know that they were concerned about how long things were taking. They wanted to get moving. Now that they had the gold within their grasp, something I imagined they must have fantasised about many, many times over the last year or so, they were eager to escape with it.

'Your concern that the police are coming is founded,' I raised my voice to ensure everyone heard me. 'We placed a call to them some time ago. Rosie ... I'm afraid I don't know her last name, is quite badly injured. But then you know that, of course.' I looked around, pausing to lock eyes with as many faces as possible. 'Who was it with the rifle?'

No response came. At least, not at first.

Irene stepped forward, making herself more visible as she separated herself from the crowd.

'Kevin told us someone was shooting,' she said.

Joshua nodded his head in agreement. 'I abhor violence. I will not tolerate it. You accuse us of attempting to kill you. You accuse us of the murder of Wayne Calder, but nothing could be further from the truth.'

228

I couldn't help the grin that creeped into one corner of my mouth, and I glanced across at Kevin who still had his deadly shotgun pointing in my direction.

'Really?' I sneered, making a point of the incongruity in Joshua's claim.

Finally, with all his peers and neighbours looking at him, Kevin's face flushed. The muzzle of the weapon wavered and then he allowed it to drop. Silently I breathed a sigh of relief, and for the first time in over a minute believed I might get out of this alive.

Fixing Darius and Irene with a hard stare, I asked him the question I really wanted to have an answer to.

'Where are my parents?'

Darius and Irene turned inward slightly, checking each other's faces as if hoping the other one might have an answer.

It was Irene who spoke, 'We haven't seen them since they were in the church. You are talking about the couple who were sat with you in the rear pew, yes? Next to the big fellow?'

Just like with their claim that they hadn't killed Wayne Calder, their words rang true. I didn't want to accept what I was hearing, but I did believe they were telling me the truth. It was desperately disappointing.

Poison and Bob were both just out of sight behind me to my left and right. The focus of the local residents had very much been on me, but they looked at Poison now when she spoke.

'I think they're telling the truth, Tempest.'

'We are,' insisted Irene. 'We haven't done anything to your parents or your big friend. You were right that we were the ones who dreamt up the

Deathling. We made the boot prints, and we spread the rumours. Joshua has been searching for the gold for over a year, carefully and methodically dividing the land around the mine into grids. It has taken him that long to find it.'

'There were landmarks to guide me back to it,' explained Joshua. 'But when I returned, they were all gone. The Fletchers had cleared the trees, and there were now roads where before there had been nothing at all. I was starting to wonder if I might never find it.'

The sound of a wailing siren filled the air, and everyone tensed. Two seconds later an ambulance whizzed past, its siren blaring and its lights flashing. I hoped it would be in time to save Rosie.

With the sage look of acceptance on his face, Joshua said, 'The police won't be far behind, will they?'

I met his eyes and shook my head. 'No, I don't think they will.'

From somewhere in the back of the crowd a small voice said, 'Will they let us keep the gold?'

The crowd parted slightly as people turned inward to see who had spoken. It was a young man in his late teens, traces of acne still visible on his chin and cheeks.

Joshua took a pace to his left, lifting his arm to place it around Irene's shoulders.

'Almost,' he said. 'We almost got it.'

'What?' snarled Kevin. 'You're just giving up? Well, you can forget that. I'm taking my share and anyone who tries to stop me ...'

I felt certain he was going to threaten to kill anyone who got in his way, but Poison darted forward, getting inside the length of his shotgun before he could lift it to deliver a hard chopping elbow to his throat.

Kevin dropped his weapon, clutching at his neck as he gagged and gasped.

'He talks too much,' quipped Poison, stepping back once more with both hands on her katana and her eyes open for any further sign of danger.

Irene turned to face the assembled villagers.

'We all agreed we would do this peacefully and without breaking any laws. The time has come to accept that the gold was never truly within our grasp.'

Joshua chuckled. 'It was a fine adventure though, wasn't it?'

Somehow, I had misread the locals completely. They had been hostile towards me because they needed to be. It was all part of the ruse to get people away from the mine and it had almost worked.

Coming from farther, away, and approaching from a different direction, we all heard new sirens as they sounded. The police were coming. They were probably going to stop at the Fox Inn where they would see the ambulance, but they would be here soon.

My heart rate was returning to normal, the danger seemingly over. Upon their admission, I could accept that the mystery of the Deathling was solved. However, that did little to end my investigation. If I accepted that they were telling the truth, and they were not guilty of Wayne Calder's murder, then somebody else was.

More pressingly for me at this time, my parents and Big Ben were still missing. Concern for them was making my legs twitch. Nervous energy dictated that I move, and the direction I chose to go in was inside the barn.

'I want to see the gold,' I announced my intention as I strode forward.

'Me too,' said Poison.

Bob echoed his agreement and all three of us moved towards the people we'd been chasing for the last three days. They parted to let us in, some of them more reluctantly than others, but Joshua and Irene were following us and that seemed to be sufficient to convince everyone to let us pass.

Inside the barn were lots of cars. Probably all of the cars that I'd seen outside the church. It struck me as a little ironic that they'd all gone for their Sunday service as if they were thanking their maker for delivering the gold finally. Had they not done so, for Kevin, Rosie, and the others were clearly still collecting it, some of them could already have taken their share and been on their way.

The cars were parked haphazardly, squeezed in wherever they could get, and it was obvious that some were already laden down with gold, sagging suspension telling a tale.

'How much is there?' I asked.

Joshua came to stand beside me, his eyes and mine on a heaping pile of glistening gold bars still stacked on the floor.

'Three hundred and forty-seven bars.'

Bob whistled, his noise one of appreciation and awe.

I had no idea what the net worth of a gold bar was in current money, but the quick glance I'd had at the newspaper article regarding the robbery listed the worth of the gold at the time at over one hundred million pounds. Now more than four decades later, I was willing to bet that it was worth vastly more than that.

'What was the plan?' I asked. 'You had all this gold. Where were you going to go with it? Surely, you knew you could not stay here?'

'We were all going to Brazil,' Joshua lamented, a silent tear slipping from his right eye. 'I don't expect you to believe me, Mr Michaels, but I'd never have gone along with the crime if I thought anyone was going to get hurt. The guns were supposed to be just for show.'

The police were going to have a devil of a time unpicking all of this. This would make national news very fast - it was the find of the century.

There was another question I wanted to ask.

'What made you choose the name?'

Joshua snapped his head around to look at me.

'Darius Cooper? I was worried some of my old gang members might still be out there waiting for me to be released from jail. They are all old now; I was the youngest of them. They might even all be dead, but they vanished off the face of the Earth, so no one knows for sure. Getting out after all those years and coming here, I knew I had to vanish if I was going to try to find the gold, so I picked a name. I guess it wasn't too bright picking the name of a famous criminal though.'

I nodded in agreement.

'Did it nearly backfire when the beetle thing got so much attention?'

Joshua chuckled. 'Yes, I was trying to be clever and achieved the exact opposite. When that blew over, I kept my head down, but Irene said we should share the secret and get the rest of the villagers involved. They helped to spy on the mine and direct me to where I could look without too much danger of getting caught.'

Irene spoke up. 'You're going to ask why we came up with the Deathling, aren't you, Mr Michaels?'

I wasn't, in truth, I was about ready to run out the door and go look for my parents. The only thing holding me back was the annoying fact that I had no idea in which direction I should run. Seeing no reason not to, I encouraged Irene to share.

'It just came to me one night,' she explained. 'My father really was involved in the original scare, but he always said it was a load of nonsense. When that poor lad, Wayne Calder, went missing, the idea just popped into my head. A few of the lads snuck out that night to dig the hole the miners found in the face of the mine. We made some 'feet' using a couple of salad bowls with bits of an old fur coat stuck to them. Mildred said their imaginations would do the rest.'

'I had searched so much of the ground inside the fence that it only left the parts close to the mine itself,' explained Joshua. 'I was starting to worry it might have been under one of the buildings.'

Irene took over again. 'We needed a way to shut them down for a few days so he could search the last few square miles of ground.'

'Why not get more of you out there?' I questioned.

Joshua answered, 'The more people on the ground, the greater the chance was that we would get caught. Besides, we had to spend

234

everything Irene had in the bank just to buy the one detector I have been using.'

I had seen what it cost.

'You really made us work hard these last few days, Mr Michaels,' Irene commented, her attitude toward me now vastly different to what it had been.

For the last minute or so as they talked, my brain had been working feverishly. I accepted what Joshua said about the dead security guard and his part in the murder, but whatever his level of guilt, four decades in jail was a tough sentence and he had completed it. Not that I would ever express my thoughts in such terms to the family of the victim, but I felt his debt had been paid.

Mostly what I was questioning was what crime any of them actually committed. Yes, they had interrupted mine operations and were guilty of vandalising mine property if one considered the fences. Other than that, and Kevin's assault on me, there really was no crime.

The police sirens, which had fallen silent briefly while they were at the inn, started up again and were very clearly coming in our direction. I did not think it would take them long to find us.

Thirty seconds perhaps.

I spun slowly in a circle, once again meeting the eyes of most of the villagers before turning my attention to Irene and Joshua.

Speaking loudly, I announced, 'I'm going outside to meet the police. I recommend that you make all your weapons vanish somewhere - the police take a dim view to people bearing arms in public. As for the gold ... Joshua, who knows that you ended up with all of it?'

The former inmate blinked in his confusion, turning the question over and over in his head before he answered.

'Well, no one.'

I tilted my head, offering him an expression that encouraged him to put two and two together.

'The police expect to find your share. You may need to move fast.' I turned away, heading for the door and led my two Chinese friends from the barn. Listening intently, I was not surprised when two seconds after we closed the door behind us, we heard an eruption of noise and a flurry of activity.

They would be watched by the police and might yet get caught with the bulk of the gold. You might want to question my motives, but I wasn't sent here to solve a forty-year-old gold robbery and it wasn't my place to sit in judgement of them. What they chose to do was down to them and I would put little thought to it once today was done.

Maybe I would drive by a few months or a year from now, just out of curiosity. Would I find a ghost town? Wouldn't that be ironic given my line of work?

Three police cars skidded to a stop in front of the barn, DCI Kirkland's face staring through the screen of the nearest one. By then my thoughts were no longer on the local residents of Playford.

There were still two murders to solve.

The barn door opened, a glance over my right shoulder revealing that it was Joshua coming outside to join me. He closed the door and came to stand by my right shoulder.

He was looking at the police and not at me when he spoke, 'You are not what I expected, Mr Michaels. If you will permit me, I would like to be the one who explains all this to the police.'

I answered with a sweep of my arm, inviting him to do as he requested.

'What about your parents?' asked Poison. 'And Big Ben,' she added.

I licked my lips, finding something distracting to do because I didn't have an answer for her. For the last three days, all I had done was chase around after the villagers. Right from the very first moment, I had assumed that they were guilty, both of creating the Deathling ruse to cover up what they were really doing, and of Wayne Calder's murder.

I had been half right.

Admittedly, my client, Stefan Fletcher had been adamant they were to blame, and though I hadn't taken his assurances as gospel, I hadn't fought that hard against them either.

It had only been minutes since the error of my thinking had been revealed, but I was nevertheless struggling to come up with another suspect. Wayne Calder and Mildred Marchant - two victims in a short space of time and in a very tight geography. Were they connected or not?

Solving this now demanded I revisit everything I had seen and heard in the last few days. From that jumble I must somehow find the thing that I had missed.

While I loitered at the door of the barn with Poison and Bob, DCI Kirkland listened to what Joshua had to say. It was a confession of a sort, but not of a crime, per se.

The senior detective's eyes continually strayed in my direction. Or perhaps he was looking at the barn and wanting to get inside.

When Joshua got to the part about the gold – the part DCI Kirkland didn't know about, I saw all the cops' faces register shock. They were about to solve a crime that had taken part before any of them were born. Not that their stalwart police work had led to the result, but they would each receive some credit for it, nevertheless.

Now they were moving, heading for the barn, as Kirkland began barking orders.

I stepped to one side.

'Don't go anywhere, Mr Michaels,' commanded Kirkland as he drew level with me.

I grabbed the meaty part of his left arm, arresting his forward motion instantly. His officers swept by him and into the barn. Their exclamations of surprise came as no surprise, but they made DCI Kirkland all the more eager to see for himself.

Unused to being manhandled, the senior detective wrenched his arm free.

'My parents have been taken,' I revealed. 'My colleague too, and I think the shooter at the mine was aiming for me.' I wasn't as sure now as I had been. Initially, I believed the sniper was a villager, and doing their best to remove me from the playing board. Now I had to look at the situation differently and admit I was confused about exactly who the target might have been.

Pushing my doubts to one side, I continued to talk, 'We still have at least one killer at large.' I inclined my head toward the barn. 'The gold and all the excitement it will bring does not need to involve all your officers. If there is ever a time to share information, this is it.'

Kirkland could not help but glance inside the barn where the huge pile of gold sat. I looked too, noticing that it had shrunk somewhat since I last saw it.

'I suppose you have a theory about who the killer is, Mr Michaels?' said DCI Kirkland, as he dragged his attention away from the gold once more. 'So impress me, Mr Michaels. Who is it?'

A huff of frustrated air escaped my nose – I had not the faintest clue.

'That is what I need your help to uncover. Seriously, my parents are missing, and the only explanation is that they have been taken. You've got two dead bodies and two gunshot victims. Whether there is one killer here or two, I have gotten close to them at some point, and they have grabbed my family as collateral. They might already be dead,' the words stung me to say them.

DCI Kirkland glanced at the gold again.

'Mr Michaels you will need to file a missing persons report if your parents are indeed missing. That can be done at the station in Rye.'

'Dammit, man, you are not listening,' I did my best to keep my frustration in check.

'Oh, but I am, Mr Michaels. You suspect your parents have gone missing, but you have nothing you can present to suggest that they have actually been taken. Had you any such evidence you would have presented it already.' Kirkland was doing a good impersonation of Chief Inspector Quinn, playing the role of the politician, and edging his way towards a fat lip.

'Look,' he relaxed his stance before I could blow my top, 'I need to deal with the situation here right now. There are more officers coming from Hastings, plus my boss and his boss are on their way. This is big news, Mr Michaels,' he explained as if that was something I didn't know. 'I will divert some of my officers to assist you if your parents have not reappeared within the next hour. Okay?' When I failed to reply, he repeated himself, 'Okay? That's the best I can do, Mr Michaels. Unless you produce a ransom note or a crime scene that unequivocally shows there has been a kidnap, my hands really are tied. I want to catch whoever is behind the two deaths and the shooting today just as much as you do, I can assure you. However, since we are both currently at a loss in that particular enquiry, I hope you will forgive me if I focus on the matter in hand.' With that, he dismissed me, stepping over the threshold and into the barn, pausing only to say, 'Don't go anywhere, Mr Michaels. I will have questions for you shortly.'

The second the barn door swung shut, I ignored his instruction and started walking. I made it about a yard before I started asking questions.

'Poison can you call the Swedish, please? I need to know where they are so I can collect my dogs.'

'Of course, Tempest,' she replied, falling into step right behind me.

My feet were heading in the direction of the Fox Inn. It was a quarter of a mile distant and that was going to give me a little bit of thinking time.

To say that things had not gone to plan was too big of an understatement. I had been worried enough about my parents when I thought the local residents had them. Now the level of concern I felt filled my thoughts and made it hard to focus on anything else.

'Babette says they're still at the inn,' Poison let me know. 'They said the paramedics are just about to take Rosie and Gable away. They are being optimistic about their wounds.'

That was good news at least.

Feeling pressure to get back to the inn, not least because I believed Babette and Hagan would want to follow Gable to hospital and I needed to rescue my dogs first, I broke into a jog.

Poison and Bob fell into pace next to me.

Falling into a rhythm and letting my breathing even out, I pushed thoughts of my parents to one side and focused on Wayne Calder. His death was how it all started.

He went missing and then the hole appeared in the face of the mine. The villagers seized upon the opportunity to scare the mineworkers, but the killer then furthered their macabre tale by bringing the body back to the mine and dumping it there to be found.

My thoughts turned to my clients. I had a responsibility to inform them about the latest development. The guards at the mine would have told them about the shooting, no doubt, and chances were that Stefan had tried to call me this morning. Or perhaps not if Colin had already told him about my phone.

I would call the mine from my room at the inn to confirm they were there, and that would be my next stop. The drive would give me a little more time to think.

We were just in time, for as we closed the final hundred yards, the paramedics were loading the stretchers into the back and getting ready to go.

Babette spotted me and looked relieved.

'We found the landlord and put your dogs in your room,' she rushed to say. She was heading for the passenger's door of their truck at the time and clearly didn't wish to hang around.

'Are they okay?' I called out before she could shut her door.

She paused with the door open. 'Your dogs? Yes. Sorry, we have to go.'

The roof lights on top of the ambulance began to whirl, strobe light bouncing off the windows of the inn and the windscreen of the Swedes' truck.

Hatchett and Mistress Mushy reappeared. They had blood on their hands and clothes, as did the rest of us – bullet wounds tend to be messy.

The ambulance pulled out, Hagan following on behind in their truck. Babette slammed her door before he got to the road, and we were alone in the carpark once more.

'I need to get cleaned up,' observed Mistress Mushy, grimacing at her outfit. 'And maybe just set fire to my car,' she added though I was certain she was being flippant.

The others mumbled words to the same effect. They were all covered in blood and dirt. Were I not so concerned about the whereabouts of my parents, I might have gone up to my room to get cleaned and changed too. As it was, the only thing I was going to do was get the keys to my car and head to the mine.

Not having a phone was a major inconvenience. I found it quite telling just how reliant I'd become on my handy piece of technology. The ability to make phone calls when I required was something I had taken for granted, and now denied the opportunity to do so, I was quite irked.

I followed the ninjas inside the inn and up the stairs, stopping to fish out my keys and enter my room as ahead of me the young ninjas went into theirs.

Bull and Dozer bounced out of their bed. Happy to see me, they trotted across the room wagging their tails. I gave them both a pat, scooping and plopping them onto the bed so I could inspect them to make sure they were indeed as I had left them. While the escape from the mine and the hidden gold had been adventurous for me, they had of course never left the Swedish truck.

I fetched them each a gravy bone and patted them on the head. While they crunched those up, I used my laptop to find the number for the mine, and using the phone in the room, phoned the main gate. The man who answered, one of the skeleton crew of guards still at the mine, was able to confirm that both the Fletchers were indeed on the premises.

That being all I needed to know, I ended the call, promised my dogs I would not be long, and grabbed my keys.

Did I really need to visit the Fletchers in person? No, probably not, but I needed to get out – staying at the inn would drive me nuts, and I believe my brain tends to join the dots faster when I am distracted.

My car hadn't moved since I first arrived on Friday, there hadn't been any reason to turn the engine on since then. Mostly this was because Big Ben's truck offered a superior mode of transport.

I slid behind the wheel and turned the key. Seconds later, I was on the road and making my way to the mine. It was pleasing to be able to deliver some news to my impatient clients. Whether they reopened the mine and brought their staff back would be down to them to decide. However, all the nonsense about a supernatural beast could now be cleared up.

Piloting my car on a route I now knew quite well required only a fraction of my brain, the rest of it I dedicated to reviewing the clues I had seen this week.

The feeling that I had already met the killer stayed with me and was made worse by the knowledge that if anyone had my parents, it was going to be the person behind the murders.

My parents and Big Ben would not take off without good reason, which was why I felt certain they were being held captive. That their situation might be worse than that was not something I allowed myself to dwell on.

My brain swirled as my car ate up the miles.

The guard waved me through, raising the barrier as soon as he recognised who was behind the wheel of the car. I drove in and around, parking next to the little headquarters building where the Fletchers' offices and boardroom were located.

The guard must have radioed ahead, because the door to the building opened before I could get out of my car, and Stefan Fletcher appeared in the doorway. Colin lurked just inside, looking furtive, as always.

'Good Lord, what happened to your face?' asked Stefan.

'A minor altercation with a few of the locals in the pursuit of a solution to your case,' I explained.

'You have something to tell us?' Stefan asked, making it obvious he expected good news. 'We heard sirens in the distance. Did you manage to catch them in the act? Which of them is the killer?'

His questions came one after the other, no time in between for me to offer an answer to any one of them.

Using an arm to usher him back inside the building, I said, 'Things have proven to be a little bit more complicated than you might imagine.' I left it at that, my cryptic answer drawing a questioning look from both men.

'We are all ears, Mr Michaels,' encouraged Stefan. 'Please do not make us wait.'

Leading the way, Colin took us past his father's office and into the conference room.

As always, it was Stefan who took the lead. 'So what is this all about, Mr Michaels?' he asked. 'If you are not here to report you have solved the case, what is the reason for your visit?'

I spotted a jug of water and a tray of glasses in one corner of the room and was suddenly overcome with the need to quench my thirst. During the drive over, I had intended to figure out what it was that I wanted to tell the Fletchers at this point. However, concern for my parents, and the natural but annoying need to imagine all the terrible things that might be happening to them had dominated my thoughts.

I used my need for a drink as an excuse to pull myself together and work out what I wanted to say.

Turning to face Stefan Fletcher, I drank my glass and placed it back next to the jug.

'What do you remember about the Union Bank Robbery?' I asked.

His brow wrinkled in question. Colin, far too young to remember the event, looked from me to his father and then back at me again. I think he was about to ask a question when his father spoke.

'The gold robbery?' Stefan attempted to clarify. 'Is that the one you're talking about?'

I nodded my head. 'Exactly right. You remember I asked you about people on your land using metal detectors.' I let that sentence hang in the air for a couple of seconds to see if Stefan would put two and two together.

'What's going on?' asked Colin, completely confused.

It was at that point that Stefan's brain supplied him with the answer.

Staring at me with a dread look on his face, Stefan explained, 'It was a gold bullion robbery, son. They got away with millions in gold bars. And they were never caught. Except ...'

'Except one of them was.' I reminded him. 'One man was caught and convicted of the murder of a security guard during the robbery. But you're right that the gold was never recovered.'

Stefan sagged, grabbing the edge of the table as if he needed it to keep himself upright. He stared down at it and then looked up at me.

'You're going to tell me that's what someone has been looking for on my land, aren't you?'

Colin's eyes widened. 'What?'

Over the next couple of minutes, I explained all about Darius Cooper, whose real name, of course, I also revealed. Both men listened intently as if I was weaving a tale and they needed to hear the conclusion. They marvelled at the concept that they were sitting on an absolute fortune in gold worth more than the GDP of many nations around the world.

When I got to the part about the locals confessing to the Deathling ruse, and that they came onto mine land to leave the strange footprints and dig the hole in the face of the mine, Stefan went nuts.

'I knew it!' he roared. 'Those miserable, murderous ...'

I cut him off, 'They didn't kill anyone.'

Stefan blinked at me, his brow wrinkling once again as he tried to make sense of what I had just said.

'But you just told us they confessed,' he challenged.

'To looking for the gold that Joshua Curly buried, yes. To coming onto mine land to interrupt your operations so that they could look for the gold, yes. To making up the whole ridiculous story about a supernatural creature, yes. But they did not confess to killing Wayne Calder or Mildred Marchant.'

Stefan threw his hands in the air. 'I don't believe this. If they did one thing, then they did the other.' He was looking at me like I was stupid. 'If they are guilty of all that, you can bet they are guilty of murder. All that gold? That would be enough to make anyone want to kill.'

Colin clearly agreed with his dad. 'They pulled the wool over your eyes, Mr Michaels.' He nudged his dad's shoulder. 'Didn't I say hiring him would be a waste of your money, Dad?'

'Changed your tune again, have you?' I spat, the frustration I felt over my missing parents bubbling over in an uncharacteristic outburst of vitriol. 'Last night you were all concerned about my health.'

'Last night?' questioned Stefan. 'He was at the theatre with me last night.'

'No, Dad,' Colin leapt in fast to correct his father. 'That was Friday night, remember?'

The urgency in his voice, and the panicked look that shot between them, hit me like a jolt of electricity. They were lying.

Stefan hadn't been at the theatre with Colin at all! His son provided him with a false alibi! And he did it because he knew his father was guilty!

'What show did you see at the theatre?' I spat my question at Stefan. The terror on his face was all the answer I needed.

248

My brain ordered my feet to move without me even needing to think about it. My right hand came up as I advanced on the senior Mr Fletcher and started to rage.

'You're the killer! Once you killed Wayne, killing Mildred was easy, wasn't it?'

Stefan tried to back away, his feet propelling him backwards, but I grabbed his lapels, thrusting my head forward so my face was inches from his.

Colin, as one might expect, attempted to intervene. As he came towards me, I kicked out with my right foot, striking his leg just above the knee and sending him to the floor.

'Where are my parents?' I roared. 'What have you done with them?'

I was beyond reason. This was not the first time in my career as a detective that I had been hired by the person responsible for the crime, ridiculous though that sounds. Just like the last occasion, Stefan Fletcher had hired me with the belief that he could convince me to follow a false breadcrumb trail. He wanted me to find evidence that would prove the villagers to be guilty and was upset that I had not.

Stefan was attempting to mumble something. I was holding him rather tightly, my knuckles digging into his throat, but I wasn't about to let go even if I was cutting off his oxygen supply.

'Where are my parents?' I demanded again.

However, I should have been paying more attention to my peripheral surroundings. Colin was back on his feet, and I had given him too long to prepare his attack this time.

249

Sensing him coming for me, I pushed his father away, roughly throwing him to the floor, and turned to face the threat. I expected Colin to attempt to punch me, or perhaps try a kick, and had my hands ready to parry a blow. This time, I was going to put him down properly. Then I would call the police from a landline. I could see one just a few feet away.

What I had not anticipated, was that Colin would not attempt to hit me at all. Instead, he selected a winning strategy, and threw their heavy crystal award at my head.

I had enough time to mutter a curse word.

The sound of distant voices, as if I were listening to them underwater, filtered into my brain. It took me a few seconds to work out what I was hearing. Or rather, who I was hearing.

That tiny snippet of information almost certainly saved my life.

Lying still on the carpet in the Fletchers' boardroom, I listened in to what was being said.

'I had to give you an alibi, Dad,' insisted Colin. 'The police were looking at you. You were home by yourself, weren't you, and they would have taken that, and the report that you threatened to kill Mildred, as sufficient cause to arrest you.'

'But I was innocent, son,' Stefan pointed out. 'Why on earth did you kill her anyway?'

'Because I knew it was what you wanted, Dad,' replied Colin, sounding irritated and as if his father ought to be grateful. 'She had been a thorn in your side for months, Dad. I did us both a favour.'

I heard someone's feet shuffling, then Stefan began mumbling.

'I don't believe this. I don't believe this. This can't be happening. What are we going to do?'

'Dad, please stop worrying. The police have absolutely no idea. And if they come around asking any questions about Mildred Marchant's death, I have two ticket stubs from the theatre that prove we were there.'

'Two ticket stubs? How?'

Listening to Stefan Fletcher, it was obvious he had played no part and had no idea until now that his son had killed Mildred. I had got it wrong

251

too. My assumption was that Colin provided the false alibi because his father was guilty, yet in fact Mildred Marchant's death had been some kind of macabre gift.

'I went to the theatre, Dad. I bought the tickets, made sure I was seen and would be remembered by speaking to several people working there. Then snuck out and returned home without ever going into the show. I even paid for seats in a box so that were anyone to really investigate this, there wouldn't be anyone from the seats around us reporting that we were never there.'

'You thought of everything,' Stefan remarked though I did not think it was intended as a compliment.

I had a full confession to Mildred Marchant's murder. All I needed now was to get up off the floor and escape. But my head was banging. The heavy crystal award had struck my skull on my right temple. I could not tell how long I had been unconscious for, but I did not think it was very long. A minute maybe.

Regardless of how I felt, no one was coming to my rescue, and getting out of my current predicament would fall to me. Even though Poison and the other ninjas knew I was going to the mine, they had no reason to report me missing, or to suspect that I might be in trouble.

When DCI Kirkland came looking for me, he might follow onwards to the mine, but that was not going to be anytime soon. So if I was going to get out of this, I was going to have to do it myself. Ordinarily, I would favour my chances against two soft civilians. However, on this occasion, I worried that I might be a little off balance and woozy when I regained my feet.

Accepting my fate, I started to tense my muscles. I intended to get up and moving as swiftly as possible, but just as I counted down in my head, Stefan asked another question.

'Oh, my goodness! Colin, did you also kill Wayne? Oh, my goodness, you did, didn't you? That's why you didn't want me to hire a detective.'

'It was an accident, Dad.' Colin protested. 'And we both know with our safety record that if I reported the accident, the HSE would come in and shut us down.

Stefan began mumbling again. I could not see him, but I imagined Colin's father holding his head in his hands and shaking it, as he disbelievingly absorbed what his son was telling him.

'Oh, no. Oh, no. Oh, no, this cannot be happening. How? How did Wayne die?'

I heard Colin sigh and relaxed my muscles again. Not only did I now know what happened to Mildred Marchant and who her killer was, I was about to hear exactly what happened to Wayne Calder.

However, when Colin spoke, he mumbled, and I was not able to make out what he said. Frustrated, I strained my hearing, hoping that his next words would better inform me.

Mercifully, his father, Stefan, hadn't heard what his son had said either.

Colin repeated his words, 'Someone ran him over, Dad. I came out of the office to check production on B face, and found him lying on the ground. There was no one around, and I could not tell how long he had been there. He'd strayed out of the safety area, out beyond the lights.

Goodness only knows why, but he was so very obviously dead. I think maybe one of the earth-shifting trucks got him.'

'Why didn't you say anything, son?' asked Stefan.

Colin groaned, the sound one of disappointment as if he wished he could turn back the clock.

'Because of the HSE, dad,' he remade his earlier point. 'We are hanging by a thread, Dad. We've borrowed so much money to get this plant working and had nothing but trouble and additional costs ever since.'

'You're right, son,' agreed Stefan.

'If anyone had come along, I'm not sure what I would have said, but I was able to pick his body up and put it in the boot of my car before anyone saw. I was going to find somewhere to bury it, but the next morning that hole appeared in the face of the mine and the locals were all talking about this stupid Deathling creature. I knew how much you wanted to get back at the locals, so I brought his body back and let rumour do the rest.'

Lying there on the carpet while Colin filled in all the blanks, I couldn't help but want to chuckle at how convoluted it had all been. How was I supposed to work it out for myself? The villagers had latched onto the missing person and decided to resurrect a local legend. At the same time, because they did that, Colin decided to use the local legend as the killer, which in turn caused his father to hire me. Then, having already got his head around dealing with dead bodies, Colin chose to kill Mildred.

I don't think I ever would have solved this case. However, now I had all the pieces I could ever need, I was feeling ready to put the case to rest.

Rolling from my side onto my front, I put my hands underneath my chest, and got to my feet. My sudden burst of movement caught both the Fletchers by surprise. They were standing not two yards from me, both reeling backwards in shock.

I had all the advantage I needed. What I did not have was full control of my faculties.

That I might feel a little woozy had occurred to me, but it was much worse than that. The room spun before my eyes, and if I hadn't put my head down, I am fairly sure I would have fainted.

Someone ran from the room, and twisting my head to follow the sound, I spotted Colin's back exiting the door.

Great, the coward had chosen to save himself. The police would catch up with him soon enough. Facing me, as I slowly brought myself up to full height, was the innocent party, Stefan. He hadn't committed any crimes that I knew of, but regardless of that I wasn't going to let him get away.

My determination on the matter swiftly met with a roadblock when Colin ran back into the room holding a rifle. Seeing him, yet another piece of the puzzle slotted into place.

It hurt my head to speak, but I did it anyway, 'You're the one who shot two people this afternoon.' I stated. It was obvious to me now and that was not the only thing I could see with greater clarity. 'You came to my room to kill me last night, didn't you?'

Colin's face split into a sneer. 'It's a bit late to work it all out now, Mr Michaels.'

'What are you doing, son?' begged Stefan. 'Where did you get that gun?'

Ignoring the second question, Colin focused on the first.

'We have to make him disappear, Dad. He knows everything. But he's the only one who does. He's going to have a nasty little accident. The HSE won't be able to blame us this time. He's a well-known snoop, Dad. His body will be found all ground up in the crusher.'

I genuinely expected his father to argue. But I guess he had a lot riding on the success of this mine and his investment in it.

'Yes, son. I suppose you are right.'

They were going to demand that I go where they tell me, and I was going to have to comply. I suspected that were I to fight, Colin might just shoot me, or brain me again. If I were unconscious or incapacitated, I would have no way of spotting and taking advantage of an opportunity if it was presented.

Out here at the mine, we were miles from anyone. The only people around who could save me were the guards, and they were at the gate more than two hundred yards from my current location. The Fletchers would be wise enough to pick a route that would ensure nobody saw us.

I had solved the case, sort of, I suppose, but I wasn't going to get to tell anyone about it.

With Stefan leading the way and Colin following on behind with the gun pointed at my back, I once again asked a question I dearly wanted an answer to before I died.

'Where are my parents?' It was aimed at Colin this time since I now knew that he was behind not only what happened to Wayne Calder, and the murder of Mildred Marchant, but also the gunshot wounds to Gable and Rosie in his attempt to murder me.

His voice growled out a response, 'No talking.'

The Fletchers took me a different route to one that I had been before, exiting the rear of their offices to arrive facing the mine itself. To my left, some of the enormous earth moving machines were parked, and straight ahead was one of the rock crushing plants.

I could tell what it was because I'd seen such things on television. Huge mechanical diggers would load the rock into the earth movers which would then bring it to the crusher. Once there, it would be tipped into a hopper that would feed the rock in a steady stream onto a series of conveyor belts which would in turn carry the rock up to the crusher.

On the other side of the machine another series of conveyor belts carried the now crushed rock away where it was collected by a new set of earth moving machines to be taken to the next stage in the process.

It was to that crushing machine that we were heading. I stumbled, the move deliberate on my part as I tested to see what Colin might do.

The answer was that he jabbed me hard in the back of my ribs not far from my spine. The blow was hard enough to elicit a grunt of pain. I regained my feet and continued walking.

I didn't have very long. The crusher was less than a hundred yards away now, and once there Colin could knock me out and throw me onto the conveyor belt. I suspected that would be his preferred tactic rather than attempt to get me to climb up the steps at the side of the machine to then be pushed in the top.

A glance over my shoulder confirmed that he was bright enough to not be too close. Had he been within grabbing distance, I might have spun around, swiping the muzzle of the rifle away so I could then attack him.

However, the distance between us meant that any attempt on my part would almost certainly just result in me getting shot.

Yes, an autopsy might reveal that I had been shot before I went in the crusher. And that could in turn lead to an investigation and a conviction. But I would gain little from it.

Ten yards from the crusher I was still to figure out any course of action that might avoid my death.

Stefan darted forward, mounting the machine to open a panel. Inside were the controls.

Colin commanded, 'Stop.'

I did as he said, nervously looking about for anything that I might use to gain some advantage or give me a chance at survival.

The machine rumbled and came to life.

Stefan climbed back down, walking in a broad circle around me to come alongside his son.

'It's all working, son. All you've got to do now is load him in.'

That the father proved to be just as at home killing people as his son was something that might have caused me to remark on another occasion. As it was, I didn't see much point in speaking.

Any second now, Colin was going to order me to walk forward. So I pre-empted his command, making my way over to the crusher. The sides were taller than I had thought, and there was no way for me to get in without climbing.

The Fletchers obviously knew that too, because they had followed me over.

'Go on, up you go,' ordered Colin, twitching the barrel of his gun as a gesture for the direction he wanted me to go. The noise from the crusher was loud enough to make talking at conversation level impossible and he'd had to shout.

I turned around to face him and was about to argue when I heard something. Reacting to it would have tipped my hand, if indeed I had a hand to play. I couldn't be sure what I had heard – the crusher made it hard to hear, but a faint stirring of hope swirled through my belly.

If the Fletchers had also heard the sound, they showed no sign, and I turned my head away again lest they attempt to follow the focus of my gaze.

Without argument, I twisted around, stumbling slightly once more in a bid to show that I was still woozy. I had not recovered from the blow to my skull, however I was feeling much better than I had. All I needed was a distraction, and listening hard for the noise I thought I heard, I hoped I was going to get one.

I climbed slowly, feigning that I was struggling with my balance. With my head down, I glanced under my arm, checking the relative positions of the two Fletchers, and beyond them where disappointingly there was still nothing to see.

A shot rang out. It went over my head just as Colin had intended, but made me jump, nevertheless.

Colin had to shout loudly so I would hear him.

'Get a move on, Mr Michaels.'

'Or what?' I goaded him. It was a dangerous tactic, but I didn't need much more time now. Having climbed several steps up the side of the giant rock crushing machine, I had an elevated view. It meant I could see something that was very satisfying indeed.

'Or I'll shoot you, Mr Michaels,' Colin assured me with a self-satisfied sneer. I believed him. I didn't doubt him for one moment, in fact. However, I didn't think he was going to get the chance.

The sound I had first heard perhaps thirty or forty seconds ago was increasing in volume as the machines generating it came nearer. A cloud of dust followed them, and I could tell it was no more than a few seconds before they would round the side of the office and be visible.

'You think you're going to get away with it, don't you, Colin? I'm afraid you are about to be very disappointed.'

Colin Fletcher's brow ruffled as a frown crept across it. He was questioning why I was suddenly so confident, and it was unnerving him. However, it did not deter him, I watched as he lifted the rifle up into his shoulder ready to take the shot.

At that exact moment, the first motorcycle came around the side of the office and into view. The change in volume was suddenly sufficient for both the Fletchers to hear it.

The first bike leading the charge was followed closely by two more. Two more followed them and then two more and then yet more as an entire motorcycle club came roaring towards Colin and Stefan Fletcher.

The mine owners' heads whipped around to see what was making the loud rumbling noise.

Sitting astride the lead motorcycle, Brother Moose spotted me, and waved an arm that instructed his followers to charge.

I took a moment to raise a fist high above my head in salute, ran two steps down the machine, and threw myself into free air.

The motion of Colin's body as he twisted to see what was coming had diverted the muzzle of the rifle away from me, but now it was continuing the circle and would soon be aiming at the motorcycle gang coming to my rescue.

There were enough of them that the target they created was unmissable.

So it was with quite some satisfaction that I slammed into Colin's shoulders and flattened him to the dirt. Before I had even fully hit the ground, my legs were lancing out to take care of Stefan too.

Colin was a big enough fellow that my first hit had not been sufficient to put him down for good. He still had the rifle in his hands, and yet again showed clear thinking when he rolled away to get distance between us.

A sharp elbow to Stefan's jaw took the fight out of him. But when I scrambled around to finish the fight with Colin, I found the muzzle of the rifle once again pointing directly at my head.

I could see he was going to fire and attempted to scream a warning. It came too late though, and he pulled the trigger anyway.

The bullet struck the piece of gypsum jammed into the muzzle. I hadn't seen it happen, but the barrel had to have dug into the ground when I knocked Colin down. Unable to escape the weapon, and possessing far too much explosive energy to simply stop, the bullet exploded the barrel of the rifle. Pressure from the gases created when the bullet was fired had nowhere to go, and this caused the breach to explode as well.

The blast caught Colin in the face, throwing him backwards in a spray of blood that came mostly from his hands as several of his fingers were severed by the force of the gun coming apart.

His squeal of pain was inhuman.

To my left and right and straight ahead, motorcycle after motorcycle skidded to a halt. The large, powerful, chrome-covered machines glistened in the afternoon sun, until the cloud of dust they kicked up followed them in to obscure the air.

'Tempest!' I heard my mother's voice shout. The sound jolted me. I was startled to suddenly have her calling my name. She hadn't been taken by anybody!

That being the case, I expected my father to be with her.

My mother called my name again, and then appeared, running towards me, her footsteps hurried by a mother's worry.

'Brother Weasel,' Brother Moose's deep voice rumbled as he stepped off his motorcycle. 'I see you've been getting into trouble again. A couple of our honorary members begged we lend a hand when they couldn't find you this afternoon.'

'Oh, Tempest, I've been so worried,' cried my mother and she put her arms around me and pulled me into a hug.

To my left, two of Brother Moose's fellow gang members, Brothers Bear and Elk, began tending to Colin Fletcher. His face was a bloody mess, but his hands were worse. His father, Stefan, was being helped to his feet and checked for weapons by yet more of my motorcycle gang brothers.

Big Ben arrived along with my father aka Brother Sasquatch and Brother Grey Fox.

263

'Whatcha been doing, Brother Weasel?' ask Big Ben. 'I'm guessing you finally figured out who was behind the murders?'

My father looked at Colin and Stefan Fletcher, his brow furrowing in confusion.

'Didn't you say it was the mine owners who hired you?' he asked. 'Why would they do that if they were behind the murders?'

I let a long sigh escape me, my shoulders sagging as I deflated. The case was over. Somehow, more by accident than by skill this time round, I had come out on top. The mystery of the Deathling, the eerie looking hole in the ground and strange footprints had all been explained. The odd behaviour of the local residents was no longer a mystery. And I could confidently tell DCI Kirkland exactly what had happened to both Wayne Calder and Mildred Marchant.

I would explain everything shortly but first I wanted to know what had happened to my parents. When I demanded they fill in the blank of the last few hours, it was my father who took up the narrative.

'Something happened at the church,' he explained. 'Not long after you snuck out, someone near the front handed a note to the vicar.'

'It was ever so strange,' commented my mother, interrupting my father because she didn't like him talking for very long without her getting a word in. 'He wrapped up the ceremony without even pausing for communion. He read the Lord's prayer and invited everyone to sing a final hymn.'

Eager to move things on, because I didn't really need all the detail about what happened at the church service, I prompted dad to continue with what he was saying.

'We looked around for you outside, but there was no sign of you,' he explained. 'The congregation all got into cars and drove off, leaving us standing around outside the church. We were going to call you, but then remembered that your phone is broken. So we walked back to the inn hoping that we might find you there.'

'Only with such a lovely day,' my mother added, 'we decided to take a scenic route through the woods.'

That at least explained why I hadn't seen them when I ran to the church and then back to the inn. The scenic route would have been down to my mother, of course, but it didn't matter now.

'What happened then? How is it that you came to be with the Whitstable Riders Motorcycle Club?' I wanted to know.

'Well, son,' dad started, 'There was no sign of you, and we started to worry that maybe someone had grabbed you.'

'I knocked for Poison and her friends,' said Big Ben, 'and since they weren't there either, and we had largely been fighting an uphill battle, I thought it might be a good idea to find some reinforcements.' He then angled his eyes towards my parents. It was a silent message, telling me that what he had actually done was get my parents out of the area.

A siren wailed in the distance, serving as punctuation to end that conversation.

I took that a stage further by introducing a new subject. 'Did you have any trouble getting in?' I aimed my question at Brother Moose.

He chuckled. 'The security guards seemed disinclined to open up for us.'

I suspected that was something of an understatement, but the arrival of the police was not only welcome but necessary.

I asked Big Ben to go back to the guard hut at the main gate. I would have done it myself, but my head was pounding so much I worried it might explode if I tried to do anything. The guards needed to know all was okay following the invasion of the mine premises by a motorcycle gang. I also hoped he could scare up a first aid kit for Colin, and maybe some painkillers for me.

With my pulse returning to something close to its usual slow pace, I noticed the jacket my mother was wearing.

She had gone to church this morning wearing her best Italian heels, a prim, older woman's suit and thick tights, plus a hat and matching coat. Now she was adorned in black leather with tassels down the sleeves and legs and had a mottled red bandana around her neck

She saw the curious look on my face as I studied her outfit.

'Do you like it?' she asked, clearly pleased with her new look. 'Brother Moose found them for me.'

Standing just behind her, my father rolled his eyes and mimed putting a gun to his own head.

'What's happening?' I asked, feeling a little off kilter with my mother's attitude. She had always been vocally condemning of dad's minor foray into the world of motorcycle gang membership.

It was Brother Moose who answered. 'We decided it was time to join the twenty-first century, Brother Weasel. We need to be a more inclusive club so when the opportunity arose today for us to sign our first female member, we could hardly say no.'

266

I felt like the world had decided to start spinning backwards on a whim just to see what that was like.

'Isn't it fun?' asked my mother. 'I'm Sister Brown Owl.'

Amanda snuggled into my chest, her feet on the footstool as she lay across the sofa with a dachshund on her lap. The dachshund in question was Dozer who almost always picks the best spot. Bull was curled up by my right hip, out cold, or so it seemed though I knew he would be instantly alert if someone touched the fridge door.

My eyes were getting heavy, and I knew I would be asleep if I gave into the desire to let them close. We would go to bed soon though any fun activities would have to wait until I had some more energy, and slightly less painkillers running around my body.

I'd been checked out for concussion while we were still at the mine and given the all clear, but told to avoid driving, operating heavy machinery and alcohol after they administered some elephant strength paracetamol.

DCI Kirkland was among the first to arrive at the mine when the call came out that it was under attack by a gang of hell's angels. He and his officers were geographically closer than anyone else the police dispatcher could rustle up. However, having discovered my wilful decision to ignore his demand to remain at the barn, he was only too pleased to respond.

He figured if there was trouble, I was more than likely at the epicentre, and I guess I couldn't fault his thinking because he had been right.

In the period that followed, a light drizzle descended on the area, dousing us with rain. We moved inside, by which I mean me, my parents, and those who had to stay.

Brother Moose, having established there was no reason to keep him, had been cleared by the police to leave. There were some complicated handshakes and the tooth-rattling rumble of three dozen large motorcycle engines before the Whitstable Riders rode into the actual sunset. It had been quite the sight to see.

Inside the Fletchers' Mine offices, the police were already going through everything. Colin had been taken away by the paramedics with an officer to accompany him, and Stefan was in custody. My testimony was going to convict them both.

In Colin's office, they found four library books relating to the Deathling. I chuckled to myself when I heard. How easy could this case have been if I had just convinced Victoria to reveal who had taken those books out.

She would have told me if I had asked her, I was certain, but I questioned if she might have forced me to pay a price first. It would not have been one I was willing to pay.

They had also found evidence of desiccant in the boot of Colin's car. I was in the loop enough, since it was going to be my testimony that sent them to jail, that I got a call from DC Kirkland to confirm Colin had confessed to everything. He'd panicked when he found Wayne's body and hid it in the boot of his car. Out of sight, it began to leak fluids which dripped out to leave a foul trail. Worse yet, it had been attracting insects and animals.

He bought the desiccant to absorb it, only later realising how he could use the withering corpse and the locals' daft legend to his advantage.

I kissed the top of Amanda's head, getting a smile in return when she tilted her head up to meet my eyes.

A yawn split my face.

'Bed?' Amanda enquired, turning her head to check the time by the clock on my wall.

It was a concept with merits. As she cleared away our empty coffee mugs and loaded the dishwasher, I let the dogs out to the garden for a final time.

It would be Monday when we woke in the morning, and a fresh week that would bring new cases. Amanda had wrapped up her Gargoyle case successfully on Saturday morning – at least she had most of the weekend off – and had already looked at what case we might tackle next.

The pick of the bunch, she said, was to do with a dead author. His wife wanted to hire us, and it had all the hallmarks of an interesting investigation. Plus, it was in London, and I was still doing my best to avoid running into Ian Quinn.

I had liked punching him a little too much and couldn't be entirely sure I wouldn't do it again just for the heck of it.

We would discuss it in the morning. For now, it was time to get some sleep. However, trudging up the stairs with Amanda a few steps ahead of me, I happened to notice her shapely derriere.

Maybe sleep could wait.

The End

Author's Notes

Hello, dear reader,

This book took me a month to write which is about the longest I have taken to write any book in the last two years. Partly that was because I found the story hard to tie down. I started out with what I believed was a very distinct idea for what the story was going to be. It came to me one day when I walked into the living room to find my son watching Scooby-Doo. The two minutes of cartoon I caught formed the basis for an entire story.

However, when I came to craft the tale, I found that I needed more meat than a child's animated story could provide. Hopefully, you were satisfied with the end result. I wanted a blend of humour, which Big Ben does a great job of supplying, and action, which is easy to come by in these adventures.

I mention tactical red light, but I cannot remember if I have ever explained that before. It's fairly simple. If you turn on a torch (flashlight) at night, it is visible from a long distance. For soldiers, identifying your location to people who want to shoot you, is a bad thing. By comparison, red light – nothing more than a piece of red plastic over a standard torch – is only visible if you are within a few yards, yet it does a perfectly good job of illuminating that which is close to you.

Another term I believe I need to explain is hamlet. I know this because I had a whole bunch of people message me about the word a few years ago when I first employed it. In England I doubt there are many adults who would not know exactly what it means, but in other parts of the planet the word is unknown unless they believe it is a play by Shakespeare. It is nothing more than the word used to describe a place on the map that is smaller than a village.

Typically, a hamlet is nothing more than a collection of houses with a shop, if they are lucky, but distinctly without a church. I cheated a little and put a church in Playford because it suited the story.

Twiglets get a mention when Big Ben punches Hatchett in the face. If you don't know what they are – I suspect they are not an item that makes it beyond the UK borders – they are a savoury snack. They fall into the love them or hate them category, of which I am firmly rooted in the latter camp. I'm not sure I can even manage to describe the taste, though if memory serves from the last time I was foolish enough to pick one up many years ago, the flavour is much akin to the gunk you find at the bottom of old beer fermentation barrels.

The Saxon Horde, otherwise known as the Staffordshire Horde, is something you can Google if you are sufficiently interested. Over four and a half thousand pieces of gold and other precious metals were found by a member of a metal detection society in 2009. Great Britain is a place with several millennia of history, so I find it unsurprising that we have treasure buried beneath our soil just waiting to be found.

It is mid-September in 2021 as I write this author's note. The weather is just starting to change, heralding my favourite time of the year. I never really thought about why I liked autumn until my wife commented on how often I employed the word 'autumnal'. For a time, it became a running joke in our house.

I believe, now that I have forced myself to consider it, that I like autumn because of the smell. Summer is over and the flowers have faded. The leaves change colour and that gives depth to the landscape. Living on the side of a steep hill, I have the opportunity to see for miles each time I leave the house. It's the smell though, more than anything that I like and I cannot explain why.

I think it is something to do with the rain, and how after the heat of the summer, it changes everything about the world outside.

The next book in the Blue Moon series can be seen on the next page. I have a plot in my head already and a distinctive idea for how the story will feel for the reader. I want to go just a little darker. I have done this in the past, cutting back on the humour to deliver a grittier, spookier mystery and I believe that is what I will do for the next book.

However, as always, I won't really know until I write it. Before I get to that story, I have other books to write.

Until the next time.

Take care.

Steve Higgs.

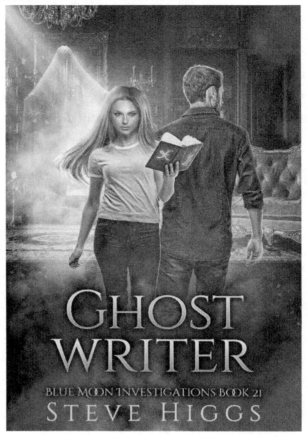

In the nation's Capital, someone is re-enacting the murders from a series of grisly horror books and all the evidence points towards the author as the perpetrator.

The big problem with that? He died a year ago.

In suspicious circumstances.

There were rumours of murder, but no arrests followed the original investigation. Now the victims are those who were closest to him, and it looks like the author has come back from the dead to exact his revenge.

Hired by the author's wife, who fears she may be next, Amanda and Tempest head to London for a case that will challenge the premise on which their business is built: the supernatural does not exist.

You're going to want to sleep with the light on.

The paranormal? It's all nonsense, but proving it might get them killed.

A FREE Rex and Albert Story

There is no catch. There is no cost. You won't even be asked for an email address. I have a FREE Rex and Albert short story for you to read simply because I think it is fun and you deserve a cherry on top. If you have not yet already indulged, please click the picture below and read the fun short story about Rex and Albert, a ring, and a Hellcat.

When a former police dog knows the cat is guilty, what must he do to prove his case to the human he lives with?

His human is missing a ring. The dog knows the cat is guilty. Is the cat smarter than the pair of them?

A home invader. A thief. A cat. Is that one being or three? The dog knows but can he make his human listen?

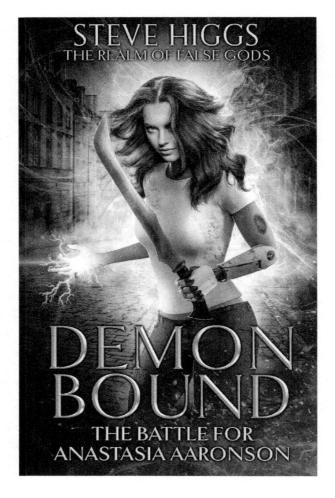

She's got a magical hand cannon and is carrying God's sword. That makes her tough to beat, but when the devil himself sends the four horsemen of the actual impending apocalypse after her ...

... let's just say all bets are off.

With a demon at her side, who she's not crazy enough to trust, Anastasia is going after the missing armour of God.

It would be an easier task if anyone on Earth knew where the angels hid it.

She'll recruit help, but can she get to the armour before the horsemen get to her?

Be ready for a wild-assed ride!

More Books by Steve Higgs

Blue Moon Investigations

Patricia Fisher Cruise Mysteries

Mission for the Maharaja

A Sleuth and her Dachshund in Athens

The Maltese Parrot

No Place Like Home

Patricia Fisher Mystery Adventures

What Sam Knew

Solstice Goat

Recipe for Murder

A Banshee and a Bookshop

Diamonds, Dinner Jackets, and Death

Frozen Vengeance

Mug Shot

The Godmother

Murder is an Artform

Wonderful Weddings and Deadly Divorces

Dangerous Creatures

Albert Smith Culinary Capers

Pork Pie Pandemonium

Bakewell Tart Bludgeoning

Stilton Slaughter

Bedfordshire Clanger Calamity

Death of a Yorkshire Pudding

Cumberland Sausage Shocker

Arbroath Smokie Slaying

Dundee Cake Dispatch

Lancashire Hotpot Peril

Blackpool Rock Bloodshed

Felicity Philips Investigates

Get sneak peaks, exclusive giveaways, behind the scenes content, and more. Plus, you'll be notified of Fan Pricing events when they occur and get exclusive offers from other authors because all UF writers are automatically friends.

Not only that, but you'll receive an exclusive FREE story starring Otto and Zachary and two free stories from the author's Blue Moon Investigations series.

Yes, please! Sign me up for lots of FREE stuff and bargains!

Want to follow me and keep up with what I am doing?

Facebook

Printed in Great Britain
by Amazon

39102684R00159